DEAD

WOMAN

WALKING

DEAD
WOMAN
WALKING

JESSICA MANN

The Cornovia Press

SHEFFIELD

Published by The Cornovia Press, Waterthorpe, Sheffield.

ISBN 978 1 908878 06 9

Berlin, Germany, December 1938

In the small hours of a winter night the main railway station was usually at its quietest, with a few officials on patrol, and prostitutes, policemen and delayed passengers sharing the benches. The tramps and beggars of earlier years had disappeared, for sleeping rough was forbidden.

This night was different. A great horde of men and women holding children by the hand, or carrying them, surged towards the most distant of the platforms where heavy wooden barriers prevented them from reaching the train. They waited, docile and mostly silent. Almost any words could be dangerous. The adults and children alike had yellow stars sewn onto their coats or jackets, but handwritten labels were pinned to the children's clothes. On each label was written the boy's or girl's name and parents' names and home address.

Uniformed men demanded papers, read each word on each page with contemptuous, leisurely attention. Questions were asked, answered and asked again. Each response was low voiced and humble, insults, imprecations and instructions received with deference. Any flash of defiance or doubt was enough to have the speaker turned away. Those who reached the platform were relieved but not happy – in fact, as unhappy as they had ever been in their lives.

The adults weren't allowed near to the train carriages, but were held behind another barrier where they had to let go of their children, who were received by a team of foreigners, mostly English. They helped the older brothers and sisters with the little ones, and jollied along the children who were in tears. "It's not for long," they would say, or, "Your mummy will join you in no time, you'll see her again soon."

The mothers and fathers craned for a last sight of their sons and daughters. Some kept rigid wide smiles pinned to their faces, and forced false cheer into their voices as they called goodbye and be good and have a lovely time and we'll be following you soon, see you very soon. Others couldn't control emotion, passionate hugs and kisses followed by unstoppable tears.

It took two hours for the train to be fully loaded. One of the foreign ladies passed through every carriage, counting. She had reached number three hundred and six when one of the older girls stood up politely, made a little bobbing curtsey and said,

"Excuse me, honoured lady, I have found a little one."

"A little one?" The lady's German was primitive but that much she could understand. She looked at the girl with a mixture of pity and impatience. There wasn't much time. The girl bent to pull a sort of laundry basket from under the seat. In it lay a sleeping child. Eighteen months, maybe two, she was breathing heavily, her cheeks scarlet and damp, her dark curls matted against the skull.

"Isn't this your little sister?" the lady asked.

"I haven't got a little sister."

"Any of you?"

There were fourteen children in a compartment designed for eight, miserable looking little creatures, several of them clutching onto the neighbouring child. They had been made to leave comforting toys behind. Crammed against the wooden barriers, several of the mothers and fathers were holding teddy bears and dolls, embracing them, sniffing the familiar smell, as they craned to see their own children at the train windows.

The engine gave a piercing hoot. The lady said,

"We'll be off in a minute. I must finish counting. I'll find her family soon, but for the moment could you keep an eye on her, my dear? What's your name – oh I see." She checked the older girl's name tag and bent to read the word on a piece of card pinned to the sleeping child's knitted jacket. "Just until we're under way. I don't think she'll wake up actually." This wasn't the only little one who'd been given a dose of mummy's sleeping draught, she thought and added, "It says she's called Fidelis."

It's been years since I saw Liza but I recognise her voice at once. Someone must have died – that's the usual reason for time-expired acquaintances to call. And in fact, someone had died. But it wasn't in the usual course of events. When I put the receiver down, my husband François asks,

"Who was that?"

"A woman I knew in Edinburgh, back in – God, it must be half a century ago. When I was married to Hector."

They say that every cell and fibre of the body is shed and renewed in seven years. And there's no doubt that our minds change and brains develop – at least, mine have. So I'm not in any way the same Isabel as the young woman who was married at twenty one and a mother at twenty two, and that Isabel was a totally different person from the child whose experiences were imprinted on her mind. A formless lump of clay, moulded into an image, could still change shape again. But the Isabel of the 21st century – that is, I myself – have become set in my ways. And I often forget how everything has changed. It's seeing the new passport photo or not being recognized by an old acquaintance that rams the truth home – or, for that matter, arriving in Edinburgh after one hour's flight rather than rolling up, exhausted, after driving for double-digit hours on single carriageway main roads.

At least the grey stone terrace where I lived half a century ago looks exactly the same as it did then, in fact probably exactly the same as it did a hundred years and more before that. The Dorneywoods haven't ever moved and time telescopes in my imagination as I name check the brass door plates, push the polished brass bell and wait on the top step. Liza Dorneywood and I used to leave our babies out here in their coach built prams, back in the days when it was not illegal or even frowned upon. Now those babies have turned into middle-aged pillars of the community with children of their own who wouldn't be left unprotected for a single moment.

The old latch-lifter on a wire has been replaced by an electric buzzer but the black door still opens onto the traditional common stair. We used to take it in turns to polish the brass name plates and sweep the sixty treads, worn into shallow curves after more than two hundred years of use. Panting my way up now I simply can't imagine how I ever ran up and down carrying groceries, pushchairs, suitcases or struggling infants.

Liza is waiting at her open front door to greet me. The door that had been my own, across the landing, is closed. Just as well. Better to remember my first home as it was when we were young and broke and used cloth-covered orange boxes as tables and such real furniture as we owned was bought, scratched and battered, at junk shops in back lanes.

I'd knocked so often at the Dorneywoods' door in those days when Liza seemed a fount of all knowledge about child care or housekeeping or, in fact, adult life. She'd been, as we put it nowadays, my mentor and a trace of the old deference survives even now, I realize, as we hug and kiss, exclaim and reminisce and tell each other that we haven't changed at all, not a bit.

In fact, Liza's hair is white, her face crumpled, her figure spread and her ankles swollen. She's an old woman.

I'm not – not quite yet. I glance anxiously into the Alice Through The Looking Glass mirror that's still above the drawing room mantelpiece. I'm not fat, my hair's dyed a natural sort of russet – even if that's not the colour nature once made it – and layers of cosmetics disguise at least some of the blotches and wrinkles.

We ask after each other's families. The Dorneywoods have five grandchildren, we have seven. We enumerate all their talents and successes.

Liza tells me about her health problems. I say I'm very well thank you.

We ask about each other's husbands. Liza hasn't met François but she has watched one or two of his programmes. Her own husband is slowing down, she says, but spends as many days as he can on the golf course.

Liza doesn't ask about my writing since she disapproves of it, having mistakenly identified a character in my first novel as herself, taken violent offence and announced that she wouldn't have my books in her house. But she wants to know more than I can tell her about the people-tracing service I'd set up five years before. I can't possibly list my clients or divulge anything I've discovered about their backgrounds.

"I've heard you talking about adoption on the Today programme," Liza says. In fact I've broadcast about my work several times, ever since a celebrity whose birth parents I had traced credited me in her interviews.

Liza hasn't mentioned my first husband but her careful tact is unnecessary. "How's Hector?" I ask.

I will see for myself this evening, she replies, and would I like to be shown to my room? It has a pink carpet and an embroidered blue bedspread, colours picked from the flowers in the chintz curtains and wallpaper on which pink roses climb through blue trellis. There's a tray with cups and tea bags, a little electric kettle, copies of Ideal Home and Edinburgh Today, a pile of newish novels – none, of course, by me. The window faces onto the same view that I saw from our own living room all those years ago. I plonk myself down on the little pink velvet chair and wonder whether I'm the same person as the bored young wife and mother of pre-women's lib days.

Later, my black suit hanging in the wardrobe for tomorrow, floral tribute ordered, I put on a silk shirt and trousers and go back to the drawing room where I find I'm overdressed, having come prepared for Edinburgh worthies to be more formal than we are in London these days. Senior judges and elderly captains of industry (which is what my old Scottish acquaintances have turned into) sit round the kitchen table in casual clothes. They see each other often, their conversation is the cosy, repetitive exchange of old friends – or perhaps I mean of old people. At least some of them, unlike Liza, read my books though I'd rather not have been told that the solution of the latest could be guessed as early as chapter three.

I'm pleased to see Hector, though dismayed by his high colour and the blue tinge to his lips. We had never really quarrelled even in the last days of our marriage, which ended not with a bang but a whimper. So we stand apart in a window embrasure and discuss the middle-aged pillars of society we still refer to as 'the children'. One son is a publisher, one a gardening contractor. Our daughter was the only one to do law like her father but she went to the bar in England not Scotland so would never have to appear before him. We are anxiously discussing our non-reading nine year old grandson when Liza calls us for dinner.

With the starter (crab, still in its M&S container) I'm surprised by how little has changed. There is still a constantly changing population of Mormon men in the flat across the street, and they still set out every morning in their dark suits to spread the word. And the Saturday night soak's still there. He passed out once a week, regular as clockwork, after he'd left the bar opposite and snored the night away on our front steps. The garnish of avocado, so commonplace now, is a reminder of more primitive days. "D'you remember, a friend brought one up with her on the sleeper and none of us had the faintest idea what to do with it." Was it fruit, was it a vegetable? A new taste. We weren't sure we liked it.

Game pie and an interlude for discussing an arcane dispute about fishing rights somewhere in Perthshire. Then more reminiscences.

My friends, in whose lives there has been more continuity than in mine, have a clearer memory of what happened nearly fifty years ago, and even before that. As they age they talk increasingly often about their earliest years. But this time memories are not quite so ancient. They reminisce happily: remember the family at the other end of the street? The ones with eleven children? Remember the impoverished dowager duchess who lived round the corner? She made an inevitable stir in the neighbourhood — titles still really mattered in those days — even though she wore a duffle coat and college scarf to queue at the bus stop across the road on her daily way up to the university where she was taking a degree with fellow students of her grandchildren's generation. And Madame Doubtfire's junk shop? Liza bought an opera coat there, upon which all her clothes were devoured by the moths that came with the gorgeous velvet garment.

Another thing Liza remembers is that I kept a diary. "Do you still?" she asks.

"No, my life gets turned into fiction instead," I reply.

I started a daily journal at the age of eleven, when Pop told me keeping a diary was a way of making sense of the world. The final entries date from the late 1960s. I read them before this trip north, having not opened the little volume for 40 years, during which I had completely forgotten almost everything written in it. Almost everything I thought I remembered was subtly different in the contemporaneous account.

Nobody mentions Gillian Butler until cheese (a careful selection, one hard, one blue, one runny and all perfectly *à point*) is put on the table along with some elegantly carved and arranged tropical fruit.

Hector clears his throat loudly. Then he taps a fork on the side of a glass. He may not be the oldest person here, nor in fact is he the only judge, but he is the senior one and after a decade on the appellate bench he has an automatic authority.

"Now: we must discuss the body recovered from the quarry at Mainpits."

A general murmur of agreement.

"Right, well, I spoke to the Chief Superintendent who's in charge down there. The human remains have been underwater for decades, in fact since 1964 if the identification is correct. But they will be doing all the usual tests and even without them, there's the car. I think we can be confident that it's Gillian Butler."

"The poor woman."

"She was so pretty, do you remember?"

"And her poor husband. At least he's well out of it now."

"Nobody has ever admitted to seeing her after she left that evening. I've noted down what we all seem to recall. The Brownes' dinner party."

"Gillian stayed on when Euan Butler left early to catch the sleeper."

I interrupted to say, "With Doctor Berlin. They shared a taxi to the station. I'd quite forgotten, but now you say that I can see them leaving the house together with their luggage. Funny, nobody carries cases now, do they? I wonder when rolling luggage began, can you remember?"

Hector brushed my irrelevancies aside. "Gillian left when the others did and drove home and there's nobody who remembers seeing her after we did. We're the last people who admit to having seen her alive, at dinner with the Brownes."

Which was, of course, what the old people at Liza's table had in common: another table, another meal, but under this same roof, getting on for half a century before.

1964

Hector and I were lucky to start our married lives in Forth Place. Bang in the middle of Edinburgh's New Town, it was a beautiful place to live – still is, in fact, since Hector never moved out.

Our brass nameplates were screwed to the door pillar. Mr Dorneywood, Advocate, Mr Drummond, Advocate. Hector already knew the Dorneywoods well. Liza was a few years older than me and had two small children. She took me under her wing, showing me the way around, introducing me to Edinburgh worthies and Edinburgh customs and, when necessary, showing me how to cope with domestic emergencies.

Mrs MacFarlane was our downstairs neighbour. She was the widow of a Wee Free cleric from the Hebrides who took in lodgers by arrangement with the Royal Infirmary – no followers, no noise, no electrical appliances and baths twice a week. The series of young medics who stayed there must have kept very peculiar hours since I'd never knowingly seen one.

Above the Dorneywoods lived a very old lady called (according to her brass plate) Gordon. I never met her, though once through her open front door caught a glimpse of walls closely covered with dark oil paintings of glossy cows and wet fields and leafy trees all in ornate gold frames. She kept herself to herself to such an extent that I didn't know she had died until, on our return from a weekend in the Highlands we saw there was a new brass name plate: "Mr Browne, advocate." Another lawyer. He wasn't a local man. It must have taken some nerve to force his way into the exclusive society of Edinburgh lawyers, I thought.

Some months later Mrs Browne appeared.

I'd left the children with Hector's sister Diana so as to get my hair set for the do we were going to that evening – I forget what it was. I opened the street door and saw a young woman sitting on the bottom step of the common stair. She was wearing a blue maternity smock over a blouse with a pussy-cat bow, had a leather handbag dangling from her elbow and a cigarette in a tortoiseshell holder between her fingers.

"Hullo," I said.

"Hullo." The outer door slammed leaving us in the municipal bulbs' dim light. "Oh! Please – your umbrella!"

"So sorry, did it splash you?" I stopped twirling off the raindrops.

"It's very bad luck to have it open indoors!"

"Really? Well, don't worry, the common stair is technically part of the pavement, if you go by the local by-laws," I said, but snapped it closed all the same. "Are you're waiting for someone?"

Mrs Browne said she was lurking out of the way because her husband was upstairs having a consultation with solicitors. "He says they won't think he is serious if they hear me in the house."

"That's going a bit far!" The Scottish legal system, and Scots law too, were quite different from the English; advocates didn't get together in partnerships or shared chambers, but worked as sole practitioners from home. When solicitors or clients came for meetings, the advocate's family had to keep quiet and keep out of sight, though as I told her, "I do have to keep the children from playing right outside my husband's door but I don't actually go into hiding."

"He likes me to go out when they are there. But I…" She stopped speaking and burped, with her hand in front of her mouth.

"Are you all right?" I asked

"I just feel a bit sick." The voice trembled, the corners of the mouth turned down. "In fact," she added, "I feel sick all the time."

"Oh do you? Bad luck!"

"Nobody told me it was going to be like this." She was crying now, her hand fumbling in the bag for a handkerchief. "The doctor said it would stop after three months but it hasn't."

"It's horrible isn't it?" I said with feeling.

"Somebody told me smoking would help."

"Didn't for me."

"Nothing really does. And I can't rise above it all, whatever anyone says, I just can't. My mother-in-law said…she thinks it's my fault. James says I'm making a terrible fuss."

That was the first, but very far from the last, time that Hannah Browne told me what her husband said. James had told his wife to snap out of it. James thought she shouldn't confide in outsiders. He had a list of assumptions and shibboleths, which his wife faithfully quoted.

My child isn't going to be born in some filthy public hospital, my wife will give birth in her own bed. Eating in the kitchen is not done. I can't be expected to get my own meals/ buy food/ do the washing-up. My wife wouldn't be seen dead wearing slacks. A lady wears a hat to church. Of course we are going to church, that's what one does on Sunday. A gentleman wouldn't be seen dead pushing a pram.

I was cautious about getting too close to Hannah, partly because Liza Dorneywood didn't take to her. "She's sly. You can see her, butter not melting in her mouth with that mother of his, but the expression on her face when nobody's looking – I'm surprised the old woman isn't turned into stone."

Hannah was a pretty girl, with round yellow-brown eyes, blunt, well defined features and curly hair even darker than mine. Her skin seemed tanned and bright even in Scotland's winter, whose chill made my light complexion chapped and dry. She was obviously just the right sort of person for love at first sight and a whirlwind romance. She told me that James took her to a dance at the Caledonian Club, to the theatre for a musical, to a London Scottish Hogmanay Ball. Then he came down to London again for a flying visit with a ring in his pocket, three diamonds in a row on a platinum band that had been his grandmother's. He proposed, on his knees (bare below the kilt) seven weeks after they met. They had a very quiet wedding in Edinburgh.

That did surprise me. I'd guessed from her 'received standard' voice that she had a conventional background with parents who would put on a show. "Didn't you want a big wedding, with all the trimmings? Bridesmaids, all your friends…?"

But Hannah said her parents were dead, you couldn't have a big wedding without a father to lead you up the aisle. At the ceremony in Edinburgh, she had been given away by a senior advocate who had been James's pupil master. "I had a lovely dress, Mother Browne took me to her dressmaker. The sleeves take in and out on poppers so I can wear it for dances. Of course James wore the kilt."

Half a century on, some of us recalled, he was wearing it again at the dinner party. The Dorneywoods were there, Hector and I, Euan and Gillian Butler, two other couples I already knew – the Stuarts and the Stewarts – and Dr Berlin, who turned out to be the latest medic lodging with Miss MacFarlane. James had gone down to the ground floor flat to beg Fidelis Berlin to help them out and apologise for the shockingly last minute invitation. His cousin Kirsty had waited until the very last moment to telephone and say that she had toothache and was going to cry off their dinner party. Disaster! They'd be a woman short. Inviting their neighbour was a real counsel of despair. He said,

"We had hoped of course to invite you properly but I'm jumping the gun."

Fidelis recognized him. They caught the same bus up the hill, she'd once been behind him in the queue for groceries. She said,

"I am free this evening, as it happens. If you're sure…"

"I'll be eternally grateful if you can come."

Fidelis had been to several wine-and-cheese parties given by medical colleagues and had learnt that everybody's house was freezing though for some inexplicable reason nobody else seemed to feel the cold. So she had bought some warm fabric in Jenner's, and sewed it into a floor length skirt and matching stole and with it wore a high necked black jersey and a wide patent leather belt. She had them on that evening, even though it was early July. She expected to be the only comfortable person in the room.

A female doctor was still unusual enough to make several of the guests do a double take. She was tall and dark, with a long strong nose and an assessing expression in her eyes.

"Goodness," one woman said in a high, clear voice. "Are you a Stewart?" The emphasis was on the royal name, the intonation incredulous, implications are obvious: she was not one of us. In fact though her voice had a Welsh lilt she was obviously Jewish.

"No, why?"

"You're wearing the Royal Stewart tartan."

"Is that what it is? I made it out of a blanket I got in Jenner's. I just liked the colours."

A tiny exchange, dredged from the memory of an unexceptional evening a lifetime ago. Reminded by the notes in my diary I found other details coming back. I remember helping pull someone's boots off in the little bedroom (which was already decorated as a nursery) and being told that she loved walking when it was raining, so she and her husband had come on foot.

"Oh!" Hannah darted into the room and moved the black pumps from the bed to the floor.

"What's wrong?"

"It's bad luck to put shoes on a bed."

"Golly, it's ages since I heard that, my old granny used to tell me the same thing. She said it was because that's where corpses are laid out."

I remember the Butlers arrived late. Gillian apologized a little, Euan not at all. Red-faced, with tufts of ginger hair on his otherwise bald cranium, he had recently become a judge and the other men were deferential. He handed a package wrapped in brown paper to James.

"It's nothing much – but I had a couple of good days on the Tweed."

James dropped the package onto a table. "Fish," he said.

"It was a whopper."

Hannah began, "But James mustn't…"

"It's most kind of you," James said, turning away. "My dear, put the package in the refrigerator." We all followed him into the drawing-room. Goodness, how hard Hannah must have been working. Three cut-glass decanters of sherry, dry, medium and sweet, stood on a polished silver tray; there was gin and tonic, vermouth, dry and sweet, and a choice of varieties of single malt whisky. She'd bought expensive flowers and arranged them elaborately.

I was shivering. Even if there had been central heating, which actually hardly existed in these houses in those days, it would not have been turned on in July. We huddled into our cocktail dresses, whispering about the symptoms of pregnancy, the men haw-hawing about some case with which two of them had been involved.

The room normally used as James's study smelt comfortably of pipe tobacco. It had been turned into a dining room for the evening, with all books and papers removed from the table where he normally worked and lawyers and clients would sit. Now the glassily polished mahogany was laid with lace table mats, damask starched napkins, silver candlesticks and decorative but not useful ornaments; at each place were three wine glasses, a tiny silver dish containing butter, a little goblet holding three tipped cigarettes and a small silver ashtray. One of the men picked up his side plate to look more closely at the gilt crest. Before he could comment, James said, "Montrose. A connection on the distaff side."

A connection to a Duke, even on the distaff side, evoked respect.

I remember the details of the table setting and menu because they were almost ludicrously over the top, even for those more formal days. As a birthday present from her mother-in-law Hannah had done 'the bride's course' at the domestic science college in Atholl Crescent. It was a very different way of learning to be a good wife from my trial and error. Hannah was shown how to make porridge, iron a shirt, make silver shine and glasses gleam, how to cook several of what they called old-faithful recipes, mince, fish pie, roast pheasant with all the trimmings and other elaborate dishes suitable for a dinner party. The Atholl Crescent brides were encouraged to keep their own cookery scrapbook, not like the tattered folder into which I shoved torn-out newsprint, but a tidy leather-bound volume. Hannah's scrapbook contained recipes for soufflé made with Arbroath Smokies, prawns in pink mayonnaise served on a bed of lettuce in a Coupe Jacques glass, herrings with chopped plumped California prunes, and hare pâté. Interleaved were advertisements cut from magazines for kitchen scales, solid stainless steel tea sets, universal can openers and one minute marmalade. At the front Hannah had stuck in an article cut out of the Scotsman by its discursive cookery correspondent who called himself Gastrologue[1]. The piece was called 'the night the boss comes to dinner' and recommended a simple menu because "nothing is more nerve-wracking than running backwards and forwards, face reddening and make-up deteriorating, between the sitting room and kitchen and trying to be hostess and cook at once." This was not advice that Hannah had taken tonight, instead she'd planned an ambitious menu. There was home-made liver pâté with curls of golden French toast; there was a saddle of mutton served with bashed neeps; there were isles flottantes, little mounds of meringue floating on smooth yellow custard; there was a savoury consisting of prunes and bacon.

The talk did not flow easily until the men got onto their shared profession and in particular its personnel. The conversation even became quite animated when James mentioned a woman they all knew, who wanted to become an advocate. Someone mentioned Dr Johnson and

---

1   It was, in fact, Stuart Piggott, the Professor of Archaeology at Edinburgh University.

dogs on their hind-legs preaching. We all, men and women alike, took such comments for granted, as we did the fact that Hannah was performing the tasks of cook, parlour maid, footman and butler, carrying in the elaborate dishes and handing them round in the kind of unobtrusive manner that implied her having to do so was a temporary, slightly embarrassing blip. It was Fidelis, since she didn't know the rules, who got up and said, "Here, let me help," upon which Liza and I also seized platters to carry out. The kitchen, in stark contrast to the clean and tidy reception rooms, looked as though it had been the scene of a hard-fought battle. Liza began to scrape and stack plates.

"No no, we can't do it now," Hannah said anxiously. "I must make the coffee. Please go back."

I picked up the package of salmon the Butlers had brought. "Hadn't I better just put this in the fridge?"

"I have to keep it separate from the other food," Hannah replied. "James is dreadfully allergic to fish, he nearly died last year. I can only eat it when he's not there."

Back to the laboured conversations. I picked at some grapes until Hannah came back and sat down, only to heave herself onto her feet again and say, "Ladies, shall we?" The men stood up, helped to pull back our chairs, and waited while we walked out of the room. There was a tray on a side table with four glasses and a decanter with a silver label on a chain round its neck. I don't suppose the engraved words said 'men only' but the message was perfectly clear.

In the drawing room, Hannah poured coffee into thimble sized cups and offered cigarettes in a silver box. Gillian Butler began,

"So, Dr Berlin…" – the formality keeping her at a distance – "tell us about yourself. You're a doctor?" The high, chilly voice emphasised that Gillian, the Edinburgh worthy, was speaking to an outsider, but Fidelis answered readily enough in a deep, calm voice.

What sort of doctor? Still not fully qualified! Oh. So what was she intending to specialise in?

Fidelis did not yet know whether she wanted to be a general practitioner or a specialist. She had done accident and emergency work, nearly completed her surgery rotation here in Edinburgh, and she was going to be in Oxford after that.

And what about her own family? Where was she from? What was her background? Was she – only this question was implicit, not uttered – was she a threat to our husbands' fidelity?

"I grew up in south Wales but I don't know who my parents were, I was adopted,"

"Oh!" A hand over her mouth, eyes large and glistening. "I'm so sorry. Were you a foundling?"

"No, I came to England as a small child with the kindertransport."

"The what?"

"Really, Hannah, you must have heard about them," Liza interrupted. "There are others like you in Edinburgh, Dr Berlin, other people who came on the kindertransports." Turning towards the supercilious Gillian, she said, "Think of Otto and Trudy."

"Well, but they know exactly who their parents were, they found them again after the war."

"I don't understand," Hannah said. "What's the kinder...what was the word?"

Fidelis Berlin said, "Let me explain. You know, of course, about what happened to Jewish people during the war."

"I think so." The tone was uncertain. "I mean – well, I wasn't old enough to really follow."

"When Adolf Hitler came to power in Germany in 1933, he and his Nazi party began to attack Jewish people. They made laws that stopped Jews working, gradually, over five years, more and more laws – Jews were sacked from their jobs, there were more and more things they weren't allowed to do – and they were physically attacked too. By 1938 it was pretty obvious that Jews just weren't safe in Germany any more. Lots had left already as refugees, but there weren't many countries that would let them in."

It was a saga I knew only too well since my own parents had left Germany as refugees before I was born, but the other women were listening to the story as if they had never heard it before.

"Did we let them in?"

"Well, there were limits on the numbers, but this country was very generous, and especially to children. It was a movement to save children even if the parents couldn't be saved. Trains were sent to fetch the children from Berlin, there were volunteers to look after them on the journey, and then more families volunteered to take them in when they arrived in England. Which is what happened to me."

"They had labels tied onto their clothes when they arrived, all their details were written down," Liza said.

The doctor said, "You're quite right, I had a label. But it only had my first name on it, so there's no way to trace any family. Presumably one of them put me on the train."

"Surely somebody would have noticed."

"Apparently not. It must have been chaos. In any case, what could they do? Those poor, tired, well-meaning volunteers with a trainful of miserable children – I don't blame them."

"The possibilities of muddling the children up must have been endless," Liza agreed. Then Gillian Butler said,

"They should have used tattoos. Just a simple number. Nobody could lose that." This ingenious suggestion momentarily silenced us all. Then Liza gasped,

"That's an awful thing to say!"

"Hitler thought of that idea first," I murmured.

But Dr Berlin hadn't taken offence. "You have to remember they were saving our lives."

"Didn't you try to trace your family afterwards?"

"After the war? I was seven years old."

"When you were grown-up. Haven't you been back to look."

"Back where? I wouldn't know where to begin."

"Even hearing German spoken might revive some memory," Liza said.

"You could be right I suppose. Maybe I will. As a matter of fact it's never seemed to matter very much." There was a different expression on her face, surprised, thoughtful, as though a brand new idea had come into her head.

I can still feel the flush of shame that made me, for the only time that evening, actually warm: I belonged with the rootless Jew, not with these ladies of the establishment. As if she was changing the subject Gillian began to talk about the importance of the link between mother and child, between father and child, the disaster that would ensue if it were broken.

"You'd put your head under a train to save your children, you'd die for them."

"Or kill," said Liza with a sinister gleam in her eye. "I'd kill for my children and kill anyone who came between us."

"That's a bit much!"

"A lioness protecting her cubs, that's me. I bet that's all of us if the truth be told."

"That's why I'm so busy with my charity." Gillian told her (by now, to me, well-known) anecdote about her son having his tonsils out and not being allowed to visit him. "Mothers With Children In Hospital, it's so important." She made a rehearsed speech about motherhood, quietly watched by Fidelis Berlin, who had never known its benefits. Gillian quoted Bowlby, Winnicott and other child care gurus, describing the harmful consequences a single night away from its mother might bring. (Fidelis looked quite mentally healthy, I muttered, unheard.) It's essential for mental health that the infant and young child should experience a warm, intimate and continuous relationship with his mother. Separation is harmful to inner stability and future psychological development. It makes the child feel acute anxiety, excessive need for love, powerful feelings of revenge, guilt, repression...

"I always think you overstate it," Liza remarked.

"Me too," I said.

"But you both subscribe to the charity!"

Liza said, "Yes, it's a good cause, it's just that I don't believe my boys will turn into axe murderers if they can't see me every minute of their day – after all, we've got a babysitter right now."

"But they are in their own home and familiar bed."

"They stayed with their grandmother last week, is that going to warp their little minds?"

"Without you?"

"Yes, we had a week down south, it was lovely."

"Oh did you?" Gillian Butler enthused. "We always used to go to the south west ourselves, before we had the villa, these days we go to France, but I did love it. Whereabouts were you?"

"Ilfracombe."

"Oh. Devon. We used to go to Cornwall, the far far west, the real Cornwall. It was quite unspoilt, you'd never be surprised to see a pisky or a witch – they haven't been dragged into the 20th century yet. Some of the farms – so primitive! The walls of the fields and houses are built out of boulders the size of a...a barrel. A dustbin. Enormous, as if they were growing out of the earth itself. Very primitive, like the people."

"The people? What d'you mean, primitive?" I asked, rather offended on their behalf.

"They aren't quite in the modern world. For instance, last time we were there – it must be, gosh, ten years ago – where does the time go? – we heard a real horror story, you wouldn't think we were in twentieth century Britain at all. A farmer died, we read about him, he'd been in prison. You wouldn't believe it, nowadays, never guess what he'd been convicted of. Owning a slave! Nowadays! In the 20th century!"

There were gasps from her audience and Gillian said triumphantly, "He was charged under the Slavery Act!"

"No – really? I didn't even know there was one," Liza remarked.

"He was a farmer, one of those messy, muddy small farms that you can't believe make enough to keep a dog alive, until you see the shiny new Land-Rover. And the slave was his daughter by one of the maids. Poor child, she wasn't christened, her birth was never registered, she was simply his property, can you imagine?"

"What happened to her?"

"The local doctor took her in for a while, pretty heroic of him if you think what a savage she must have been. I saw them in church, she was a scrawny little thing, can't have been more than eleven or twelve...I think they sent her off to boarding school. The best solution, really."

"Hannah, are you all right?"

Hannah, very pale, nodded and burped. "I feel sick after meals," she murmured, indicating her pregnancy as explanation.

"Oh bad luck."

At this point the door opened and the men, well fed, rosy and glossy, came in with the kind of swagger that implies we had been waiting for them on tenterhooks. All of us women shifted slightly in our seats to make room for a man to come beside us. James Browne sat between me and Fidelis Berlin and asked her what her next posting would be. "Are you planning to stay in Edinburgh?"

But she hoped to be in Oxford. "In fact my interview's tomorrow, I really must leave in a minute, I don't want to miss the train. I haven't decided between psychiatry and obs and gynae. But I think I might plump for the psychiatry. What you've all been saying this evening, it's given me ideas."

"About?" James asked in a forensic tone of voice.

"The parent child relationship. I haven't thought about it much before."

"Really?"

"It's rather outside my experience."

"I suppose it must be."

"And what about you, Isabel? Hannah tells me that you're terribly clever!"

"She only says that because I was at Cambridge. I'm just a housewife now."

"No career plans?"

I answered, "No."

My words were utterly truthful – then. Half a century on it's embarrassing to admit it.

Fidelis Berlin and Euan Butler left early, sharing a taxi to catch the sleeper train and we went soon afterwards because the next morning we were setting off very early for the summer holidays. Hector flopped straight into bed but I pottered around for a while before cleaning my teeth. In those apartments in Edinburgh's New Town, built as such in the eighteenth or early 19th century, the lavatories were ventilated by a small square of windows high up on the thick wall, which opened onto the common stair, sometimes emitting embarrassing sounds and smells. I was in there when I heard more goodbyes upstairs and the door of the Browne's flat slam closed. Gillian Butler was leaving with the Stewarts, speaking in a low but audible voice. "I could swear I've seen her before."

"Dr Berlin?"

"No, I mean Hannah. I can't pin it down. But it will come to me. Euan always says I've got a memory like an elephant."

Rather too loud in the sleeping house, a man's voice called "Gillian. Come on if you want a lift."

"I'd love a lift."

"It's getting late."

"Okay okay, just coming!"

I heard the patter of party shoes clip-clopping down stairs and the front door banged shut. I'd been silent and motionless on the lavatory and was now about to pull the plug when I heard another door softly closing: the Brownes' front door, two floors up from me.

Knowing that I would not have time in the morning, before going to bed I wrote a quick note to Fidelis, quite formal as was the custom in those days.

"Dear Dr Berlin, I hope you won't think I'm interfering but I had the impression at the Brownes' this evening that you might think of making further enquiries about your background. Just in case you're not already fully equipped with your own lawyers and advisers you might like to know that my father is a solicitor and one of his many specialties is making enquiries in Germany about lost property and family. If you are wondering where to start he would be quite a good place. Good luck! And have a good summer. We'll be back in early September. Yours sincerely, Isabel Drummond."

I went to bed with my head full of the last minute chores I would have to do in the morning before we left for the punishing drive south. There were still few stretches of motorway. Most roads were miles of single track on which we were inevitably and repeatedly stuck behind a heavy lorry and there was nowhere to have a pee or change a baby's nappy. If a personal hell awaits me, it will consist of endless journeys in a car full of screaming infants.

Fidelis had finished her stint at the Royal Infirmary but wasn't to start at the John Radcliffe in Oxford until November. Meanwhile she stayed in Edinburgh doing very short term locum posts which gave her widely varied experience. It was at an outpatient clinic in a village in Fife that she had her first encounter with the occult.

Michelle was fifteen, and had been referred by a general practitioner whose scribbled note said 'delusional?' Michelle was prone to going into a trance and while in that condition apparently recovered suppressed memories of horrible experiences which included spiders, worms, huge figures wearing black robes with invisible faces, and red symbols drawn on the floor; she soon added apparent memories of being touched, felt, and hurt 'down there.' During their second consultation Michelle described a table on which she was spread-eagled and tied down – at which point in her trance she came to, screaming. The nurse fetched the adult who had brought her that day, a genial, open-faced clergyman who asked to speak to Fidelis privately.

"I can't talk about my patient," she said, and Michelle said,

"That's okay Miss, you talk to the Reverend, he'll tell you what's going on."

The Rev Jeremy Bennett, smiling and calm, explained to Fidelis that he was a witch finder.

"I beg your pardon?"

"A witch finder. Now Dr Berlin, I can see that you find that an exotic notion but my profession is an ancient one, much older than yours."

"A witch finder. Right. I see. And…um…how do you do it?"

"Not, I assure you, by looking for a Devil's teat or a sixth finger or by other such physical signs. We don't throw the poor woman into a pond and see if she floats, nothing so primitive, ha ha! But you must understand, the devil walks on earth still, and has his worshippers still.

The black mass is still celebrated, up and down the land. Satan still walks."

"Satan? Black mass?" Fidelis did not know how to reply. She wondered whether this man should be the patient rather than his young charge. He went on,

"This poor young woman is one of those who has been subjected to the vilest of treatment. I can hardly describe it, even to a medic like you – impregnation with the sperm of an animal! The sexual abuse, the cruel rituals!"

"Michelle told you all this, has she?"

"She has suppressed the memory, as such young women invariably do, for otherwise they would not be able to live in a world that had treated them so cruelly."

Fidelis felt at a loss. This deluded man was not her patient; if he had been she would have certified him. Instead he was free to spread stories of this poisonous nonsense. As she sat there apparently writing, the possible future rushed through Fidelis's mind: hysterical girls claiming to have experienced everything this pillar of the community described; their parents panicked; police investigations, prosecutions, prison sentences, children taken into care – somehow she had to stop him. After he left she listened to Michelle, who by now had remembered more details of her experiences. Naked, spread-eagled on a cold table, tied down, a woman in black with a cat sitting on her shoulder and men with huge 'things' coming towards her – at which point Michelle screamed and slumped in a chair as though she'd fainted.

The Reverend Bennett was in the waiting room when Fidelis came out. He started forward eagerly. "You'll be reporting this to the social services then?"

"Haven't you done it yourself?"

"It would be more persuasive coming from a medic, after all you have examined her."

The protocols were perfectly clear. At this point Fidelis should write a report for the social services department and also for the police; she should ensure that this juvenile was removed from the environment where such things happened to her.

That is to say, she should do those things if she believed the allegations. Fidelis found herself absolutely unable to get her head round these accusations. Physical examination of the girl showed no signs of any abuse though she was not a virgin.

That weekend Fidelis took Saturday off and caught the early train to London. She'd been dubious about going so far just for a party but it would be a golden opportunity to ask Benjamin Perkins' advice. Unlike most of her friendships with men, this one had not begun with an affair. He was a full generation her senior and their relationship, originally that of teacher and pupil, now was more like that of a father and daughter; sleeping with him would have would have felt like incest, and all the more so since he had married Rosa, who was Fidelis's contemporary. Fidelis was anxious for his approval. She dressed carefully (because he noticed women's clothes) in a Jean Muir shift under a Bill Gibb coat, and moderated her language.

Fidelis knew that Benjamin Perkins had been a historian before he started his medical training but had no idea his dissertation had been about witch-hunts in early-modern Europe. "Just the person I need!" she said cheerfully. They had met for tea in Brown's Hotel, and in its incongruously cosy surroundings he told her about the brutal methods by which supposed witches were identified, listing the meticulous examination of their bodies in search of a 'Devil's teat', the immersion in water to see if they floated, or keeping them awake for days and watching to see if a 'familiar' appeared. "It was all simple and primitive and the end was burning at the stake."

"What about the Black Mass?"

"It was only invented in the 19th century, and as for white witches and Wicca – well, that's a very modern phenomenon."

"I know. I've seen a leaflet about it." Fidelis had read the bland prose that explained that Wicca was nothing more than the 'native spiritual path of Britain' which teaches that the individual controls her own destiny. Far from casting magic spells, Wicca relied on willpower. That might be helped along by 'visualisation exercises' which included such rituals as writing down and burning the wish, burning a candle while thinking of the wish, circle casting and pentacle drawing. "I don't know where my clergyman witch-finder fits into all this," Fidelis said.

"What have you done about him so far?"

"Kept it quiet as far as I could. Just imagine the panic, the publicity – there'd be mass hysteria. A witch-finder indeed! The man should be defrocked."

"I'm not disagreeing, Fidelis, but you do realize that there are still active witches."

"Self-styled."

"Remember when I did a locum in Cornwall?"

"I certainly do, when you came back you said you'd been the only psychiatrist west of the Tamar."

"No paediatricians either, or traffic lights, or moving staircases."

"You're making that up."

"No, honestly, it's really backward. And I came across a coven of witches. I tell you what they are, they're simply people who are trying to exert some control over a messy and random world. They don't need the rituals or the words, call them spells if you want to, and if they've got familiars or fetishes it's to focus their attention as a rosary does."

"But they believe in their powers themselves?" Fidelis said.

"Of course. But then so do faith healers and homoeopaths."

"You make it all sound very simple."

"I know but I think that is the explanation, whether they mean to do harm or good. The women I met were rather like conventional do-gooders, but they called themselves white witches. They let me watch one of their midnight masses in a stone circle on Bodmin Moor."

The waiter brought more hot water and for a moment there was silence between them. Then Benjamin said, "I get the feeling that this is upsetting you. Is that why you came all this way?"

"Oh Benjamin, you read me like a book."

"So what is it that is worrying you?"

"That's the trouble, I don't know! It's the idea of a Black Mass, I can't pin it down, there's something at the back of my mind that makes me feel sick and frightened and lost when I think of it. And yet I know it's all silly, as you have been saying yourself…"

"Nothing is silly that affects you so powerfully, but the question is why."

"If only I knew!"

"Clearly this is not the moment to try to find out. So all I'll say is that those I saw were perfectly harmless – well, obviously they couldn't do any harm even if they wanted to, but the point is they didn't want to. I tell you what it was most like – a Women's Institute meeting. The only difference was, this lot didn't have clothes on. But as for your witch-finder, he's the one who needs to be certified, not her."

We stayed in London with my parents, had a long weekend in Wiltshire with Hector's favourite cousin and then drove on for our fortnight's real holiday in Cornwall. I found the cottage through an agency recommended, as it happens, by Gillian Butler. Sunset Cottage was in the Land's End district, nestled in a fold of the hills and facing west, with a glimpse of the sea from the bedrooms upstairs, and a face on view of the prolonged summer sunsets reflected in the distant water. One's memory shows only the principal highlights of such holidays, as if we'd spent fourteen days on the beach in blazing heat. It takes the scrawls in my diary to remind me how many days consisted of grumpy outings to 'wet weather attractions', and that in two weeks, our family of five had to visit one of the local doctors' surgeries three times. I'd asked our landlady for advice, and been told the life story of all three medics who worked within reach. Dr Williams, a local man, Dr Tierney, old, with shaking hands but X-ray eyes, Dr Pettifer, "a long streak of nothing, he is – now, my dearie, if only you could have seen the old doctor, Dr Maberley, sad…"

"What's sad, Mrs Tresize?"

"Nothing went right for him after that girl…"

A long anecdote about a good-for-nothing little madam, adopted when she was nine or ten by the good doctor and his wife. "All down to her, it was, the Tregidgas, they've farmed at Roscollow for centuries, they had their own ways, tradition – miscarriage of justice…" As the incoherent saga led our landlady down unconnected alleys, it came to me that I knew what she was talking about. This was the story Gillian Butler had heard when she stayed in a rather grander rented property in the next village. The illegitimate child of a local farmer, born on the farm, her birth never registered, so nameless and numberless, never sent to school or inoculated, but instead put to work on the farm, used in loveless sex by the farm workers – her half brothers, her unadmitted cousins – abused by the farmer's wife and legitimate children. It had been slavery indeed, ended when the girl threw herself on the doctor's mercy. Cleaned up, caught up – for she was very quick to learn – done up – "You wouldn't have known her, that little madam" – she was still at some fancy boarding school when her benefactor, the doctor, died, and she never came back. But her story was still told; so was the story of her farmer father, who came out of prison and hanged himself in the cowshed.

Mrs Tresize couldn't see what her neighbour had done that wasn't what his ancestors had always done. "We have our own ways," she said. "Don't need folk from up-country telling us what to do."

"Where is she now, what happened to her, Mrs Tresize?"

"I wouldn't know, madam, but she was as clever as a cartload of monkeys, that one, knew how to get what she wanted, wrapped the men round her little finger. Poor Dr Maberley, he was that bamboozled. And as for the Tregidgas, they've all gone. Driven out of the parish." A nasty story, made nastier by its teller's loyalties. A truth that was stranger than fiction.

Hector and I decided to move on rather sooner than planned because of the incessant rain, drove to Plymouth and took the ferry to France. We had a couple of weeks in the Dordogne followed by a leisurely drive north stopping with relations and friends. So we were away for nearly the whole of the long legal vacation, and out of touch in a way that one can hardly remember or imagine now.

Then came the hassle of organising everything for the new school term and a new au pair (Polish, this time) and general catching up. So the Brownes' baby, born in late August, was nearly six weeks old by the time I went to visit them.

In those days middle-class women expected to stay in bed for a ludicrously long time after having their babies – with warnings of prolapse and worse if one disobeyed – though six weeks was over the top. All the same, that's where Hannah still was. James's mother, who looked capable but exhausted, warned me that she was still feeling very poorly. "It's the bairn, of course, but she's got herself that upset about everything and anything, politics, the test match, the nuclear bomb, even Mrs Butler. Did ye no' hear about her? Run off! What kind of a person must she be, to leave her man like that?"

Nowadays of course, someone would have sent a text or an e-mail or I would have read the story on Twitter. It's hard to think myself back into a time when we only telephoned long distance in cases of life or death. People did write letters but as it happened either nobody had written to us or the mail had gone astray for we'd missed all the gossip about Gillian Butler leaving home.

Several people told us the moment we were back, still talking about it weeks later, still speculating about the whole imaginable list of reasons for a wife to walk out. We'd never known the Butlers well so it didn't mean very much to me and I couldn't see why it should to Hannah either. It seemed to me that she must be suffering from nothing more – or less – complicated than post-natal depression. I found her in bed. The baby lay in a lace-hung cradle wearing pink from top to toe. She had a thick thatch of darkish hair and her eyes were already topaz brown.

I said, "What a lovely baby. What's her name?"

"She's called Allegra. James chose it. He says it means happiness."

"He must be thrilled."

"I suppose he is."

"What are you saying, Hannah, of course he is," Mrs Browne said severely.

"But he can't get a night's sleep, with her crying."

"I don't suppose you can either," I said.

"Actually, I'm not sure how interested he is in babies."

"This wee one will be a dote, you'll see, once she starts responding," James's mother said firmly.

I said Hannah must be tired.

"Indeed she must," Mrs Browne agreed and began to tell me how many people had come to visit. "I've heard that when Mrs Dorneywood had the twins they said 'no visitors for a fortnight', at least that's what Mrs Butler told her. Mrs Dorneywood waited until she felt strong enough, which was very sensible." She picked the baby out of the cradle. "Time for your bottle, isn't it my wee bairn," she said. Once she was out of the room, Hannah said,

"When I watch him going up the hill towards Parliament House every morning I'd swear he was glad to escape, the way he walks, sort of eagerly, bouncing up and down. And then when he comes back down in the evening he looks so dejected. It makes me wonder if he really wants to come home."

"Hannah, what nonsense!" I exclaimed. "How can you say that, with that lovely baby?"

"I know he always wanted children, right from when we…"

"When you first met? How did you, actually?"

"Through his cousin, we lived in the same hostel in London, both our secretarial colleges had recommended it. They'd found me a job too, I was a copy typist in a fruit import business. And then James came to London for a conference with this English lawyer, and he dropped in on Marie, and she wasn't there just then, so I said he could wait till she got back and then…"

"The rest is history," I said.

"Isabel, can I ask you something?"

"Of course."

She went bright red and spoke in a very low voice. "How soon after having a baby do I have to let him…well, you know what I mean? He wants to…you know – and I thought, after all this, can't I – do I have

-25-

to…"

"You know what, this is something you should ask a doctor."

"I couldn't possibly. Dr Sturrock? No!"

"Well, there's a woman doctor under this very roof, at least there was. I haven't run into her again since your dinner party, do you know if she's still around?"

But Hannah certainly wasn't going to consult our neighbour. Standing at the window after the baby's afternoon feed, she'd put her down in the muslin draped cradle and then waited for James to come into view. She watched her husband walking down the hill, his bowler hat at a jaunty angle, his tightly rolled umbrella swinging at his side. He crossed the road and disappeared from sight immediately below. Hannah went to her own front door and opened it. She heard the door onto the street slam closed, three floors below, but then another unexpected sound: a triple knock of knuckles on wood, a door opening, low voices murmuring and a door closing. She waited again. He was not coming up the stone stairs. He had gone into the ground floor flat. He was visiting the doctor.

Hannah's mother-in-law had hinted as much. She'd been given a warning by the landlady: the lady doctor was no better than she should be, a temptress, a Jezebel.

Fidelis went south again in September. She treated herself to a sleeper though even a third class ticket was more than she could well afford. She soon regretted spending her own money in order to endure ten hours on a hard bunk under a scratchy blanket, breathing in the tobacco fumes from the man in the lower left and in the small hours when the old lady below was snoring, beating off the man from the upper right.

Fidelis was on her way to see the lawyer I'd recommended to her – my father. He knew much more about cases like hers than the Cardiff generalist her foster parents had consulted.

Fidelis was one of 10,000 children rescued from Nazi Germany and taken without their parents to safety in Britain. By 1945 there were millions of displaced children in Europe. Fidelis was better off than most in that she lived with affectionate foster parents and could remember no other home; but unluckier than many because her identity was lost. Her real name might or might not have been Fidelis, but her surname was certainly not Berlin since that had been chosen for her in England on her arrival from the German capital. So it was a little pointless to include her name in lists of displaced children after the war, but as her foster parents had agreed with the representative of the Red Cross, there wasn't anything else they could do.

At the time there were literally hordes of displaced persons, millions of lost families, hundreds of thousands of searchers. Nothing came of it, nor at the time did she know that the investigation into her own history was going on.

Growing up with the Christian, Fabian couple, Fidelis always knew that they were not her parents. During the early years her crippled 'Poppa' and his bustling, romantic, affectionate wife Auntie Megan conscientiously reminded her that one day her own mum and dad would come and find her. Looking back, Fidelis realized that it must have been in the middle of the war, towards the middle of 1942 that references to her parents tailed off. It was about then that the fate of Europe's Jews had become known.

During her teens it didn't seem to matter very much to Fidelis. The words mother and father meant something obscure and irrelevant. She didn't need them. Presumably Poppa and Auntie Megan must have told her that no traces of her family had been found, at some point when she was thought old enough to bear the information, but it had made little impression on her. In fact, she realized later, and was dreadfully ashamed of herself for thinking it, she probably wouldn't have been all that pleased if her own parents had turned up, needy and disruptive and embarrassingly foreign. In fact, awful confession though it was, she might as well admit that it would have been quite inconvenient. There was a lot to be said for being free from family demands, fond though she was of her foster family.

Poppa, who had lost a leg in the First World War, died in 1952 when Fidelis was 14; Auntie Megan died four years later and in sorting out her papers Fidelis found the first report of the failure to trace the family of the child known as Fidelis Berlin. Dated November 1945, it was on the Red Cross official paper, a standard printed form in which names were filled into spaces in a copperplate handwriting. Then she came across another folder which showed that in the following year Poppa and

Auntie Megan had commissioned a private search *via* the firm of solicitors in Cardiff. It was short but kind. Their investigations had been unable to add to the information, or lack of information, provided by the Red Cross. The letter had a handwritten postscript: "This is not necessarily the end for your foster daughter, there is always hope that further information will come to light. Unfortunately, unless and until it does, I know of no other avenues to investigate. I am most sincerely sorry not to have been able to help you in this matter."

By the time Fidelis went down from Scotland to consult my father, it was getting too late to trace lost families; the West German economic miracle was in full swing; and most clients came to ask if they were entitled to money as a restitution of what they'd lost. The West German government paid out millions in compensation. My father helped countless people to recover some of it, always (as he told me later) sick at heart to be weighing cash against the lost lives. Fidelis could have claimed financial compensation. But she wanted something else: to find out who she was.

There was not much hope of doing so. My father had initially returned to Berlin immediately after the war, having left Germany in 1933 as a penniless refugee, and spent the war years as an enemy alien, thirteen years later, newly a British Subject and wearing the uniform of a British Lieutenant-Colonel, he climbed into an aeroplane for the first time in his life and arrived back in Berlin as a temporary member of the Control Council of Germany, derisively known as 'Charlie Chaplin's Grenadiers.' His letters describe an intensely emotional and bewildering moment.

Everything had been reduced to ashes and rubble. Streets and buildings were hardly identifiable, the combination of such masses of debris with burnt out buildings and the utter hopelessness seemed unique. Once the initial shock had passed, he settled into his assigned apartment, with a German housekeeper (known as a batwoman or 'bedwoman'), began to find his way round and tried to make contact with people he had known. He also tried to trace people on behalf of his clients. At the time he was the junior partner in a small firm, glad of any work that came along. For obvious reasons a lot of what did come along concerned other European refugees; many of his clients were seeking restitution of property; others compensation for the careers they didn't achieve and property they had not been permitted to enjoy; and some were seeking the answers to questions about lost family. He was able to help a lot of them. By the time Fidelis went to see him most of such queries and investigations were finished, successfully or otherwise.

Obviously he never told me what happened at their meeting – he retained professional confidentiality to the very end – but his client Fidelis herself was far less cagey.

She'd expected a dusty Dickensian atmosphere and was surprised to find that the offices of Janson, Hollyokes and Arnold were shining and modern. Fidelis saw that Mr Arnold didn't resemble his daughter, but there were photographs on his desk of Isabel and another young woman (almost certainly a sister) who resembled her and an older woman who didn't.

Louis Arnold looked like a man whose pin-striped suit had been tailored in Savile Row and shoes handmade in Jermyn Street. He wore a silk tie with broad stripes in pink and apple green. In fact he seemed like the archetypal English gentleman until he opened his mouth and spoke with a strong foreign accent. He was a sharply observant man and immediately said, "Didn't Isabel tell you? I'm a refugee too, like you, I'm even from Berlin. The difference is that I left under my own steam as an adult in thirty three, and my parents escaped in time. They're in Haifa. But yours, I gather, are lost so far without trace? Sit there, there's tea if you'd like some – shall I be mother?"

He was a good listener, silent but receptive as Fidelis told him what she knew. An unaccompanied infant, a label with the name Fidelis, no other evidence at all; or if there had been any, now long lost.

"They were a bit disorganized, those people on the children-transport trains, I've met some of them over the years," he said. "But so brave and good. Far sighted too. Most people couldn't imagine that the Germans could ever set out to harm children. They thought it was simply inconceivable."

Fidelis asked him if he had heard of other cases of unidentified infants on those refugee trains. He said that he certainly had and told her that towards the end, in 1939, many parents had become desperate to save their children, having given up hope for themselves. There were stories of changed identities and stolen places on the refugee trains. "One mother, standing near the railway line at a place where trains slowed to a crawl, threw a swaddled infant with great accuracy in through the open window. Another must have managed to board the train at Berlin, for she handed her baby to a teenaged boy saying, "Hold her for a minute, will you please?", left the compartment and was never seen again. When the train pulled into Hook of Holland 24 hours later, the teenager was still sitting in the same place, still holding the baby. They had to be prised apart."

"Those poor children, what a trauma to have to overcome."

"Yes, the experience must have left its effect on a good many of them. But not all. Look, for example, at yourself."

"I was lucky with my foster family."

"That's not always enough. There needs to be a certain inherent toughness – some of the cases I've seen – well, never mind that. Let me tell you what I think we should do."

Mr Katzenellenbogen would be sent to search for information. That was what he did. Mr K haunted my childhood, turning up at our home at the oddest times. He was always awkward with me, having no idea how to talk to children, or later to girls. He looked like the ferret that he metaphorically was, a tame ferret, living in his master's pocket. My father was his master, using him not exactly as a private investigator but as a cross between a fixer and a runner, who did the things a solicitor couldn't or shouldn't do himself. A pre-war Jewish refugee himself, he had no objection to going back to Germany, so he often went on behalf of those others who said they would never set foot on German soil again. He came in useful for hundreds of post-war compensation and restitution cases, when it was necessary to get witnesses to prove that the claimants really had formerly owned the property which had been expropriated by the Nazis, or to hunt the details of lost relations or to check archives for wills and other legal documents. It was through this kind of detective work that jewels, paintings, even houses and businesses, stolen by the Nazis, were found and restored to the rightful owners, or their heirs. If, 20 years on, there was any information to find about Fidelis Berlin, Katzenellenbogen would almost certainly have found it. But he came to a dead end.

"Dear Dr Berlin, I write to advise you that in accordance with your instructions we have made further investigations into the question of your parentage. Despite careful research in the available archives Mr Katzenellenbogen was unable to identify your family. In fact he found no information or hint or clue to help him identify the baby on the kinder-transport. While I sympathise deeply with your desire to find or at least identify your family, I would be lax in my duty if I failed to advise you that there is little hope of acquiring further information and that I do not recommend investing further money, time or effort in the search." In his even, intelligent handwriting my father had added a postscript on a separate sheet of paper. "The only conclusion has to be that your identity was purposely hidden by the person, whoever it was, who smuggled you onto that train. There could be many reasons for such an action – a marital dispute for example – and one has to remember that the people involved cannot have dreamed that this parting from their children was more than a temporary measure. They all expected to be reunited when the emergency was over. What actually happened was unimaginable before as it still is afterwards. I am so sorry not to have better news for you. If there is ever anything else I can do for you, do not hesitate to ask."

"I don't care a bit," she told her friends. "I'm me, I'm free and whatever my nature, my nurture made me." In the swinging pendulum of psychological fashion this was a period when nurture was definitely regarded as the predominant influence. All the same, there must have been some submerged fear of what nature might have endowed her with, for Fidelis was to make life-choices, subconsciously or perhaps purposefully, that meant she was never sufficiently committed to any man to have his child.

Hannah hardly set eyes on Fidelis again before she moved away from Edinburgh, but she listened obsessively for her husband's return home, making sure he wasn't inveigled into the ground floor flat. It must have been an uncomfortable household, the wife resentful and suspicious, her husband frustrated, both of them insane with exhaustion. The eighteenth century builders had effectively soundproofed the separate apartments, with thick floors and cinders as noise insulation, so one normally heard nothing from above or below. But sound floats between open windows so I knew only too well that Allegra cried at night. And cried...

She would have been about three months old when I met James Browne as we were both coming into the house, and he told me that Hannah had gone through to Glasgow to stay with his mother that morning. She needed a complete rest.

Hector would have exclaimed, "Thank God for that." I merely said, "That sounds sensible."

"Dr Sturrock thought a change of scene would do her good. She hasn't been herself at all. And my mother's happy to take care of the wee one."

He was a short, square-shouldered, sandy-coloured man, with fierce blue eyes, his chin jutting forward, his fists clenched. Why didn't he come away in and have a drink? I offered. Keep me company for a while as Hector was in court in Galashiels and would be back late. I poured James whisky, plied him with peanuts, and he sat quiet and observant as I came in and out of the room, repeatedly called away to turn off lights and say goodnights and sort out fights and all the other rhyming rituals that go with motherhood. Relaxed, perhaps, by these intimate glimpses, James became all confiding.

He told me about himself, details he'd probably soon regret imparting. He wasn't a public schoolboy from a landed background but wished he was, wished he'd inherited wealth and social status. In fact he came from what he called 'a good family' which had distant kinship with grander people. He was very proud of his family tree. He hadn't been to public school but to a city academy. Then came military service. "Just caught the tail end," he told me. "Germany in forty five – the less said about that the better."

But as men usually do, he said more. He'd been in the army of occupation. He'd seen things, done things – unspeakable. Indescribable things. Belsen.

He veered away from that subject to describe German hausfraus scavenging in gutters and children who stood offering for sale a single button, a bunch of dandelions, themselves. He mentioned the British servicemen sentenced to firing squad execution after raping German girls. "The soldiers always missed. The Tommy wouldn't shoot his mates. So the officers had to finish them off."

"It preys on your mind?"

"Sometimes. I do have bad dreams."

"But you got a medal, DSO wasn't it? Hannah told me."

"She talks too much."

"But they don't give out the Distinguished Service Order for nothing. Of course Hannah's proud of it."

He took a swig of whisky and said, "When I was demobbed I had a medal, a scrap of stone from Hitler's bunker, an army revolver, some friends who were going into the law and not much else. So that's me, if you wanted to know."

"You've done very well for yourself then."

"Aye, well enough – so far."

All the old furniture, the silver, the oil paintings, came from salerooms; the flat in Forth Place was heavily mortgaged. None of that worried him. James knew that he was an effective advocate and a good lawyer. He made a lot of money every year, would make more and in the not too distant future the signs of prosperity would be based on reality, a healthy bank account and all debts repaid; and when he became a judge, the title. "You needn't say anything about this to Hannah, mind, it would only worry her, especially now. She's very vulnerable, very sensitive, and so needy. She lost her own parents, you know."

"I noticed she hadn't mentioned her family but I didn't like to ask."

"She was an adopted child and her adoptive parents both died the year she went to college. She was all alone in the world when we met. I tell her we have to have a large family to make up for it, especially as I'm an only child too."

"Does she want to have a large family?"

"I think she's a wee bittie scared just now." He breathed heavily in and out, stood up, sat down, met my eyes, looked away. "The idea of going through all that again…"

Oh God, I thought, here it comes. This is what he really wants to talk about.

"She had a bad time."

He burst out with what sounded like a rehearsed speech. He'd fallen in love with Hannah at first sight. He knew fine he was twice her age but if ever there was a lassie needed looking after, she was the one. They kissed and held hands while courting, heavy petting (in those days few young people went 'all the way') and then when it was their honeymoon she'd been so bashful, shy – you wouldn't actually say she rejected him, but there was something wrong, after all it wasn't as though he was completely inexperienced.

"She just doesn't like it!" he burst out in the tone of an aggrieved, disappointed child. "Will she come round in the end? What do you think – as a woman – I can't force her!"

I uttered platitudes about youth, inexperience, the memory of childbirth and love conquering all.

"Women forget, don't they? It's nature's way."

Even in those days, still in my docile phase, I was thoroughly sceptical about nature's way. What does Mother Nature care about her children's health or happiness? Nothing. Nada. Zilch. All that matters to her is that they are conceived and born, never mind in what squalor. Left to nature, where would I be? Not here! Not like this! Without interference one of my babies would have been born dead, strangled by the umbilical cord, and I'd have died myself in delivering the next one if I hadn't had an emergency Caesarean. And if we'd survived at all, nature would already have turned me into a toothless hag, and my children would have been scarred by smallpox or died of it.

And it was nature's way that killed James Browne that very evening. If I had only asked him to stay and have an omelette with me he wouldn't have died. I felt like a murderer.

Usually if he was on his own James went to the New Club for dinner but after our unsatisfactory and embarrassing conversation on a subject for which we both lacked the vocabulary, he apparently didn't feel like company. Having said goodbye to me and climbed the stairs to his own home, he had decided to make himself a meal. There was cold ham in the fridge, and butter and tomatoes, and in a painted pottery dish with a lid shaped like a sitting hen, some unidentified paste, flecked green with chopped parsley and red with paprika, tasting and smelling powerfully of garlic. James laid the kitchen table for one, with a cloth, silver cutlery, good china, a starched napkin, and a crystal wine glass. He'd put out a decanter of claret, a toast rack, butter in a silver dish and the pâté in its gaudy container. He had served himself a good-sized scoop, piling high his triangle of toast with the savoury concoction, and he had eaten, according to the pathologist, about four ounces before apparently realising that the pâté contained fish.

His body was found in the passage between the kitchen and the telephone in the hall. The sudden, violent anaphylactic shock had killed him.

The procurator fiscal suggested later that the pottery dish misled him: he must have supposed that the pâté it contained was made of chicken or turkey. Where it had come from was anyone's guess. The widow insisted that she would never have brought anything made of fish into the house. Nor, obviously, would James himself. Had it been a present? Probably. At that stage, so soon after the baby's birth, lots of visitors arrived with gifts of food. The Brownes' larder contained boxes of chocolate, jars of marmalade and jam, containers of soup, two rich fruit cakes, some home-made shortbread and a casserole dish full of mutton and barley stew.

The police interviewed as many friends and clients as they could find, but nobody admitted having brought the terrine to the Brownes. Subsequent analysis proved that the pâté had been made of some freshwater fish, pike probably or something else sufficiently tasteless to seem, in combination with herbs, spices and garlic, to be meat.

How unspeakably mortified James Browne would have been to know that after he died Hector had to organise a whip round among their colleagues to collect cash for the dead man's dependants; and to know that without that collection his wife and daughter might not have eaten that week. His secret was out: and it was a shaming one in that society. Not so much the pretence of being richer than he was, which was normal and natural, not at all the fact that he was a self-made man – which was to his credit – but that in living above his means and dying unprepared, he'd left his family destitute.

2011

The service in St. Giles is macabre: not a funeral, since the recovered bones are in a police mortuary, not quite a memorial service either, because so few people in the congregation ever knew Gillian Butler, nor a celebration of a life cut short so early. A lot of people have come, but the majority of them, I'm pretty certain, out of simple curiosity. There is no reception afterwards, so Liza Dorneywood takes me directly from the cathedral to the airport. She drives badly, never indicating, seldom changing up from second gear. Gritting my teeth and trying not to look at the road I say,

"What now, do you think?"

"Let's hope it doesn't take long for the police to discover what happened and who did it. We're in for a pretty uncomfortable time otherwise as the last people who saw her alive."

"Though we weren't the only ones."

"The last time anyone saw Gillian was that evening in James and Hannah Browne's house. Hector says the police don't seem to think there's a connection but they haven't got anyone else to focus on."

"There was someone else at that last dinner too."

"The lady doctor, I know, she's on the list, but she was just an outsider, not one of us. I never did understand why the Brownes invited her.

But as it happens the police have already eliminated her from their inquiries. She was definitely on the sleeper train that night, she was in Oxford before Gillian disappeared and apparently she can even prove it. Doesn't that seem extraordinary after all these years? Something to do with keeping a diary and claiming expenses for travelling."

"I wonder what happened to Hannah Browne," I said. "Did you ever hear any more from her after she left Edinburgh?"

"I had always thought she must have gone back to her family – didn't someone say she came from Cornwall?"

"I think so – but I can't remember any details. Any name – somebody must know where she is."

"Actually that's exactly what we thought you might find out."

"What?"

"People-tracing is your specialty, isn't it? At least it's what it says on your website."

"You want me to track Hannah down?"

I fix my gaze on my lap to avoid the sight of Liza's erratic lane discipline. It comes to me why they are all in a hurry to find Hannah Browne and what they want from her. She was the outsider – perhaps the destined scapegoat. Liza says,

"Isabel – we'll pay the going rate for finding..."

"Don't be silly."

"But we need you to do this. Look at it from our point of view – think of the scandal, think of the effect on Hector's reputation, that must be important to you even if it's only for your children's sake. Look what it's doing to us – you could see how upset my poor old boy was this morning. He's not a well man. We've got to get to the bottom of what happened that evening, where did Gillian go afterwards, how did she get there, what was the connection between Gillian Butler and the Brownes."

"After all these years? It's a bit late."

"But we didn't know that Gillian was dead till now."

"You all thought she'd gone off with some man."

"And wouldn't have blamed her either."

"How's that?"

"Her husband was a bully. Emotional and physical." Correctly interpreting my silence, Liza goes on, "For heaven's sake, Isabel, you've been a social worker..."

"Well, not exactly. Not qualified."

"Never mind, he wasn't the only one, you know perfectly well that it wasn't unusual then, so we all just thought Gillian'd had enough. Like we did when you walked out on Hector."

"That's completely different. Hector never…never…not one single time. You don't think I'd have stayed with him for one single day if…"

"Ok, ok, I believe you. But Euan Butler was different. The thing is though, he expected Gillian to come back sooner or later, when she'd made her point. That's what we all thought too. So nobody really looked for her very hard."

"But surely, after a while, when nothing was heard, there must have been an attempt to find her."

"I don't know if Euan tried anything. We didn't see much of him after she'd gone, I never liked him, to be perfectly honest I always thought he was a bit of a brute, and I'd have run away myself if I'd been married to him. And if he tried to put the authorities onto finding her, well, they'd have said she was free white and twenty one. Do you remember that saying?"

"All the same…"

"Actually, I do remember somebody coming to ask about her, but I've no idea if he was an official or a private detective, but either way, if she'd chosen to bolt it wasn't up to the police to drag her back. Or to anyone else, it would have been straight nosy-parkering interference. People have a right to drop out if they want to."

Liza's tone is a message in itself. She evidently disapproves strongly of my new job too. I find myself wondering whether she has a personal reason for it.

"Of course. It's one of the basic principles I operate on," I said.

"Anyway, we all just thought she'd met someone else."

Instead of which…

Trainee divers had come upon the remains, no longer a body but a disarticulating skeleton. Skin, hair and fabrics had long since disintegrated though various objects which had fallen off the woman's remains were dredged out of the silt on the quarry's floor. The wedding ring which was the initial means of identification with, engraved on the inside surface, the words 'Gillian Euan always'; a silver necklace; a belt heavy with brass studs and loops; a large stone, still held inside the net of an indestructible nylon bag, the bag itself still looped round the belt. She'd been weighted down to ensure sinking and drowning. Or, she'd weighted herself down.

I could think of a lot nicer reasons to be reminded of my younger days than by the discovery of the rotting remains of a human being. But now we knew what had happened to Gillian Butler, it was surely a relief in a way. For isn't knowing always better than not knowing? Or at least that's what we tell ourselves nowadays. We didn't when I was young, an era when people were mealy-mouthed and hypocritical and anything unpleasant or embarrassing was *best left unsaid*.

When I left him, Hector blamed "those bra-burning harpies" and if he could he would have cited the women's movement as the co-respondent in our divorce. The new feminism was the cause of the break up of families, the corruption of society, the infection of women like me with silly, selfish ideas – and so on, and on. In fact he wasn't and isn't the hidebound old buffer that makes him sound – even before the days of women's lib I wouldn't have married him if he had been. I think it hurt his pride less than blaming the man I left him for. And finding Hector in bed with one of his clerks gave me a better justification for breaking up the family than my dazzling but superficial lover. He didn't last long but I wasn't going to crawl back home with my tail between my legs.

In those days, before the general loosening up of society's rules, being the guilty party in a divorce would have put paid to Hector's chances of becoming a judge. I didn't want to do that to him. So we agreed to meet in London, at the home of his sister, my best friend at college. It was through Antonia that I had met Hector, and I'm glad to say we are still close despite my divorce from her brother. Their other sister, who is called Diana, has never really forgiven me which is perverse because she hasn't been a model of virtue herself, whereas Antonia has stuck faithfully to her husband through thick and thin – and there has been a lot of thin.

Of all the many entertainments and encounters I've had in her house, this one was by far the most uncomfortable, before or since. To discuss purposely breaking the law – any law – was a kind of torture to Hector. But if the powers that be discovered we'd colluded in reaching a harmonious agreement, we would never have got a divorce and his career would be ruined, exactly the opposite of what happens in the 21st century. Nowadays we'd be required to show we had tried to reach agreement, we'd be offered mediation and exhorted to 'be civilised.' Back in the 1970s divorce was still supposed to be a confrontation between antagonists.

So it was in the strictest secrecy that we made a deal. I'd be found in bed with another man and Hector would divorce me for adultery. I'd be the one who committed the 'matrimonial offence' and his reputation would remain unblemished. He'd also be let off any legal obligation to support me, which was all right in theory, but in practice meant that I wouldn't be able to afford to have the children with me, if he failed to keep to our verbal and unrecorded agreement.

Oh, the hoops we went through in those days, trying to square the circle of modern life and old-fashioned practices and prejudices!

In the end we sorted it out by dint of metaphorical smoke and mirrors and using Antonia as a cash conduit. It worked out all right. But the effect of that experience was to reinforce my scepticism about the legal system, lawyer's daughter and ex-wife though I am. I've certainly never felt guilty when I've had occasion to circumvent it.

We were still being taught to lie when I was starting out as an adoption counsellor. It was after I'd moved south with the children and before the days when there were strict requirements for social worker's qualifications.

It had not occurred to me as a profession I would think of going into. But I needed a job and, because the chairman was a friend of my father's, I was offered one with a private adoption society. They don't really exist any more, but were still going strong at the time. I believed and piously spouted the doctrine I was taught in the short, informal training: that nurture was paramount, not nature. We advised parents to tell themselves as well as everybody else, both in public and in private, that an adopted child was their own. On the list of things that I couldn't forgive Hector for was his saying, (repeated to me by our daughter) that if his cat gave birth in the stables it didn't make the kittens into ponies.

But it wasn't long before we were told to use a different new line:

children should be told they had been 'chosen.' A few years on, and there was another change of fashion: they had to be given all the information the adoptive parents had. So far, so possible, as far as I was concerned. I baulked at but obeyed the next new dogma: that children and their adoptive parents should be of the same race. But after that we were informed that adopted children should be kept in contact with their birth parents throughout. That was the point at which I left the profession.

I've gone private – as a matter of fact I've become a kind of detective. The clients who come to me now are relics of the earlier era when an unmarried woman's pregnancy was a disgrace. Adopted people employ me to find out whose child they would have been, and birth mothers commission me to track down their long-lost children. Then I act as a go-between or shield. I make the initial contact, facilitate the first meeting and protect my clients as best I can from predatory or publicity seeking or disappointing blood relations.

Sometimes the task simply involves clerical drudgery, looking up registers and electoral rolls, but equally often it's serious investigation, sometimes recalling a plot of one of my own novels. It can be exciting and then I feel like a private eye. So Liza Dorneywood was right to assume that I knew, if anyone did, how to find people. She was wrong to imagine that I would leave it there. I'm far too curious, even nosy. I want to assemble a complete dossier – where they had been and what they'd been doing, and why and how. I've learnt things about human behaviour I never could have imagined. I've discovered far more techniques and tricks than I ever use. Do I need a justification? Hardly. But if I do, then let's say that the information comes in handy for my crime novels.

I could never have written fiction set in Edinburgh when I was married to Hector; or at least, I could never have published it. I wrote the first book in a white heat of terror and energy the summer after we parted and before we reached an agreement. Cambridge degree or no, as far as official qualifications went, I feared I was unemployable and I'd lost my meal ticket. I'd started the job with the adoption agency by the time the book was published in the following spring. Most reviews were complimentary but it's the unflattering criticism that engraves itself on a writer's heart. For years I felt hurt and mystified by Liza Dorneywood's announcement that she would never have one of my books in the house. I forgave her one summer when I had a sudden, blinding revelation. I had been re-reading some of my own old work, before writing an article about it for an online magazine.

I've always said and believed that what I write is not in any way autobiographical, that I never portray real people in my novels, that the whole point of writing crime fiction – at least the whole point for an upright, uptight author with no personal experience of crime – is that it's fantasy, every episode invented, every character imagined, with no connection to one's own life.

My first book, written forty years ago, has become a period piece. The world is so dramatically changed that I sometimes can't believe my own memories. Pre-women's lib, pre-computer, pre-credit-card, pre-car culture – the world of my youth is a foreign, primitive land. If you think I'm exaggerating, just read a novel from those days, not necessarily one of mine.

Writing the above, I pause and spend a couple of hours reading one of my own books – and have a sudden, extremely unwelcome revelation: I have been kidding myself all these years. Suddenly I see likenesses in my characters to people I'd really known. My words, which I would have sworn had been spun out of my imagination as baseless fantasy, in fact describe a real place, which was as it should be. But it was shocking to recognize some real people, even, to some extent myself. The story is told by a single, secretive woman, the daughter of an established Edinburgh family. Her brother is married to a Cambridge graduate from the south of England who plays a minor role. In that character, I now see my own, much younger face.

After all these years of protests to the contrary, it has to be acknowledged that subconsciously or unconsciously or perhaps just carelessly, I'd based that first book on what I knew. No wonder Liza had taken offence, if she saw herself in one of the less attractive characters; no wonder Hector's younger sister remained so unforgiving, even after he had forgiven me and married again.

And what about the other books? Have I been deceiving myself about all of them?

Or is the solicitor murderer in the sixth book uncomfortably like one of my father's junior partners? Is the gutsy girl (who saves the day in the only thriller I've attempted) based on a BBC news reporter I'd helped with adopting a child? Or the well-known woman psychiatrist in books 10, 12 and 13 – had I pirated what I remembered, and what I've read since, about Fidelis Berlin?

Frankly, yes. The mystery was not what I had done, but why it had taken me so long to recognise I did it. It was a bad moment. This was not my self-image! Luckily however it looked as if I've got away with it without any repercussions.

However the very last thing I want is to meet my involuntary models in the flesh.

Then one day I go to a party launching a feminist concert series.[2] On my way in I glance at the list of those present. The moment I see her name written down I turn towards the door intending to do a runner, and find myself chest to chest with our host. Beside him is another guest whose name badge is pinned to her jacket.

Is there the slightest chance that she won't know my name? Or that she hasn't read any of the books in which her alter ego appeared?

Some hope!

I'm shaking and sweating with social embarrassment.

It feels shocking, almost indecent, to confront her in the flesh, and all the more so because she looks dismayingly like the description of my fictional heroine. An old woman, but still energetic, upright and involved. I thought I'd made up such attributes as thick well cut blue-grey hair, tanned complexion, and a clear, assessing gaze. Disconcertingly, here they are. She's even wearing the kind of clothes I'd imagined, a sculptural skirt and top by Yohji Yamomoto.

"This is…" our host begins.

"No need to introduce us," she says. "We knew each other a long time ago. Anyway I know exactly who Isabel is. And she knows more about me than I know myself."

My cheeks burn. Then she goes on,

"Don't worry, I was flattered, I only wish I was really as successful as your heroine. And as for her adventurous sex life…!" She breaks off and we both laugh, myself from relief.

All the same, the parallels are disconcerting. I discover that she lives on the third floor of a white stucco terrace overlooking Regent's Park, which can't be very different from the flats I invented for her. Unlike my character, she has been married, though she has no children. And she's published numerous papers and books, but none turned into a bestseller, unlike my heroine's.

"Sadly – I was quite envious of my doppelganger when I read that."

I am speechless. She goes on,

"But it's not really quite coincidental, is it? You know that we met many many years ago…"

"In Edinburgh."

2 An unusual concept, especially when you count up the number of orchestras or groups led by, or named after or even performed by women, and until you check how many programs consist of work by women. You've guessed; the total is zero.

"So I must have stuck in your memory."

"Actually," I admit, "I didn't make the connection until quite recently."

I start to tell her about the discovery of Gillian Butler's body at which she suggests that we leave this reception and find somewhere quiet to talk. So it's over red wine and lasagna in a comfortably old-fashioned establishment that still has carpets, tablecloths and chianti bottles wrapped in straw that we remind each other of that distant evening in Edinburgh.

Fidelis can just about recall that there was a dinner party, but not much about it. She does remember getting to know Hannah Browne though, and that not long after the baby was born Hannah broke off all contact. "She thought I was having an affair with her husband. What was he called? John? Jack?"

"James."

"That's it. James Browne. She was quite mistaken, you know, though he did once ask my advice about Hannah."

"Did you say she accused you of sleeping with him?"

"She did, but I hadn't."

Hannah wouldn't speak to her, cut her dead if they met in the street or on the common stair. Fidelis was so busy that it hardly registered, and when she did notice, was too busy to worry about it. Her last few weeks rushed by, and as soon as her year at the Royal Infirmary was at an end she moved back to England, some locum jobs and her next training post, in psychiatry.

"I wondered if I should go to James Browne's funeral, I read about his death not long after I'd gone south. But then I decided it would upset Hannah, even though she'd been mistaken, it would be tactless to turn up."

My reply is interrupted by the jingle of my mobile phone. "I'm so sorry, I won't answer." I reach down to turn it off, but Fidelis says, "Don't worry, I don't mind. Go ahead."

"Isabel. Isabel, is that you? Can you hear me?"

"Yes, Liza, loud and clear", I reply, pressing the 'reduce volume button' and gesturing apologies to Fidelis. "Is something wrong?"

"Yes, it's about…it's Gillian Butler. Well, her remains – I can't bear to think of it. It's about what happened to her. I had the police here. My dear, it's all so awful. She was killed, Isabel, murdered, it's been confirmed."

"That's dreadful…"

"It doesn't bear thinking about. All those years…"

"Did they tell you what happened?"

"No, but it's in the papers. She was hit on the head with something like a cosh. And I can't tell you what they're insinuating about us all, it's simply awful, the Scottish papers – there's no respect any more!"

"About you all, Liza? What do you mean?"

"Senior Judge's Salad Days. That's one headline. Another says Judicial Wild Oats. It seems too peculiar for words but I think they are actually implying that it's something to do with us."

"Sounds libellous to me. Actionable."

"Hector says arguing or saying anything at all would only make matters worse. And Fraser agrees. But Isabel, we all think that Hannah Browne, if that's still her name, might have some idea of what happened that night. One of the girls thinks she and Gillian were close. And frankly, by now, we're desperate. I do hope you're a bit closer to tracking her down."

I'm not yet, in fact. My initial inquiries produced zero result, which wasn't surprising since Hannah Browne had almost certainly remarried with a change of name at least once. I put the phone down and say to Fidelis,

"Quite a coincidence. That was somebody asking if I'd found Hannah Browne."

"Is she lost?"

"I'm sure she isn't, my not being able to find her doesn't mean she's disappeared. But with a surname like Browne – and it hasn't been a priority. But I'll find out where she went, there's always a paper trail these days. It just means going back to when she left Edinburgh all those years ago and following from there."

"I can save you some trouble. I saw her several years after that, in Somerset."

From The Argus, September 10 1979

Witch Mother gets Life

The mother convicted of killing her four children during a magic ritual was today sentenced to life imprisonment at Cambridge Crown Court. Rowena Jones, 44, who described herself as a licensed practitioner of pagan ritual and Wicca, had pleaded not guilty by reason of insanity to the charge of murder. Jones was charged with child neglect in June 1978 when a psychiatric report by consultants at Addenbrooke's Hospital suggested that she might be a danger to herself or others. But after a later examination by another consultant psychiatrist, Jones was released on bail on 23 January this year. The dead bodies of her children Kevin, 7, Rosie and Rachel, 5, and Maggie, 3, were found in her house on February 3. Elwyn Jones, 49, said, 'If I'd had the slightest idea that a mother could do such a thing I would never have let Rowena take them out that afternoon. But professional psychiatrists thought she was safe to be in the community. They made a tragic error of judgement. And so did I.'

"A sad, silent psychiatrist sat solitary and suffering by the sandy sea shore." She repeated the words in a whisper several times until they did not make sense any more. Then she muttered, "Fidelis feels feeble, foolish, frightened." The sea was calm and grey; the beach deserted. Nobody came here at this time of year because there wasn't anything to do. But Fidelis had nothing to do but think. "Fidelis thinks thankless thoughts."

It was a long time since Dr Fidelis Berlin had been completely unoccupied. Recently, a natural tendency to prefer work to idleness had become an almost frenzied determination to channel her thoughts away from what she found unthinkable. But when her thoughts returned, as they obsessively did, to what had happened she couldn't see where her behaviour had gone wrong. Would another woman have shown more perception, more foresight, more sympathy? Might another woman have seen what was coming? But Fidelis was not another woman. She was the same cerebral creature who had turned into that sad, silent psychiatrist, she was the product as well as the producer of her professional principles, she was the woman, whose thoughts were thankless.

Fidelis had not believed in the occult and the dead children were the result of her incredulity. She had set their mother free to kill them.

She had deferred the start date for her new job and although she was not yet due to finish the previous one, she couldn't face going back and had vacated her flat and put her furniture in store. She needed some time off, time to think things out, to put herself on trial since nobody else was going to.

Rosa Perkins, her finger always on the pulse of her friends' and acquaintances' activities, inevitably heard that Fidelis was taking time off and offered the loan of the Perkins' holiday home near Nancemere. "It's pretty uncomfortable at this time of year you'll find, so you'd be doing us a favour – keep it warm and aired for a while."

The cottage was on the edge of a small town, which before the Norman conquest had been a centre of European learning and drawn students from all over Europe, still prosperous in the Middle Ages, but left behind in the 19th century when the expansion of a deep-water port in the neighbouring town had drawn all trade away. With prosperity went modernisation; the place had never been pulled down and rebuilt. Nancemere had come to a halt before Queen Victoria came to the throne. It was somewhere to retreat to, to hide in, which was lucky since that was what Fidelis had set out to do. As she got used to Nancemere she discovered something about its history, including the fact that others had used it as a hideout. A gang of bank robbers were arrested in a house they had bought in order to create a hiding place in its chimney. Allegedly, showers of gold had fallen out when the police took a crowbar to it. Further back, in the 19th century, a notorious adulterer had retreated to Nancemere. It all made the place sound like a punishment station.

Was part of her penalty the primitive discomfort of a cottage without any mains services? She did vaguely remember Benjamin referring to it as 'a stone tent' but hadn't quite expected to cook on bottled gas, drink water which was probably contaminated and wrestle with an open fire. There were mice. On her first night a bat had flown in through the tiny window and landed on the bed, blindly struggling. When the rain was very heavy the septic tank overflowed and stinking liquid came bubbling under the back door.

Fidelis had made no attempt to make the place seem like home. She did clean it, she took her washing to the launderette quite often, but she had imported none of the pottery, pictures, ornaments, the woven fabrics and the sheepskins, the blue-and-white china or the rocking chairs which she would normally not live without. Least home-like of all was the silence. Fidelis, who normally lived in a cloud of classical music, did not turn the radio on and had not brought a record player. And she did not sing.

The barrister who had been briefed to represent her at the enquiry was an old friend. Desmond had come to visit her once. As they lay together in the damp, lumpy bed, he remarked that she was inflicting on herself the punishment which no lawyer would ever say she deserved.

"For God's sake go out and get a hi-fi," he exclaimed. Fidelis made no answer and he changed the subject, drinking without comment the builder's tea, eating the processed cheese which was all that Nancemere's little shops provided. The nearest supermarket was 50 miles away. Afterwards he sent her a ham, a Cheddar from Paxton and Whitfield and a reading list. "You've spent too much time with a small section of humanity. Time to read about different kinds of predicament."

War and Peace and *Anna Karenina*, *Middlemarch* and *North and South*; Fidelis had read all of them at school, conscientiously and without feeling. Forcing her way through them again was no more difficult than any other of the tasks she was setting herself these days. Much more difficult were the modern novels, family sagas and sensitive stories by other women about shipwrecked marriages. Such little problems. Desmond had sent some lighter reading, a couple of crime novels which Fidelis didn't open, and a naval adventure set during the Napoleonic Wars called *Master and Commander*, which was so absorbing that, while she was reading it on the muddy beach, the tide rose without her noticing until she felt the icy water on her feet. She read *The Golden Notebook* and felt unsympathetic towards the problem of not being able to get down to one's own work. Fidelis's research beckoned and tempted. She longed to concentrate on its objective problems. But she was carrying out her self-imposed punishment. Her sentence was to make herself come to an understanding of how she had gone so catastrophically wrong. Because of her misjudgement, four children were dead and their mother in prison, or a secure hospital, for life.

Desmond insisted that she had nothing to blame herself for.

"You couldn't possibly have known that that woman would do such a thing. Had she ever threatened her children, said a word or dropped a hint?"

"I should have been able to tell. What was I there for otherwise?"

"It's not your fault. She gave no hint of it, everybody says that, even her husband."

Her husband didn't bear thinking of. He'd thought the worst day of his life was the day the family court awarded custody of the children to their mother. How could he have imagined a day when the police would come to his door?

He didn't even blame Fidelis. He was dignified in bereavement and hadn't castigated or pointed the finger of guilt, not at the social workers, not at the judge, not at the psychiatrist whose evidence had swayed the judge. And because he didn't, the psychiatrist herself did.

She'd been specialising in psychiatry for several years, and recently taken a specific interest in the parent/child relationship. She'd published articles and lectured, and had been appointed to a consultant post in London due to start after Easter. "If I couldn't recognize that the woman was quite deluded there is something wrong with me. I'm not trust-worthy,"

This time Desmond had come down bringing dinner (smoked salmon, Chablis, marrons glacés). He said mildly, "I thought that for centuries the whole point of witchcraft was concealing that one had anything to do with it. If they could hide it from witch-finders they can hide it from people who aren't even trying to find them."

The mother had seemed tense, which was natural in the circumstances, but not deluded, not dangerous. "But I knew she'd taken an interest in witchcraft, the husband mentioned it. Wicca, he called it."

"Which doesn't have to be any more sinister than belonging to the Women's Institute. You know that, Fidelis, I don't need to tell you. You've got to stop beating yourself up."

"How to recognize your own mental illness: feelings of excessive shame or anger when reviewing past débâcles," she quoted sourly. "That's what the Oxford Handbook tells psychiatrists."

"What does it tell them to do about it?"

"Realize that to avoid mistakes one would have to give up medicine."

"Is that helpful?"

"It also advises confiding in someone you trust."

"That's me. Which being so, Fidelis, let me reiterate: if the police didn't find any wax images, and the social workers and doctors didn't, and neither her husband nor the children ever mentioned them, you could not possibly have known. And even if you had some inkling that the woman was going in for magic spells, they could perfectly well have been harmless – I mean, obviously they were harmless, but she might have meant no harm."

Fidelis was realising, perhaps for the first time, that she had not chosen a profession that involved messing with other people's minds because she was empathetic or sympathetic towards them but because by nature she was apart, separate, watching other people as though they were specimens.

Not surprising really, she told herself, it's exactly what you'd expect of a patient who was separated from her family at an early age. But now she wondered whether the studies she had immersed herself in had taught her the lessons that she needed. The novels she was reading were a corrective. Understand Emma Bovary and Emma Woodhouse, and she might understand herself better too. Perhaps she would even learn to think with her guts and not her brain, to be spontaneous. What was it one of her many men had said? It was some piece of clever wordplay to do with fucking and sucking. Fidelis sucked out his soul to examine and once she'd analysed it didn't need him any more.

She was walking a lot this week. If one walked briskly enough, she found, one could concentrate the mind on nothing at all, letting serious thought be short-circuited by the chaff of idle reflection: that the sea was blue, the sky dappled, the turf soft beneath her feet. She thought about clothes, and what she would buy when she went back to London, and whether she was really the right type to wear this year's tiered skirts and flower pattern blouses with contrast piping – and then noticed what she was thinking about and at the same time realized that she had been unconsciously humming a tune from *Cosi fan Tutte*.

Fidelis realized she was ready to end her self-imposed exile and go back to work, though chastened and more cautious. She turned back towards the town, and stopped at a small shop to buy a paper. About to pick one up, she snatched her hand back on seeing that the lead story in nearly all of them was again about the witch-mother who had sacrificed her own children. Another woman was there peering the headlines. She looked familiar but Fidelis wasn't in the mood for social chit-chat. She was backing out of the shop, without noticing that above her head was a little mirror placed to allow the person behind the counter to see shoplifting customers. An unforgiving gaze was fixed on her reflection. Fidelis was thinking that in future she would take what her patients said not more seriously, since she had always taken their words seriously, but as fact not fantasy. She would act on allegations of abuse. No more children would die on her watch. She was half-way down the motorway when it came to her that it had been Hannah Browne in the shop this morning. "So that's where she's ended up. She'll think I was being stand-offish. We should have met while I was staying there," Fidelis thought. But it was a momentary distraction from thinking about her new job, and soon forgotten.

2011

I'm an ardent libertarian and deplore state interference or surveillance. That said, even without access to police records, or access to a person who has access to them, it's astonishing how much information there is out there.

In 1979, the year that a woman became Britain's Prime Minister, Mrs Hannah Browne was arrested at a women's lib rally. She gave her address, and bail was paid by a Mrs Loretta Payne living at the same address, a farm in North Somerset.

It might have been a farmhouse in the past but now was simply a substantial country house reached down a badly maintained lane. There was space for a dozen cars on a gravel forecourt overgrown with weeds though mine was the only one parked there. The paint on the green front door was blistered and cracking, the bell didn't work and the lion's head knocker was a solid lump of tarnish. The door was opened by a skeletal young woman with Slavic cheekbones, wearing jeans and a pink t-shirt. Lithuanian, I guessed, or Polish. I gave her my card which on one side says *Isabel Duhamel, People Tracer*, and on the other, *Isabel Arnold, Writer* – explained that I was hoping to be given the address of somebody who had lived there many years previously, a Mrs Browne, and could I perhaps have a word with her employer. Her accent was thick but the words were fluent. Mrs Payne was at home, and who should she say wanted her? Congratulating myself on the unexpected ease of finding this informant, I went into a large light room. A green baize table, four upright chairs and two packs of cards were set out in front of a blazing wood fire. Two pink velvet sofas had been pushed back and on one of them sat a woman with white hair and many deep wrinkles, wearing a blue vintage coat-dress, which I immediately envied, and several strings of large pearls. She was holding a telephone handset.

"Oh," she said, her voice husky but audible, "I thought you were…

oh dear, am I having hallucinations? You may be the answer to prayer! Do you play bridge?"

"I can, not very well but..."

"And if you do, will you? One of my four has just rung, to cancel. She says she's on granny duty which I have to say I think is a poor excuse."

"Well – I was planning to go back to London after..."

"Don't. Stay. You can stay here if you like, God knows there are enough beds."

"But Mrs Payne!" I heard the bossy tone in my own voice. "You can't invite a complete stranger to stay – how do you know I'm not an axe murderer?"

"Because I know exactly who you are. I've seen you on television – and I've read all your books too. You can spend the evening telling me why you're here. Meanwhile I can hear my friends coming."

An ancient couple tottered into the drawing room. Mutual introductions and explanations were hurried through; the green baize table was the old peoples' magnet.

The bridge I normally play is casual and conversational, more an excuse to see friends than a serious competition. After a couple of games I said, "I'm nowhere near good enough to play with you all."

Mrs Payne made no bones about it. "You're not, are you? Never mind." I fancied that I could see the words *better than nothing* hovering on her lips.

Two hours later, just as I was realising that I had not brought enough money to pay my losses, Mrs Payne slapped her hand against the green table top and said, "Enough. Lucky we agreed not to play for money."

"Lucky indeed," I agreed.

"But..." the old lady began. Then she said, "You're kicking me. That hurt!" She bustled to her feet looking indignant and as they went out to the hall I could hear Mrs Payne trying to soothe her down.

"It's not as though she needs the money," Mrs Payne said as she came back into the drawing-room. I replied that I was embarrassed: I ought to pay my gambling debts. "Nonsense, nonsense! It was really kind of you to enable us to have our game. Now Magdalena is going to show you upstairs, the room is always ready in case one of my daughters comes down unexpectedly."

It was a high ceilinged pink room with a high mahogany bed covered in a lace counterpane and lace doilies under a series of pink china containers on a mahogany chest of drawers. An equally old-fash-ioned bathroom held a huge bath and a lavatory encased in a wickerwork armchair. The view outside was spectacular, a wide expanse of well cut grass sloping downwards towards the sea.

When I went back into the drawing room, Mrs Payne was standing at the window. Without turning round she said, "Please help yourself to a drink."

On a silver tray were bottles of spirits and fortified wines. I didn't like to ask for an ordinary glass of wine – Mrs Payne was of a generation that drank wine only at meals – so took some sherry, which was stronger than I remembered. At this point, when I'd been in her house for hours, I was able at last to raise the subject that brought me to Somerset. Mrs Payne did not hesitate in her reply. "Hannah Browne? Of course I remember her, of course I know who you mean – not that she's called that now."

"Are you in touch with her still?"

"As a matter of fact, now you come to mention it I haven't heard from her in some years. We used to exchange Christmas cards, but I'm not sure where she is now." She took not a sip but a swig from her gin and tonic. "She was by far the best I ever had."

Prompted by my questions, Mrs Payne told me what had happened. Hannah had come to work as a companion/home help, through an agency. There had been no need to interview her in advance because the agency cost a fortune, and one of the things one was paying for was being spared the selection process. Any carer the agency sent was guaran-teed to be able to cope with the details of any assignment. Electric cooker, Aga, gas stove; big car, Land Rover, little old runabout; walking the dogs, feeding the cats, calling the plumber, answering the telephone, laying the table; knowing when to tactfully disappear to eat on her own, or when her employer wanted company. 'We service people', was one of the agency's tag lines.

Hannah Browne's previous charge, though very frail when she arrived, survived for several long, complaint-filled years before dying in his sleep one night. The next day his family swooped in and cleared the place like locusts. Hannah was evicted immediately. Her savings had grown to a healthy sum, but so had house prices. In order to have a roof over her head she had to take the first job the agency could find that star-ted immediately and had accommodation for her daughter and a decent school nearby.

"Very bright girl, Allegra, and mature for her age – a real little madam actually – she ups and announces that if her mother thought she was going to move to any tinpot school in some tinpot country town she was much mistaken. She'd been offered a scholarship at Greenland's and she could board there. Hannah was upset at first, she missed the girl but then she began to make her own friends. It was the time that women were marching for liberation – I was already well past it but that kind of protest was a kind of rite of passage for younger women."

"Yes, I remember."

"So many women were so very naïve in those days. I remember, quite early on, there was a rally here, in the town. I wanted to go myself, just because I was interested, but I'd broken a couple of bones in my leg skiing and I couldn't manage very well on my own. So I asked Hannah to come with me. It was a real eye-opener for her. She said she'd never seen so many women together, all so self-confident too! I could see what she meant, a whole lot of women who seemed really sure of themselves, it was unusual in those days."

"Yes, I remember," I said.

"We went round the stalls, you know the kind of tat they were selling, charms, bead necklaces strung on leather shoelaces, herb scented candles, hand-made, fringed leather purses, books, pamphlets. Posters were plastered against every available flat surface.

Hannah seemed mystified. "Like a fish needs a bicycle" – what did that mean? A woman needs a man, a house needs a wife, like a fish… Hannah didn't get it. She went into a tent whose placard said 'Self knowledge is queen.' There was a coat stand, a couch, a cheval glass and a hand mirror. But it wasn't anything to do with clothes or make-up, it was about looking at one's own body – down there. She never had, and was disgusted and mystified by the pictures on the wall, which showed lots of different patterns and arrangements of pink and brown, wet and dry, hairy and bald. Above them was a banner reading 'There's no such thing as normal.'

"It was all rather unsettling," Mrs Payne remembered. Hannah became restless. The job was too easy for her. She had become self-reliant as a widow and had no problem with local emergencies – she had coped with much worse than the neighbour's cattle in the rose garden or the gardener falling out of an apple tree. When the woman who came in to do the heavy cleaning complained that the washing machine was making a peculiar gurgling noise in its insides; when the man who delivered the daily papers backed his car into the pond; when a high wind blew half a dozen slates off the roof, Hannah knew what to do. She always coped. But one could see that she felt restless. Rootless, perhaps. And lonely. The trouble was, Mrs Payne explained, "I was working all the hours God sent. I was a writer myself, you know."

"I didn't know – I'm so sorry."

"No, how could you? I wrote as Delphine Savage…"

"Oh, I had no idea…"

"I expect you thought I was long since dead."

I'd loved Delphine Savage's trilogy, set during the English Civil War, when I read it as a schoolgirl. I hadn't thought of it for years, but now felt I could truthfully say, "I've read your books. I adored your cavalier, dreamed of him when I was a teenager."

"I was working on a sequel set in the reign of Charles II, but my late husband wasn't happy if I let things go, that was why I needed a housekeeper. And Hannah was really excellent so it was worth making an effort to keep her sweet. But she missed her daughter. I was only too pleased she was at boarding school, a tiresome child in my view, she behaved as if she was so much superior to her mother. She even dared to patronize me! So we showed her."

Mrs Payne laughed, a rippling gurgle of amusement. Her skin was a network of fine and deep lines, her eyes were sunk into the skull and her lips thinned, but suddenly I could see what this nonagenarian had looked like when young: beautiful and mischievous.

"How? What did you do?"

"Well, it began with encouraging Hannah to join in a bit locally. I sent her off to political meetings, consciousness-raising sessions, 'Get to know your body' classes, a poetry group, even a witches coven. It seemed to be a good way to meet people, but…" the ancient voice cracked and hoarsened, "it ended in tears."

"Witchcraft?"

"Lots of those women would have done anything to get out of the house in the evening. It didn't mean anything – except, perhaps, to one of them, a very intense young woman, what was she called…? Rose? Violet? No, that's it, her name was Daffy – Daphne, I suppose. Or Daffodil? Anyway she and Hannah palled up. I was surprised at first because they were so different. But it was nice for her to make friends here."

Mrs Payne described a tall, pale woman, her hair a great cushiony bush of wiry red curls. She had a brooding, compelling presence that intimidated both patients and doctors at the GP's surgery where she was the practice nurse; but when she chose she could be magnetically charming. Other women were drawn into her circle, seldom risked her displeasure by missing meetings and came away from them in some way surer of themselves. "I'm a good friend and a bad enemy," she would say, and there were several women in the neighbourhood who were careful not to offend her. At the same time they insisted that one woman's miscarriage was nothing to do with attending a Black Mass; nor was another's diagnosis of breast cancer in any way connected with a letter she had written to the local paper saying that children and vulnerable adults needed protection from local blasphemers and the lunatic fringe.

Daffy frequently insisted that "Each one of us is our own priestess," and carried a list of spells in her fringed, folk-weave bag.

Animal Spells, Banishing Spells, Cleansing Spells, Court cases and Justice Spells, Death Spells, Ghost, Necromancy, and Vampire Spells, Divination Spells, Domination and Influence Spells, Dreams, Astral and Nightmare Spells, The Evil Eye, Fertility Spells, Safety Spells, Gamblers Spells and Charms, Healing Spells, Hexes and Curses, Invisibility, and Transformation Spells, Love and Seduction Spells, Good Luck and Ill wishing Spells, Love, Marriage Dissolution Spells, Financial Spells, Pregnancy and Childbirth Spells, Protection Spells, Psychic Powers, Summoning Spirits, Unblocking Spells, Weather Spells.

Daffy told Hannah and Hannah told Mrs Payne that witchcraft, Wicca, was the ancient wisdom of women which a male dominated society feared and suppressed. It should be celebrated, not concealed. Perhaps it was that very respectability that robbed the procedures of any power they might have had. How could Hannah work a spell, when she was every inch an aspiring Sloane Ranger in her flowery Laura Ashley blouse with a corduroy skirt and flat shoes with brass snaffles, and hair held back by a velvet band? The Wicca meetings, as described to Mrs Payne, and as she described them all this time later, sounded like a cosy book group or some other equally innocent excuse for women to go out and meet people.

"All the same," Mrs Payne said, "a few years later something awful happened. It was like the Salem witch hunts, people were consumed with irrational fears. It's a dreadful story actually, it distresses me to think of it." Her hands and her lips were trembling. "Even now I still feel ashamed that I didn't even try to get involved at the time. I knew all about it, I should have done something – though I don't know what. Or how. That poor woman's life was ruined. Her whole family's, in fact."

"Which woman, Mrs Payne?"

"Sandra, she was called. The district nurse. She and Hannah didn't get on, there was some misunderstanding about a previous meeting. I'd heard them arguing after Sandra had dealt with my leg but I didn't like to pry. And then, as my grandson would say, everything went pear-shaped."

The more senior one became in a profession, Fidelis realized, the less opportunity one had to use professional skills. Head teachers rarely taught; senior partners concentrated on admin rather than individual clients; and consultant psychiatrists saw fewer patients. Fidelis's advice was sought, her recommendations acted upon, but she made them after reading the documents, and very seldom set eyes on the individuals concerned. It didn't seem to be a very satisfactory system but it was the system, and as one of her colleagues said, writing a report for the court about the needs of children in a matrimonial dispute was a nice little earner. She did it, of course, with the utmost care, conscientiously reading every word in the documents, and not allowing herself to wonder how many of the mothers' or fathers' allegations were pure, vindictive invention, by someone who knew that the mere suggestion of ritual abuse would probably be enough to dish the rival parent's claim.

'Ritual Abuse' was in fashion as a matrimonial or parental offence – difficult to understand or prove, but internationally accepted as a real and unforgivable phenomenon. The very idea was disgusting, but Fidelis never brushed the allegations aside, instead taking them as seriously as possible. Fidelis's foster mother would have said that it "gave her the willies." Desmond, who had many times cross examined expert witnesses, said she needed to visualize what went on, and brought a home movie to show her.

"Thou, thou who, in my capacity of Priest, I force, whether thou wilt or no, to descend into this host, to incarnate thyself into this bread – Jesus, artisan of hoaxes, bandit of homages, robber of affection – hear! O lasting foulness of Bethlehem, we would have thee confess thy impudent cheats, thy inexplicable crimes!. We would drive deeper the nails into thy hands, press down the crown of thorns upon thy brow, and bring blood from the dry wounds..."

"Do turn it off, I get it," Fidelis said. But Desmond replied,

"There's more.'"

"Cursed Nazarene, abstractor of stupid parities, impotent king, fugitive god!…O Infernal Majesty, condemn him to the pit, evermore to suffer in perpetual anguish. Bring Thy wrath upon him, O Prince of Darkness."

"Nobody could possibly take this seriously."

"You need to get yourself into their mindset."

Fidelis's foster parents had been tactful about taking this Jewish child to Christian services, but she did sometimes accompany them to chapel as a child and rather enjoyed hearing the hymns belted out, the polite, prescribed and private prayers. Remembering it now, she wondered whether she had believed any of it. Scepticism was her natural environment. Certainly by the time she was 13 or 14 she was an atheist. "You'll go to hell," a girl at her school had warned as, "You've had a chance of salvation and rejected it."

Apart from that she hadn't much experience of religious ardour and in fact was never quite convinced that it was what fired missionaries or hell-fire preachers – was it an excuse or a justification, or a genuine motive? A lifetime of singing sacred music had embedded the language of Christianity in Fidelis's subconscious, but the words didn't carry an emotional charge. Her voice worshipped while the mind remained engaged only with the sound, not its meaning. Perhaps it was a question of upbringing. The Methodists of the Welsh valleys did take the rituals seriously, but also remained matter of fact, restrained except when it came to singing. She remembered her foster parents coming back one day from a service conducted by a revivalist preacher and the polite but dismissive way in which they had spoken of his enthusiasm.

Perhaps you could only get into the mindset of devil worshippers if you had yourself ever worshipped God. To Fidelis, their rituals seemed squalid, inelegant, but above all silly. She pressed the remote control and the scarlet room and its black robed participants disappeared from the screen.

"No, you've got to see a bit more," he said, "There's a goat."

"Must I see the goat?"

"And an altar." He turned the machine on again and pressed fast forward. "This is the bit."

A naked girl, a robed man, candles and other ecclesiastical paraphernalia. An audience, or congregation. They should have looked sinister in their black robes, but those who needed glasses still wore them, one set of bare feet poking below the dusty cloth revealed chipped pink nail varnish, another revealed a big bunion and corn plasters on the toes. They all looked ridiculous, from the small stout female to a tall, cadaverous man with acne. Or perhaps not ridiculous: pathetic, as they shuffled and leant forward to get a good view, to experience some kind of ecstasy, which was presumably the object of the exercise.

The focus moved to a full frontal shot of an erect penis, another, from below, of spread legs and a shaved vulva. Whoever was wielding the camera showed as much as possible of the ritual coupling, a remarkably unerotic sequence. The female remained motionless with none of the thrusting and squirming that in blue movies was supposed to signify ecstasy. She served as a receptacle, nothing more, and did not show any physical reaction when, the sex-act completed, her partner scooped some liquid from her vagina with a kind of spoon, deposited it in a silver bowl and, dipping his finger into it, signed the foreheads of some of his congregation with a five cornered star. The whole scene was a parody, not only of the Christian Mass but of any ritual.

"I was expecting an orgy. This is really dull."

"You'll get a better orgy in a student hostel any Saturday night. Think Sunday worship compared with a pop concert. Ritual has lost its power in our society. There is no need to dress sexual urges up in liturgy any more."

"Unless your urges are illicit."

"Exactly. Which is where the hysteria about children comes from, because nothing else is illicit any more."

"Hence the decline."

"Anyway, in the same way that electric light abolished ghosts, science banished mysteries."

After all, Fidelis thought, why subject yourself to the boring task of memorising rituals, of reciting interminable formulae, why lay yourself open to the threat of gruesome punishment, why expose yourself to the threat of reprisals, when the sex and drugs and out of body experiences (if they existed) were available without archaic rigmarole? In a society where such things were no longer forbidden the incentives for participants must surely have diminished.

The on-screen picture had shifted to a presenter, a serious, knitted-brow sociologist. "The real point about the occult ritual," he said, "is that we know, and you know, and participants are beginning to know, it simply doesn't work."

Sandra knew that she'd regret staying so late but she couldn't bring herself to leave. It always seemed so easy, so, quite simply, *nice* to be with a
group of women. Obviously one didn't like them all equally. For
example, Sandra didn't have very much time for the woman who kept a
sweet-smelling gift shop in the High Street but whose own house was a
slum. Sandra had been so shocked by the condition in which the
woman's ancient father was living that she had got the social services on
the case. And actually, Sandra wasn't really one of Daffy's devotees, having seen how brusque she could be on the job. But whispered gossip
warned that it could be a mistake to defy or annoy her, and after several
years one could see that her bark was worse than her bite. Anyway, the
meetings were fun and the other women were nice. This evening Sandra
had been the one to let off steam. She was fed up with having to do all
the dirty work at home as well as having a full-time job, fed up with the
doctors who thought nothing of asking her to make them tea just
because she was the only woman in the room, and fed up with the teachers who assumed there was a menial future for her girls simply because
that's what they were. It was all very well for Keith to make fun of her
women's groups, but he didn't know what it felt like to have to spend
your life fighting for your rights. It was preaching to the long-since converted, but it was good to get it off her chest all the same.

Keith was still awake when she got home, complaining that he'd had
to spend the evening looking after Mel, who wasn't feeling well. "They
had their jabs today and the nurse was mean to her – she said."

"Which nurse?"

"Called Daffy, she said."

"Oh."

"Mel did a picture of her – God knows where that kid gets her
ideas. Have you had a look at her drawing book? Creepy imagination
she's got, you'd think the nurse had been torturing her."

"She's at our meetings." Sandra didn't discuss her interest in Wicca
with Keith, it wasn't the kind of thing he had any patience with. "The

consciousness raising sessions," she had explained, though that idea was not much more to his taste.

"Consciousness crap – it'll be a women's lib march next," he said grumpily.

"I might at that."

"I'd never live it down. I don't know what the world is coming to. I wish you had never met those bra burners. All that feminist crap."

"That's where you're wrong, the spells we tried tonight were for catching men – and we nearly made a medieval love potion."

Keith growled, "For God's sake pack it in, I need my sleep even if you don't."

But Sandra did need her sleep and hadn't had nearly enough of it when she was woken by the knocking. She groaned, muttered in Keith's ear, "It'll be for me, go to sleep again," and rolled out of bed. The knocks became louder and continuous. "All right, all right, I'm coming." Were they nuts, waking the whole street like that? She dragged on her dressing gown as she went downstairs. The central heating didn't switch on until seven and it was freezing cold. Taking the key off the hall table, she realized that the banging was now being made by some heavy implement, and as she moved towards the door it splintered before her eyes like the moment in a horror movie when the enemies are suddenly within.

In the gap where her front door should be she saw the burly shapes of several men in uniform. Two ran upstairs. Behind them came two women, one a policewoman who took Sandra's arm and moved her roughly to one side, the other a mumsy person in jeans and an anorak who was guided by a uniformed officer saying, "They'll be upstairs, miss."

The children! She turned to try to follow the woman. She saw Keith on the half-landing, standing between two policemen who were holding his arms. He was wearing pyjama bottoms and nothing else, struggling against his captors. Sandra realized that she had been screaming all the time without being aware of it. Her throat was sore. One of the policemen was reciting something. She didn't listen because upstairs she heard the door of the girls' bedroom, Kimberley and Mel were crying, calling for her.

"I've got to go to them, can't you hear?" but they didn't let go of her arm. "I'm here, girls, downstairs," she shouted.

"Mum, I want my mum." They had been hustled into their clothes at top speed, any old clothes, their hair not brushed, with no food inside them, they were carried screaming past their father, past their mother, out down the garden path in the middle of the night, and into a dirty little old car. As she shrieked and tried to reach them, the car, with its two children in the back and two strange women in the front, drove away.

One of the police, another woman, was speaking to her. Put on some clothes? Search warrant? She couldn't take it in. They were arresting her, she was to go to the police station, she was to be charged with – what?

There were men in the sitting room looking at books, picking up the video cassettes and putting them in a plastic box. Another man in uniform came downstairs carrying Kimberley's riding crop in a polythene bag.

"Keith." She tried to speak but no voice came out and she realized she had been screaming so loudly that her throat was rough, sore. Where was he? And then he came down the stairs, he'd hustled into some sort of clothes, the trousers he'd worn yesterday and a sweater, shoes with no socks, his thin ginger hair standing on end. Policemen were holding his arms behind his back and then he'd passed her, with a desperate silent stare and she saw handcuffs. She felt her own knees trembling.

"You'd better get some clothes on," the policewoman said. Unresisting, Sandra allowed herself to be led up her own stairs. She went into the bathroom. Someone had peed and not pulled the plug. The policewoman didn't let Sandra shut the door as she sat on the lavatory herself. Her mind felt paralysed. She put on the clothes the policewoman handed her, the pink shell suit she'd had on last night, the black lace up shoes she wore for work. Across the landing men were searching the drawers in the children's room. She didn't brush her hair, she didn't clean her teeth or look in the mirror but followed like a zombie down the stairs again, out of her own front door, into a car, guided by a hand on top of her head like when people were arrested on TV. She didn't even register that there were crowds of people in the street watching, her neighbours, her friends – she didn't notice the flashing of camera lights or the shouts from men and women with notebooks. Did you abuse your children? Do you belong to a coven? What were your rituals? Pervert. Child abuser. Do you think you'll ever see those kids again?

"As far as I know, which is quite far," Loretta Payne told me, "Keith and Sandra never have seen the children again. Of course no one knows exactly what goes on in the family court, but what I heard was that the medic – a woman psychiatrist – gave conclusive evidence that the children were in danger and the court had them put in care somewhere away from here."

"How dreadful for them if they hadn't done anything, it doesn't bear thinking of."

"It was a real tragedy, and it just shows what's liable to happen when people flirt with concepts they don't understand."

"How did things turn out for Hannah?"

"Oh, that part of the story had a happy ending."

Hannah bought herself dungarees and boots, let her hair grow into a thick frizzy cushion, and signed on to do a degree at the Open University.

"It was fascinating," Mrs Payne remembered, "like seeing a flower opening. She simply loved it, came to realize she was clever and could cope and understand. So many women had been taught to think themselves stupid – I was watching liberation personified."

"Did she stay on here then?"

"She studied part-time and supported herself by working here. It took several years, subject by subject – you know how the OU works – but she did it. In fact she finished at exactly the same time as Allegra finished at Cambridge."

Allegra and her mother both graduated with second class degrees. Allegra then became a trainee banker. Loretta Payne said, "Hannah might have stayed on, but at the time I was planning to go and live near one of my sons in Australia – that didn't work out, but it's beside the point. Anyway, I knew someone in London who needed someone like Hannah, but the story has a sad ending, that poor woman, she's had such bad luck. Oddly enough, it's quite a coincidence that you…look, I'll tell you. Sit yourself down again. We'll have supper on trays in here. It's a long story."

Loretta knew a surgeon called Raymond Cunningham, who had been forced to take early retirement because he developed a latex allergy. "Eventually he couldn't be in a theatre at all."

"I had no idea it could be so dangerous."

"It isn't usually. But this was much worse than an ordinary irritant dermatitis or even another hyper-sensitivity. He developed a type one allergy, which was bad enough – it means asthma, conjunctivitis, hives, that kind of thing, unpleasant but bearable and he carried on for a while. But then it got much worse. One single contact and he might have a massive anaphylactic shock. It could kill him."

"Isn't there any alternative to latex?"

"Of course, and Raymond's own gloves were made of synthetic rubber, but he couldn't always be sure that nobody else was wearing latex ones. Even having it in the room – in the end he had to give up. But he was miserable."

He hated not being able to use his skills. Surgeons don't have time for hobbies, he'd snapped at a well-meaning well-wisher when he retired. You could teach, another suggested. Or write your memoirs.

Another old friend took him sailing in the Ionian sea for a long summer. His daughter gave him tickets for a series of chamber music concerts. His son arrived for lunch one day carrying a kit for making a grandmother clock.

"Clock-making! I ask you," Loretta Payne said. Her voice was fainter, her lips and her left hand trembling.

"I'm afraid I've exhausted you with all my questions," I said.

"I am rather tired," Mrs Payne admitted, so she finished her story quickly, telling me that she'd sent her old friend a kind of present: Hannah. She needed a job and somewhere to live; he needed a helper and someone to live with. "I thought those two would get on," Mrs Payne told me, and added, exhausted now, "I'm one of nature's matchmakers."

I suppose I could be called a matchmaker too. I match the people I have traced together with their unknown parents or children. It's an exacting task while 'people tracing' sounds like an exciting one, and it was indeed both exacting and exciting for private eyes like Philip Marlowe. But I'm not in the least like a character in a Californian thriller. Instead, I am businesslike, accurate and base my actions or conclusions on evidence. Isabel Duhamel sticks strictly to professional standards.

Born under the sign of Gemini, the twins, I have two faces, two behaviours, two personalities. Isabel Arnold, the novelist, is a creature of imagination and invention. She can't hear an anecdote without imagining embellishments, playing with alternatives, visualizing the dialogue.

At this point you could be presented with a strictly objective list of the facts I listed in my case notebook. I prefer to offer the embellished version in which Arnold puts colour and action onto the dry bones of Duhamel's fact gathering.

It was unusual for Fidelis to be unpopular when she addressed meetings or seminars. Her reputation was good, her books and articles accessible; as a rule she was listened to with respect and even asked for her autograph. So what happened in Aberdeen was an almost traumatic experience for her.

The subject of the conference was 'Satanic Ritual Abuse And Recovered Memory.' Fidelis had prepared carefully, knowing that her opinions were controversial, and had put on the professional woman's equivalent of full body armour which was, in fact, what she had worn for her register office marriage to her second husband, a civil servant. The dark green shift dress by Joyce Ridings with very plain, very expensive silver jewellery from Georg Jensen still seemed a little festive, for it had been a happy day even though the marriage hadn't lasted much more than a year. The civil servant had loved Fidelis's imaginative variations on cooking's traditional themes, and the jolly, convivial company at her dinner table. He expected his wife to produce equally delicious meals every evening, and was appalled to find himself sent off to buy takeaways when she was busy. She was always busy. He wanted to make love when he felt like it and not when he was tired. He was often tired. The marriage lasted for a shorter time than it took to arrange its dissolution.

Single again, Fidelis could see at a glance that nobody in this conference audience was possible. Not that she expected to find anyone here, she reminded herself, or perhaps anywhere. The single life has its charms, she reminded herself as she rose to address this unpromising group.

Her subject was the danger of excessive credulity. "The very idea of repressed memory is a creation of a romantic society," she asserted. "The first references to dissociative amnesia date to the early 19th century which leads one to suppose that it is not a natural neurological function but a culture-bound disorder." As she expanded the theme, her pre-meeting nervousness proved justified. Recovered memories of sexual abuse were making therapists and writers rich, so this was not what they wanted to hear.

As she spoke, Fidelis realized that she was not saying what she wanted to say. She couldn't be, because if she were then she would not be feeling so uneasy. *What's wrong with me?*

In the afternoon the conference moved on to the subject of ritual abuse. Fidelis had tried but failed to find any hard evidence of any kind to show that children were being made part of abusive pagan rituals. "Rumours galore, and news stories full of hearsay, but actual proof? No. I believed the stories as we all did at first, I've made judgements on the best evidence, or what seemed to be. And of course I am bound to be wrong probably as often as I'm right. I made a dreadful, unforgivable mistake once, when I failed to recognize that a mother of four was on the edge. The consequences were tragic. I'll never forgive myself."

"There but for the grace of God…" someone called from the back of the room. For a moment there was silence. Then Fidelis made a gesture – *banish that thought, put it behind you* – and went on,

"Conversely, I'm still mortified when I think of a family that was split up on my advice. I thought, better safe than sorry. But later I thought they were probably innocent. When all you have to go on turns out to be gossip…"

"What did you feel like when you realized you'd been wrong?"

"In both cases, I thought I'd never work again. But you have to accept that you can't do this sort of job without making the wrong decision sometimes. Nor can you do it unless you're able to pick yourself up off the ground and carry on."

Sitting down in the front row to make way for for the next lecturer, she breathed deeply, tried to empty her mind. She had worked through her personal feelings of guilt a long time ago. So why were her hands trembling, her heart noticeably beating, her breath coming too quickly?

The current speaker, a young academic from the Midlands, was talking about the effect of taking part in or even seeing some of the more lurid rituals. A young child would forget experiencing that incomprehensible fear or horror but it would remain in the psyche, ready to be revived.

"The point is," the lecturer said, "whether or not the rituals had taken place – I won't say whether or not they had the desired effect – and even though none of us in this room would believe they could have any effect – the child who observes them doesn't really forget."

Yes she does, Fidelis thought. Nature is merciful so the victim forgets. Those who remember were not victims.

Whatever made me have that thought? she wondered, surprised at herself.

The next speaker began with a provocative statement: In the United States there was an outbreak of credulity. He had collected examples of it. In Ohio 500 square feet of parkland were excavated in a search for more than 50 bodies alleged to have been ritually murdered and buried in there. Needless to say nothing turned up. In Virginia a police lieutenant was reported as saying that the very lack of evidence for human sacrifice was evidence in itself because the groups about which nothing was known were the most dangerous of all. More dangerous still was the credence given to the purported 'survivors' whose 'revived memories' of childhood ritual abuse were increasingly being treated as hard evidence. And on the basis of such allegations of torture, sacrifices, and sexual degradation, a whole and profitable industry was being built. On this side of the Atlantic, in Rochdale, in Nottingham, in Orkney, children were removed from their family homes by officials convinced that they had been subjected to ritual abuse. Guilt was established – if only in the minds of social workers and a few medics – by a series of perverse tests: anal dilation was one, the medical procedure in itself a kind of child abuse. He showed a video of another kind of test. The child was asked to draw a picture of what happened at home. Dogs, cats, mummy or daddy, were greeted with frowns. At last a picture that could be identified as some kind of circle was produced. Bingo! The ritual dance, on paper! The accusations and implications, the assumptions, the interrogations! Innocent families destroyed!

That speech was followed by the day's climax, the star speaker, billed as a crusading fundamentalist and expert on cults. Looking him up afterwards Fidelis realized that his life consisted of travelling the circuit of police and social work conferences in the United States and now in the United Kingdom, giving seminars on 'satanic worship, mind control cults and destructive religious groups.'

Fidelis listened incredulously as he spoke about underground, secret sessions at which humans were sacrificed, tortured and subjected to hideous rituals. Human sacrifices – as many as 50,000 a year in the United States – were part of the grisly rituals. Many of the victims were children borne to order by captive women breeders.

These lurid stories horrified Fidelis simply because she did not believe a word of them. They horrified some of the audience because they did.

Fidelis thought, I can't just sit here and listen to this garbage. She seized on the moment when the speaker paused for breath.

"Do you have evidence for these claims?" she called in a clear, commanding voice.

He said, "Ah, the famous Dr Berlin, the so-called voice of reason! Can you wonder that these devils get away with their unholy work when the authorities are dominated by such *reason*?" he gave such emphasis to that last word as to show quite clearly that he meant the opposite.

"I'm not arguing," Fidelis replied, "merely asking for the evidence."

"Police departments all over the US have got the evidence and it's evidence in hideous quantities, believe you me. Anyone who's seen the bloody remains isn't going to doubt what I'm saying today. I tell you, I have prayed about this, I've been on my knees to the Lord for days at a time begging him to take this burden from me. Do you think I chose to have this cesspit of vile deeds polluting my mind? But God has called me. We must not go on closing our eyes to what is happening behind the screen of respectability. It is would be to betray those innocent children that have been sacrificed in the name of Satan."

"The proof?" Fidelis called again.

"I am the proof, I tell you, I've seen with my own eyes, with these ears I have heard, I am a witness to corruption and evil and now I must stand up to be counted."

The audience was restless. Fidelis could see one or two people getting up to go but the majority wanted to hear more. Their credulity was incredible – in fact, it was disgusting. For a moment Fidelis tried to be balanced; she knew that she had an irrational disgust for the irrational, and as far as religion was concerned, she'd always say, "it's a closed book to me." Were there more things in heaven and earth than she and Hamlet's Horatio were aware of? Probably, but Fidelis didn't 'have a God shaped space in her consciousness.'

"I'm bearing witness here, believe me," the creamy, persuasive voice continued. "And are you to be counted in beside me?"

"I don't join in, I observe; I don't believe, I analyse." Like many psychiatrists and psychologists, she was more keen to understand things than to believe in them. It baffled her that these qualified social workers and professionals in the field of child care actually seemed to credit the nonsense they were hearing. Fidelis mounted the three steps onto the platform and pitched her voice to be clear and audible. "You want to hear what this man has to say, and I can't stop you but for God's sake, don't be taken in by hysteria and rumours. You're not a mob of ignorant villagers in old Salem, you're educated professionals! Listen to him if you must but don't believe anything without evidence. Wild assertions aren't proof."

It was a losing battle. They weren't listening to her. They were hating her. She pulled the tattered shreds of her dignity around her, walked off the platform and out of the hall. The sound of slow hand-clapping kept in time to the click of her high heels on the wooden floor.

By marrying Raymond Cunningham Hannah became the stepmother of his two grown-up children. The son, Andy, was the one who had lain in wait to speak to her on the day she moved in. He wanted to be certain that she understood about his father's allergies. She listened attentively, and replied,

"I quite understand. I'll be very careful. You would go a long way to find anyone who'd be more cautious about allergies then me. I have had experience of what they can do."

"Well, good luck," Andy said, meaning it. His good wishes were less sincere seven months later when Raymond announced that he and Hannah were getting married.

"It's like the dark ages, he needs a wedding ring to get into her bed," Raymond's daughter said. She had taken to teasing Hannah about her superstitions, ostentatiously spilling salt on the table without then throwing a pinch over her shoulder, marching under ladders and never touching wood. Andy remarked, too loud,

"I just hope she's on the pill. We don't want Dad starting all over again with a new litter of sprogs."

Restarting with babies was the last thing Raymond wanted himself, but Hannah wasn't taking the pill because it made her feel sick. Raymond had seen everything when he was in practice, and he wasn't going to trust someone in her late 40s not to get pregnant, though the problem did not arise until the honeymoon, since Hannah had insisted on waiting.

It was a small family wedding at which Raymond's two children and Allegra made it pretty clear that they weren't expecting to become friends.

For as long as she could remember Allegra had felt obscurely guilty about her mother, so Hannah's announcement that she was getting married again came as a huge relief. Allegra flung herself into the arrangements, insisting on providing extras for which Hannah seemed grateful and Raymond's children disgusted – cakes, lucky tokens, a blue garter, some of the inventive sex aids available in specialist shops. On the morning of the wedding itself, Allegra turned up and scattered presents around – posies of flowers, party favours, a case specially designed for vibrator and diaphragm, little heaps of sugared almonds. And that afternoon Allegra drove her mother and new stepfather to Gatwick Airport to catch their flight to Venice.

Always careful about his allergy, Raymond got out of bed to fetch his glasses to double-check the small print on the condom packet. It was their first night together. He was naked and couldn't help noticing that Hannah was not looking at him. But he was looking at her, dark (or darkened) curly hair let out of its pins and jutting almost horizontally, soft pink skin under a demure white nightgown – a voluptuous, enticing vision in his eyes. This is going to make everything all right again, he thought.

Since 1975 anyone who had been adopted as a child has been entitled to see the original birth certificates. I'd been helping such people through the hoops and over the hurdles since I started working. The meeting of birth mother and long-lost child could be a joyous moment, but it requires careful planning and tactful intervention. Few experiences can be more traumatic than for a respectable middle-aged or old woman to be told by an unknown adult that she is his or her mother. Even when carefully prepared for, after months of gradually inching towards a meeting, the moment of confrontation is a difficult one. My job is to make it easier.

The next change of policy came in 1990. It was decided that we should extend our services to include enquiries from birth mothers and other birth relatives. Actually they were far more difficult to deal with and required more detective work and more tact. The last thing we wanted was middle aged women bursting in on a young person saying "I'm your mother". What if her child didn't know that the people he thought were his parents actually weren't? What if the birth mother was a drunk or a druggie? One has to go carefully.

Soon after the law changed, Fidelis Berlin received a summons to give evidence at a judicial review. A case from some years back in which two very young girls had been removed from their parents was to be reconsidered.

This couple, called Sandra and Keith and referred to in court as Mr and Mrs M., had been the target of one of Britain's periodical fits of irrational hysteria during a scare about witchcraft, started who knows how, and blown into a full conflagration by the press.

She had been a district nurse, he had been a bus driver. They had a house of their own (on a large mortgage) and two daughters, Kimberley and Melanie. It had been a happy little family according to them.

They never did understand where the accusations came from.

OK, they didn't deny that Melanie had drawn some peculiar pictures at her day nursery but they weren't witches and knives and altars, she'd got the idea from a programme on kids' TV with wizards and warlocks.

And it was true that Sandra had been to meetings of a woman's group where they had experimented with an ouija board. Sandra, in fact, had disapproved and left early.

Kimberley had a bladder infection. It was simply cystitis.

Melanie had been spoken to by a man in the playground at the end of the road.

Kimberley started having nightmares.

Somebody at the children's school had reported suspicions, the social services got involved and the children were subjected to a series of tests. At the end of a long morning of painting, at last a picture that could be identified as some kind of circle had been produced. Bingo! The ritual dance, on paper!

Melanie did a drawing of someone wearing a tall pointed black hat. Then she did one of people dancing in a circle. It could have been ring-a-ring-of-roses but the child had been questioned. Her sister had been questioned. Did mummy and daddy dance? Sometimes. Did mummy and daddy touch them? Sometimes. Did mummy and daddy take them out in the dark? Sometimes. Did it hurt the little girl to do a wee-wee? Sometimes.

Sandra, the mother, brought an album to court and was allowed by the sympathetic judge to hand it in as evidence. Press cuttings, hate-mail, pictures obviously taken as the hunter-photographer ran after his quarry, birthday cards with loving messages from Sandra and Keith marked 'return to sender' – and reports by social workers, medics and psychiatrists. One of the expert witnesses was Fidelis Berlin.

Whether she would have spoken so candidly if the case had not been in camera is hard to tell. As it was, she said quite straightforwardly, that normally she would have regarded the evidence she was sent as dubious and unpersuasive. She would have taken very little notice of the social workers' theories, and urged the judge to return the little girls to their family home.

"The fact is, Your Honour, I was having a crisis of confidence at one time. I had made a disastrous mistake in a similar case and frankly, I wasn't sure of my own judgement. I didn't know what to do. The parents seemed like harmless victims – but what if I was wrong – again? I dithered for days over this one. In the end I played safe and recommended keeping them in care while further enquiries were made. I never heard what the final outcome was until recently, that is."

Sandra and Keith had fought as best they could. But they didn't have the weapons, they couldn't afford a lawyer, they didn't even know exactly what they were fighting against, since nobody would ever tell them what they were accused of and what the evidence was. Eventually a pro bono solicitor got involved and after endless interviews, hearings, court appearances and arguments they were told by no less a person than a high court judge that their names were clear.

But by this time the children were settled in their new home. They were thriving. The foster parents loved them. They loved the foster parents, who wanted to adopt them. The girls had ponies and kittens and were happy at their new school.

Moving them again would be destructive and disturbing. It was a pity, not to say tragedy, and his Lordship sympathized with the parents and would cause enquiries to be made as to the conduct of the local authority. But in the end the well-being of the children was the paramount consideration. It was not in the children's best interests to have their lives disrupted again. He felt obliged to make an adoption order for Melanie and Kimberley. Afterwards, from the social workers, Sandra and Keith learned that they wouldn't be told the girls' whereabouts. They would not be permitted visiting rights. There would be no farewell meeting. Goodbye.

It seemed a miracle that they had stayed together, and that neither had gone mad.

"We set up our own little business," Keith told the judge.

They found God, Sandra told him. God had tried them.

"And how," the judge injudiciously said.

"In his infinite wisdom and mercy," they responded, in chorus.

The judicial review might have relieved hurt feelings. His Lordship hoped that it could do at least that. He regretted having no power to offer a more material compensation to a couple who had experienced such suffering at the hands of the authorities. He didn't criticise the social workers or Dr Berlin; they were doing the best they could on the evidence before them. On behalf on everyone involved he sincerely apologised to the aggrieved pair. There wasn't much else he could do. The girls had new lives. They might not even know that the names they been given by the adoptive parents were not their own.

1997

It was raining, spiteful, slanted rain that unerringly found the openings in any garment, gutters full of dirty water which the passing traffic splashed over pedestrians. The huge, brightly lit cornucopia of the Sainsbury's on Cromwell Road seemed like a kind of refuge. Allegra scuttled into the shelter of the massive store, chose a small trolley now that she was shopping just for herself and threaded her way through the late evening shoppers to the cabinet of ready meals.

"Hi Allegra, how you doing?" Julie: a secretary at the bank, who also lived somewhere near Earls Court.

"Absolutely fine," Allegra said. Why wouldn't she be fine? Look what possibilities lay ahead now that she'd unloaded Baz. About time too. She heard uncomfortable echoes of the traditional speech about giving a man the best years of one's life. The years in which she could have taken up the offer of places at Harvard Business School or Insead; in which she could have had a couple of children and got pregnancy out of the way; years that could have been time out. She could have postponed her career and travelled the world with a backpack. And what had she actually done with her good Cambridge education? Cooked and cleaned and serviced Baz, worked all the hours God sent, slaved away so that he wouldn't have to slave away. So that he could produce the great work of art.

A titter escaped from Allegra's tight lips.

"What's so funny?"

Allegra had hardly noticed that the other woman was still standing there. Julie was below Allegra in the official hierarchy and much less well-paid. All the same, she was an important figure at work, because she knew where all the bodies were buried. Julie was somebody one avoided annoying. "Nothing," Allegra said, "it's not really funny. It's just that it seems peculiar to be buying supper for one."

Julie's trolley was heaped with family packs of baked beans, kitchen paper, all the boring staples that it was a mother's lot to buy.

"Your bloke away, is he?"

"Didn't I tell you? We've broken up, Baz and me, it's over, he's moved out."

"God, I'm sorry. What a bummer."

"To tell the truth it's a terrific relief."

"You want a new model, you're in the right place."

"What do you mean?"

"In the supermarket."

"They got a special offer on available men?"

"Don't be silly, I mean the convenience food section. It's where singles hang out, didn't you know?"

Allegra didn't know, wasn't sure she believed it and couldn't be bothered to think about it after a long exhausting day. "I'm only here for something to eat," she said.

What to have for supper? Something she never had with Baz, a salad or a veggie dish: pasta. He didn't like that.

Allegra and Baz had been an item since their first term at Cambridge and even after they'd finished with University, they'd stayed together like an old married couple, but their daily lives had grown far apart. There was not much future for them together, but she had so much invested in the long-running relationship that it took her a long time to recognize the truth of the matter. Once Allegra started clawing her way upwards at the bank, going out hideously early in her short skirt and wide shouldered power jacket, with her trainers on her feet, her heels in her briefcase and her mind on the day ahead, she and Baz grew increasingly jealous of each other. Not envious; he would have hated working in a large organisation and dealing with impersonal money; while she'd had quite enough of falling out of bed in the afternoon and getting back into it just about when other workers were finishing their night's sleep. She wanted an ordered life now, she'd grown out of feeling liberated by untrammelled freedom, these days it simply worried her. So did the dirt and mess that used to be the outward and visible sign of some psychic bonfire of the conventions. Like any other little bourgeoise, these days she'd get back to the flat after work and start cleaning and tidying.

Baz couldn't see the point of dusting or putting things away – hiding them, he called it – specially things he couldn't see the point of in the first place. Why did they need a vase, a teapot, an extra rug? He said she'd sold out.

"You're quite happy to live on the proceeds," she would reply.

Then she felt ashamed of using money as a weapon. She did still believe that art was more important than commerce. She was no longer so certain that what Baz had been making was art. But Allegra had invested a lot of emotion, energy and money in this relationship. She might never have cut her losses if she hadn't left the office early – she'd cheek to cheeked with Andy at the wedding and caught his cold – arrived home mid-afternoon and walked in on Baz in bed with another girl.

Pesto, Allegra thought. I'll have pesto. Baz hated that. She asked the nearest tall person to reach a jar from a high shelf for her. Only after a pink, scrubbed, short nailed hand had deposited the bottle into her almost empty trolley did she look at its owner, a youngish man with a basket hooked over his left arm. It contained own brand cereal, peanut butter, and white sliced bread; poverty rations. He was dressed in a stiff suit with a narrow tie (neither in fashion that year) shoes carefully polished, shirt equally carefully ironed, his cheeks shaved so smooth that he had developed a rash from the repeated scraping of the razor. He had pale blue eyes, high cheekbones and very short light hair. Eastern European, she thought, thanking him, meeting his eyes; and then she realized he was the best looking man she had ever seen. She turned towards the fresh fruit and vegetables with a swing of her bushy hair, aware, but not letting herself show it, that he was moving in the same direction. Snatched glimpses showed her a chastening image. There was an expression on his face of bafflement, wonder, yearning and, she thought, a little disgust.

He must be from what until very recently was called 'behind the Iron Curtain.' To see him in the cornucopia of an ordinary Western supermarket was rather chastening. Allegra realized she had never in her life been really hungry or even gone without her favourite brands of consumer luxuries. It made her feel obscurely ashamed, even remorseful – as if she owed him something. They'd never have got talking if she hadn't felt the need to make some recompense to him, some kind of atonement for her riches and his poverty.

He spoke correct, old-fashioned English, full of complicated sentence structures and obsolete expressions. It turned out that he had learned the language largely from Victorian blockbusters. From such novels he had also derived his ideas about life in the west, though he was quickly disillusioned. The first time he came round to hers, Joachim Wenders examined everything in the flat, like an anthropologist taking in the details of an alien lifestyle.

"I am sorry it's so untidy," she said.

"Please no apologies. Disorder represents freedom, I suppose. Both are new to me."

He was a structural engineer, qualified in the old German Democratic Republic, now doing a postgraduate course in London. He'd found that he had not so much to learn after all.

"Did that surprise you?" she asked.

"Not so much. It was not all bad," he said. "In many ways we had a good and constructive way of life."

"But you aren't sorry it's gone are you? Surely…"

"What is the point of regretting or delighting? It has happened. It was inevitable. That was a regime whose time had come."

"Were you there? When the Wall came down – we were all glued to the television, could I have seen you?"

"I did not demonstrate. It is not a constructive mode of behaviour I think. I am what you call a pragmatist."

"But the demonstration worked, it did the trick."

"Like all Westerners, you are sentimental. You like to attribute the fall of the regime to events that can appear for one minute on your screen. Students, people, waving flags and chanting – that is all sideshow. The change comes with the flow of history, it is an inevitable progression."

"Well hooray, whatever caused it."

"But in losing what was not good we have also lost much that was good, it is not all glorious now. Order and discipline were no bad thing."

"Wasn't it tyranny and oppression?"

"That is what history will conclude but history is written by the victors."

She quoted some of this conversation to a colleague who had been in the middle of writing a PhD thesis about post-war Europe when his palm was crossed with the bank's silver and he turned into a financial analyst instead. He said,

"Lots of people thrived under that regime. And don't forget, where people are kept down there are other people keeping them down and thriving on it too."

Allegra knew Joachim wasn't one of them. No way. He couldn't. Never. He was too good-looking not to be good. In fact he *was* good. Honest, straightforward, conscientious, kind – as different from Baz as a man could be.

He'd moved in with her, bringing his viola and one cardboard suitcase. Allegra had been surprised that he played the viola, somehow it didn't seem to fit with her idea of growing up in the former DDR, though his style of playing, hard, accurate and insistent, perhaps did. But her thoughts flitted lightly past Joachim's background. Hadn't her father been in Berlin as a soldier in the army of occupation? Hadn't Granny Browne, right to the end of her life, thought of Germans as enemies? However much you intellectually reject somebody's views, Allegra thought, they repeat themselves in your mind, vicious, scornful, hate filled sentiments in a chorus nobody else could hear. Irrefutable accusations: you're sleeping with the enemy.

Raymond and Fidelis had served on several committees together over the years and had become good if not close friends. His own specialty being concerned with the mechanics of the human body, he was rather apt to dismiss the vagaries of the human mind. But catching sight of Fidelis on the far side of a crowded room in The Royal Society of Medicine, Raymond realized she was just what he needed. He wormed his way across the room towards her, greeted her as affectionately as she did him, and said in a low voice that he wanted her advice.

"Of course. Do you want to come to my office?"

"No, no, not professional advice. Let's go and have some dinner."

He looked weary and older than his age. Giving up his job and losing his status had knocked the stuffing out of him, Fidelis thought, and it didn't seem as if his new wife had put it back yet. They left together and went into the first eatery they came to, a French restaurant with the menu scrawled in purple ink. With bowls of onion soup in front of them, his untouched, Raymond began to talk about his honeymoon.

He and Hannah had limped back to the hotel – the Gritti – after a long day of exploring and fighting their way onto overcrowded water buses. "It all looks so peaceful from a balcony overlooking the Grand Canal, but Venice is too exhausting really. I probably made a mistake trying to talk to her before she'd had a rest. I'd ordered Bellinis. Perhaps they struck the wrong note.

"It sounds perfect, what more could one want?" Fidelis said.

"It's worse in a way when things go wrong in a beautiful place."

Another long pause. Then he went on with his story.

He'd poured Hannah a second glass and watched her relax before asking, "Is that what it's always been like for you?"

"Like what?" she asked, her eyes innocently wide.

"You know."

"I don't."

"Last night…"

"What's wrong?"

"You didn't like it."

"Yes, I did."

"You don't like it."

"It just takes a little while…"

"Do you really prefer women?"

"No – oh! That's a disgusting thing to say!"

"Then did I hurt you?"

"No, of course not, it was lovely – I'm just a bit shy, out of practice, it'll take me a little while to relax, to let go – it'll be fine, honestly!"

"Was it fine with James?"

"Of course it was."

"And before, when you were younger, nothing happened to you? Your father, a brother – did anyone touch you then?"

At this point, Raymond said, Hannah had burst into tears and locked herself in the bathroom for an hour. He couldn't bring himself to raise the subject again. But what was he to do? A subject best approached crab-wise, Fidelis thought. There could be such a thing as an excess of directness. "Do I remember that Hannah grew up in Cornwall?" she asked.

"Yes, her parents – adoptive parents, that is – lived in Penzance."

"I didn't know she was adopted," Fidelis remarked.

"It seems to upset her to think about it."

"That's probably significant," she said.

"I know. Do you think I should try to find out more about it?"

"What do you think?"

"I don't see myself spying on my wife or detecting things she doesn't want me to know about. And presumably she'd tell me if she did want me to."

"Has she said a lot about her first marriage?"

"Very little. I've heard something from her daughter Allegra…"

"Allegra?" Fidelis interrupted. "Allegra and Hannah – what's Allegra's surname?"

"Brown, Browne with an E."

"Oh – I've met them, a very long time ago, in Scotland. What a curious coincidence."

Raymond's body language made it absolutely clear that this was not a subject he wanted to discuss. The advice he had hoped Fidelis would give him was very specific and very private. Where was he going wrong in the bedroom?

"I mean to say, Fidelis, it's not as though I'm completely without skill or experience myself!"

"No", she replied gravely. "I could give you a good reference myself. Very good, in fact." She allowed a pause, while they both remembered. Then she went on, "Give it time. She's not had an easy life, she must have lots of emotional sorting out to do. This may be a problem which will cure itself."

Allegra's wedding was a low key, bureaucratic affair in a Register Office. Joachim's relations didn't come to England for the wedding so they used Allegra's ten days leave from the office to go to Germany and visit his father, uncles, aunts and cousins – his *family* – that demanding, desirable entity which Allegra had always managed very well without.

Joachim persuaded Allegra to give up work when she was pregnant. "It's not good for a mother to be out of the home all the time. I saw it so much as a boy. It was taken for granted, but I always wished it hadn't been." Allegra's heart bled for the little boy Joachim had been. Work was so much part of her personality that she had never envisaged herself without it. But she knew her job was shaky. The writing was on the wall at the bank. Better jump than be pushed.

It was unsettling to be at home. "I can't remember when I didn't have somewhere to go out to every day. I don't quite know what I'm supposed to be doing."

"You will know well enough after the baby comes." Both her husband and her mother were sure of it.

Allegra felt curiously disorientated. What was she doing in casual clothes at this time of day? Who was now sitting at her desk in a dark suit dealing with her clients? The familiar argument unfurled in her mind. And what was she supposed to do all day anyway?

With months to fill in, Allegra started writing, doodling with words at first, without any particular plan, and she was surprised to realize, seven weeks before the baby's due date, that she had completed 100,000 words: a romantic novel. Like the baby, the book was waiting to jump into the world.

She hadn't mentioned her writing to anyone else, not even Joachim or Hannah, doing it during the day when the house was empty and always listening for a key in the door or foot on the stair, ready to cover the screen with a game of solitaire. It was, she thought, the contemporary equivalent of Jane Austen concealing her pen and paper from anyone else's sight.

On Hannah's birthday Allegra took her mother on a 'girls' day out' together, a pamper day at a health spa. It was an unsuccessful birthday present because Hannah strained her shoulder in the swimming pool and by the end of the day couldn't even lift the bag containing her leotard and gym shoes.

They took a minicab home.

The cab drew up outside Raymond Cunningham's house. Allegra asked the minicab driver to wait, helped her mother out, took the bag and went to the front door. She put the bag on the step and said,

"I won't come in."

"Oh Allegra, I really can't bend down, I really need you for a few moments longer. Could you pick up those letters from the mat? Raymond must have been out all day. And look, do just take the bag upstairs, I don't think I can lift it myself."

"Horrid smell, have you got something wrong with the drains?"

Allegra said, hauling her heavy body up by the banisters. On the bedroom floor she turned sharp right, the case dropped from her hand onto the floor, she did a double-take and then shouted, "Mum, don't, don't come up, keep out!"

But of course Hannah got herself painfully upstairs, looked over Allegra's shoulder and saw the body of her husband lying on the floor beside their bed. He'd vomited and voided, and died of a heart attack (as the inquest later determined) early in the day, presumably just after Hannah went out. The cup of tea she had left him was untouched on the table.

Fidelis had been having bad dreams. At the time she was between husbands, but she wasn't alone in the house. An old friend who now lived in Australia had written asking Fidelis to be kind to her son when he came through London. Fidelis had invited him to stay, and after a while, to stay on. Aaron was six-foot two inches tall, with brown limbs and sun bleached hair and some rather arty tattoos. He ate like a horse, ran round the park like a gazelle and slept like a log, so she must really have been making quite a loud noise to have disturbed him in the small hours. The first she knew of it was waking to find herself in his kind, un-sexual arms, in her own bedroom, with tears on her face and Aaron rubbing her back and making the kind of sounds that people hiss through their teeth at horses.

"You were crying in your sleep," he said.

"Sorry I disturbed you," she replied.

"You didn't really, I was online, but you sounded so unhappy – can you remember what it was?" Flashes of misery were still going through Fidelis's mind. Something she didn't want to do, something she was frightened of doing, and always in the background a black clad figure.

Though she'd never taken a professional interest in dreams, Fidelis had undergone the obligatory analysis herself, and even tried to keep a dream notebook. It remained embarrassingly empty because, with rare exceptions, since childhood she had been unable to remember her own dreams. A friend said she was like solicitors who fail to make wills and doctors whose own families are never permitted to be ill.

"You kept shouting, nine, nine," Aaron said. "Number nine, do you think?"

"Perhaps I dream in German," Fidelis said lightly. "Which would be clever since that's about the only word of it I know in real life."

"Something from when you were very small. A memory coming to the surface perhaps."

With gratifying punctuality the baby arrived on his due date – 1st August 1998 – and so quickly that Joachim didn't get to the hospital until the moment after his son had entered the world. He made up for his absence by being at home on holiday for the next fortnight. Much to Allegra's surprise he was prepared to be a participating father (at least so long as nobody was watching) and changed nappies rather more efficiently at first than Allegra herself, wielding the wipes and baby lotion authoritatively. The first time he did it Allegra was reminded of his dexterity with the viola. "It's quite easy," he told her. Look, you hold his ankles with one hand like so – he's very dark, isn't he?"

Peter was born with a full frizz of dark hair, like his mother and grandmother, but his skin was perfectly white and his eyes were becoming hazel by the time he was six months old. Allegra adored, worshipped, doted on him, but she found life as a full-time mother unbearably boring. She hinted as much to Joachim, whose face took on the expression of revulsion Allegra had only seen once or twice before. His cheeks, his neck, his whole body seemed to swell in a seizure of disgust. At that moment the postman knocked with a letter to sign for. Allegra had almost forgotten sending her manuscript to a publisher, but this was a letter offering her a surprisingly respectable sum of money for the book.

It was a romantic novel, fiction for women. Perhaps that was why Joachim did not want to read it, even to correct her grammar and punctuation, at which, having learnt English as a foreign language, he was far better than she. When she published her third book a journalist from a

Midlands free-sheet asked her what part her husband played in her writing, and she replied rather sourly, "Background music." Looking back she realized, though she did not admit it, that about the only thing she could remember him saying about her writing was that she must use her married name.

"You are no longer Allegra Browne. To use that name would be a fraud on your readers – if you have any."

It wasn't exactly what one would call encouraging and the book came out to the usual resounding silence: or, to be accurate, short if good reviews in two broadsheets and three women's glossies, three local radio interviews and invitations to speak at a couple of literary festivals and a Women's Institute. It would have been nice to leap to stardom with one's first novel but Allegra swallowed her pride and disappointment, looked with relief at her bank statement and told herself to persevere. She installed a table in their bedroom and worked on the second book in the moments when Peter was in bed, half an hour here and half an hour there until it added up to 80,000 consecutive words almost before she had realized it. Meanwhile Joachim went out early and came back late. It took Allegra a while to notice that he was getting more and more discontented. By the time their son was two, she realized, suddenly, that he had turned into grumpiness personified. He despised English cooking, English casualness, English standards, the young! Litter, jaywalking, dirt – in fact he had become venomously critical of the Western lifestyle and London's in particular. "We could go and live in Germany," Allegra had offered several times; her work after all could be done anywhere. "I wouldn't mind a change of scene, it might be fun."

"You're so frivolous. Fun! Is that all you think of? You live for pleasure. Buying those ridiculous ornaments and clothes all the time, things, useless things, you take nothing seriously."

"I do, I take lots of things seriously!"

"Such as?"

"You for instance, and Peter. And if you'd be happier going back home…"

"How can I possibly take you there when you make it so obvious that it disgusts you."

"I don't! I didn't! You can't blame me for being shocked at the contrast between our wealth over here and…"

"You thought we weren't good enough for you."

"Well your family didn't think I was good enough for you, did they? And you didn't like it a bit when your father said I looked Jewish."

"You understand nothing about real life, you know nothing of hardship and deprivation and struggle."

"Oh Joachim, why are we quarrelling? I only suggested it because I thought you might be happier."

"Do you seriously think you would fit in there? A place which you make no secret of not liking."

It was true that she didn't like it. Joachim's father and sister were his only surviving close relations. They were not so much hostile as uncomprehending. The old man looked at Allegra as he might look at an exotic species of pest on the geraniums. But Allegra was determined not to be offended; instead she was hyper-understanding of the distortion that sixty years of totalitarianism must have wrought on a personality, just as it had on the environment.

Joachim came from a little town called Köthen in Saxony-Anhalt. He had told her several times that area had been the cradle of the Reformation, and the town itself was where Johann Sebastian Bach composed the Brandenburg concertos and Samuel Hahnemann invented homeopathy. But Joachim's home was not in the town centre where the vestigial traces of earlier civilisations still stood. He had grown up in one of the *Plattenbauten*, prefabricated apartment blocks built after the war by the city's Communist rulers. His family thought themselves lucky to have their own bathroom and kitchen and not to be sharing their tiny living room and two bedrooms with neighbours. To anybody from the prosperous west the accommodation seemed cramped, uncomfortable and soulless, quite apart from the unpleasant feeling of the invariably artificial fabrics, the ingrained smells and grime and the emptiness of daily life in which either you worked or you slept or you watched television. There seemed to be no other possible occupations. Joachim did not bring his viola on their visits to his family. Allegra wondered how he had managed to play and practice it, given that he would have been audible in a dozen other apartments. She didn't like to ask.

Not only were the physical surroundings in which he had grown up brutally ugly, but so were most of the people who lived there, and the surrounding countryside, a flat and sour blasted heath. Allegra understood that the slowness, surliness and negativity of the people she met there was not their fault. Many of them looked unhealthy, toothless, their faces pocked, slouching and too fat, and the physical surroundings were degraded by neglect. Allegra had taken to allowing her fancies more rein now that she was a novelist not a banker, and she thought of Joachim's home town as a place that had been asleep for half a century, restlessly, with nightmares: a corrosive slumber during which the fabric of the village and land around it had slid into dereliction. But it had woken up now. It would be prosperous and pretty. One might even be able to help it on the way.

"Do you think you'd find work?" she asked, and added, "I can work anywhere now, and Peter's still portable." The trouble was that she could hear the insincerity in her own voice. She had never been able to act.

"You don't really want to live there, stuck with my family and friends all day? You'd hate it! I'm not blind, I've seen the snooty expression on your face when you're over there, you have been spoilt by soft living in the west. You wouldn't last one winter."

"Well you must take Peter to see your father more often, even if we go on living in London. It is not fair on him otherwise, and you want Peter to learn German, don't you?"

So Joachim took Peter to Germany without Allegra. Though he didn't mind changing nappies in private he wouldn't have been seen dead doing so in public, or pushing a pram or buggy but it was a short flight to Leipzig and usually some woman came forward to help him. The first time they went Allegra thought she would die without her baby. But ten days later, when they got home she told Joachim,

"It was funny you know, on the first day I simply couldn't bear it, I thought I was going mad, then the next day I woke up like a different person, like I'd turned into a single woman again, I stopped listening for a baby crying, and I stayed up till the small hours watching movies and I really forgot about him. I actually made myself look at his picture and say his name first thing in the morning, like somebody saying their prayers. I must be an unnatural mother."

It was not until some time later that Allegra realized he hadn't contradicted her.

Alone in her dark bedroom, comfortable but wide awake, Fidelis said out loud, "I don't know what's come over me." Like many of her colleagues who spent their days excavating other people's thought processes Fidelis gave little thought to her own. She had far better things to think about. Post-menopausal, busy and vigorous, she was at the height of her powers and the peak of her career. She was free to please herself, her two former husbands had turned into good and supportive members of her wide network of friends, her sex life was varied, unemotional and enjoyable. With professional success went sufficient prosperity. All should be well. All would be well, but for the fact that she had apparently lost the knack of sleep.

If I were my own patient, she thought – and after a while, she added a mental footnote, "physician, heal thyself." She thought of the paper she had herself written on the subject: 'Failure of adaptation to childhood trauma in old age.' She'd seen the patients, drawn the conclusions, helped their distress and recorded the deduction, that those who had apparently had successful lives, forgetting the trauma of childhood evacuation or deprivation or exile, found themselves haunted decades later by guilt and misery they thought long forgotten.

Look at Johann, for example. He wasn't a patient but an acquaintance. Master of an Oxford college, Nobel prize winner, Knight of – the Bath? The Garter? some archaic order or other – and in fact more recently made into a peer of the realm; father of four and happily married to a bishop's daughter. Could any man be found who had better adapted himself to the circumstances of his life than he? Or who'd made a greater success of his life? Yet at the age of 70 he had begun to dream of what had happened to him when he was seven. In his dreams he was crouching in ditches under machine gun fire, pushing a pram piled high with family belongings he hadn't seen for 63 years, and beside them, his baby sister. Sometimes he was carried, great big boy that he was, by his small, pregnant mother. He didn't remember exactly what had happened between the deafening sound (literally, since he had impaired hearing ever since) and finding himself alone: no mother, no baby sister, no pram, all gone as though they had never been. He was on a boat, he thought, though even that memory was vague. Alone, dirty, bruised and in a world of silence. He couldn't say very much about the first people who had taken him in, farmers who expected the child to earn his keep; he certainly did remember the second family, a schoolmaster thrilled by the boy's mathematical ability, always encouraging and pushing him to go further. "But my real life began at Cambridge," he always said. It was what he told the presenter of *Desert Island Discs* and other interviewers as well as Fidelis herself. He'd been less reticent than usual with her, because he knew her background was not dissimilar. "He has bad dreams," his wife told Fidelis and later when they were alone, whispered, "He wakes up screaming, with his hands above his head, cowering, except that you can't cower when you're lying in bed. It's not planes or bombs, I don't think, it seems to be birds, big black birds. Actually he's never been very keen on birds come to think of it, I remember once when there was a flock of crows, we were in France – in fact, not crows they were choughs and I saw his face, he was – was it disgusted? Or was he actually afraid? I didn't like to ask."

Well, Fidelis thought again, as she had when she first heard of Johann's bad dreams, snap! Perhaps all of us who were saved back then are lying in our beds having nightmares.

Stop it! Think of something pleasant, something that makes me happy.

Holidays: the brilliant blues and greens of an Ionian island in early June, the mild water embracing and supporting her; last weekend in Paris, wearing the perfect suit, pleased with her own reflection in the windows of shops whose wares might have been designed to appeal, specifically to her. As her breathing slowed and her thoughts wandered, there were strong arms around her, holding her up high so that she saw them from above, the men in black robes like ladies' clothes, walking round and round like follow-my-leader and they mustn't touch, she mustn't be put down, they were scary – with a sudden jerk she was awake and sitting bolt upright in her bed, panting and sweating. Another nightmare.

She turned the light on and plumped the pillows behind her and picked up the current book, a novel by Margaret Atwood. She reached out for her glass of water. Before taking her sip, she muttered, "And what was that all about?" But the physician could not heal nor the psychiatrist analyse herself.

'Satan and Social work.'

A network of doctors and therapists who still believe in the prevalence of ritual abuse, seem determined to revive the "Satanic panic" – the hunt for devil-worshipping paedophiles who go round sacrificing animals and sexually abusing children – which caused such mayhem in Nottingham, Rochdale, the Orkneys and most recently on the Scottish island of Lewis. Although the allegations in those episodes proved to be unfounded, these professionals are no doubt sincere in their convictions, but campaigners fear that they will influence experts dealing with vulnerable children considered at risk of abuse and adults suffering from various forms of mental illness from anorexia and depression to self harm and drug or alcohol addiction.

Joachim had the paper spread out on the kitchen table in front of him. It was quite a long time since Hannah had actually seen him. She wasn't usually there on a Sunday because she tried to make her visits to Allegra and the baby when Joachim was sure to be out. In fact, as she stood on the front doorstep earlier on, she'd been rather dismayed to hear through the open kitchen window the slightly harsh sound of his viola playing Telemann's concerto.

It wasn't that she didn't like Joachim, or that she felt ill at ease with him, she always said, always insincerely. But, as she explained to her daughter, "I probably say the wrong thing without meaning to. I don't want to irritate him."

Allegra couldn't say that Hannah wouldn't irritate Joachim because she knew she would. He was driven mad by Hannah. She fussed; she gushed. She told Peter he was sweet, upon which Joachim would say,

"I wish that you should be firm with the child. It's not good for him to be so indulged. He must learn that life is real and earnest."

Joachim showed his disapproval of his mother-in-law by behaving as though she wasn't there, hardly answering if she spoke and reading rather than conversing. Today when she went downstairs he'd put the viola back in its velvet lined case and was sitting at the table with the papers spread out in front of him. Squeezing behind his chair to get at the instant coffee, Hannah paused to look at the picture. She leant across him and tapped her finger on his paper. Joachim jerked his head back as though dislodging a mosquito or fly.

"I knew her," Hannah said.

Joachim had not been going to read the article. He usually skipped features or profiles about women. But this one was a continuation of a news story he'd noticed on the front page. He found it unexpectedly interesting.

Profile of Dr Fidelis Berlin by Esmond Smith.

Fidelis Berlin is a world authority on the relationship between young children and their parents. When she expresses doubts about the prevalence of ritual satanic abuse, other professionals should listen. "I don't deny that it happens, but very very seldom. Who was it that said 'Given the horror that humans create all on their own, who needs Satan?' But I do think social workers, family court judges and expert witnesses should be asking themselves that question."

Dr Berlin has been in the forefront of parental psychiatry since the 1970s. I suggested to her that it was an unexpected specialty to choose, given that she never knew her own parents; in fact that she never knew any relations at all.

The infant Fidelis arrived in England on the first kindertransport from Germany in November 1938. Children travelled on those trains labelled like luggage but the particulars of this child were lost and she will never know whether the harassed staff of volunteers who greeted the pathetic refugees had reunited her with the correct label. Her age could only be guessed at. A foundling, in effect, she was fostered by Fabians and says she could not have had a more caring or kinder home and upbringing. After grammar school she went to medical school in London. So why did she choose to specialise in a subject of which she had so little personal experience? "I don't really know," she tells me, her voice deep and authoritative, the accent Oxford and posh. "I suppose it just seemed interesting at the time. It is interesting, and important too – what could be more important than the relationship between parents and their children? We need to see what's happening, or not happening, clearly, without pet prejudices or mistaken preconceptions." By mistake, I suggest, she must be referring to the mindset that sees unprovable abuse through, among other mechanisms, Münchhausen's syndrome by proxy, magic rituals, covens of witches. "We need to look at facts," she insists. Not theories, not philosophies, just what the actual evidence can show.

"What is this word, coven?" Joachim said.

"It means a group of witches."

"Witches? That is…Hexen? Hexerei?" His eyebrows met in a furious frown.

Hannah said hastily, "It's a kind of religion. An old religion. Wicca, it's called."

But Joachim had stopped listening. "I've heard of them."

"It's a woman's thing, Joachim, not for you."

"They are child abusers."

"No, Joachim, that's not..."

"We don't have such people where I come from."

"Yes you do."

"Nein. No."

"I'll show you." Hannah leant across, noticed Joachim shrink away from her – do I smell nasty? she wondered anxiously – and pulled out the tabloid she had brought with her. It took her a while to find the right page, with Joachim poised to leave the room, but then she came upon the picture again. Below a photograph of naked women dancing in a circle was a short paragraph. *"Witches have returned to the German forests, dancing naked in groups under the full moon and calling to their gods. The covens vary in size and in how seriously they take their calling but the numbers are rising, particularly among the young."*

2011

I'm trying to describe these events in chronological order, but you will understand that I am writing with authority about people and events that I only learnt about many years later. And because this is not my story, I haven't described my own life. The story of a single mother in London during the heady days of women's struggle for liberation isn't relevant; for the same reason I haven't said anything about meeting, marrying and later parting from my second husband, Marcus, or anything about François, my third. In case you're wondering, I didn't have any more children. Marcus didn't ever want any and François already had five. As I've already explained I didn't put real people in my novels on purpose or consciously, but I can now see that my fourth novel, a kind of 'bridegrooms in the bath' story was the result of my increasing irritation with Marcus, and the seventh, set in the Dordogne in a glorious summer, describes the setting of my first weeks with François – and no doubt gives away other details of that happy time.

François was the London correspondent of a French radio network when we first met. When he retired he decided to stay in London because he loved it and because his two grown-up children were working in this country too. He's in his late 70s now and beginning to think we should move to Paris because the French health service is said to be better than the British one. Sadly he is beginning to need health services.

Not being very well he spends far more time at home than I do and has quite unintentionally turned into my telephone secretary. Luckily he doesn't seem to mind fielding the increasingly frequent calls from Scotland. It was taking longer than I'd expected to track down Hannah Browne. I didn't suppose that she did it on purpose, or even that she knew she'd done it, but somehow she had left few traces, or at least few that I could find.

I told François, "Just don't answer the phone."

"Poor Liza…"

"She can leave a message."

"Anyway, what if it's a new client?"

"If they're serious they'll ring again."

"But I feel really sorry for Liza Dorneywood, I don't mind trying to calm her down."

"OK then but remind her I only started looking quite a short time ago."

"She's the kind of person who wants answers yesterday."

"I can't do it so fast, Hannah Browne has been flying under the radar for too long."

"But you will find her?"

"I hope so. And you can certainly tell Liza that."

Aaron claimed to have hypnotic powers.

"Let me try. Let me help you remember. Not now obviously but tomorrow or the next day. You've been crying in your sleep ever since I got here."

"Aaron! I haven't!"

"You have too."

"I can only apologise for disturbing you," Fidelis said coldly.

"Don't be daft. But let me help you."

"Hypnotism doesn't work on me. I'm immune."

Aaron insisted, "You'll never have closure if you don't find answers. At least try."

The following Sunday afternoon Aaron and Fidelis sat facing each other in her sitting room. They had eaten a traditional lunch – roast pork, apple sauce and all the trimmings, bought and cooked by Aaron, "It's rent in kind," he explained. "And so will this be – helping you remember." He placed her on the wing chair she usually chose, and pulled a lighter chair up so to be facing her.

"I promise you," he said, "hypnosis works with everybody…"

"That isn't so," Dr Berlin replied.

"It is, so long as they let themselves. It depends on relaxation. You have to imagine your conscious mind as a television which is programmed, and your unconscious mind like the video cassette or DVD which can be wound backwards and forwards, beyond your death even and before your birth."

Aaron went on, in what was evidently a routine spiel, "I will enable you to relax, you'll remain conscious throughout, and you'll remember what happened unless while you are in a state of trance I tell you not to. If you regressed to some awful moment, to something which brings on a trauma, don't worry, I can instantly bring you back to your normal state."

"That's lucky," she said drily.

"Close your eyes, sit comfortably." Aaron said, before moving on to the usual relaxation routine. Fidelis had heard it many times and never been any good at it. "Visualise your muscles and relax them, work down from your forehead to your neck, onto your shoulders, down your spine …"

His voice became softer and more monotonous. "Imagine you're in a train, you are sitting comfortably in a seat by the window, you're looking at a view, you see the stations and each one has a sign showing your age. You're going backwards through the years. You have a long way to go but you're really in charge of that train, the moment you press that button you can stop. You can talk if you want to – go back now, back to when you were 55, remember what your life was like then, go back further, 50, 45, 40…"

It's curious, Fidelis thought, this spiel is having no effect on me whatsoever. She felt wide-awake, and didn't have a single twinge of memory even from the most recent years. At that moment she couldn't even remember what she'd done the day before. It was a pity to seem uncooperative when he was so well meaning. Aaron intoned the decades, his voice softening as she went. "Remember what happened when you were 30." Purely out of politeness, Fidelis murmured,

"That was when my first book came out."

"25, 21…" By the time they reached childhood Aaron's voice was a whisper and Fidelis's mind was a blank. "Four," Aaron intoned, "three, two – are you with your mummy, are you holding your mummy's hand?"

This was too much. "In your dreams, matey, not mine!" Fidelis did not say the words aloud but she opened her eyes and sat up and said, "Sorry, I really don't remember anything."

"Are you certain?"

"Absolutely positive."

"Then it means there's something in your mind that's stopping you."

You don't say, she thought.

"There's a block preventing you from seeing things. You see, it's simply isn't possible to forget anything very important that happened to you, no way can you forget it."

"Look who's telling me," she thought sourly.

"Any highly charged emotion, when you enter its zone, you get a sudden shock, like an electrical charge. So I think your memory is still there, but the battery is going down, the voltage is too low to feel."

Later, sitting at the kitchen table with another glass of wine Fidelis still felt irritable and offended. Aaron had been intrusive. But he meant well. And one shouldn't discourage the young. So all she said was,

"It didn't work." And her nights were still full of horrors and terrors. Something dormant and buried had been wakened in her mind, a monster that would inhabit her dreams.

"You're like a cat on hot bricks," Hannah said. Allegra was restlessly walking up and down, putting things into the open suitcase and taking them out again, swooping down on Peter to give him an impassioned hug, refolding his clothes.

"Sorry," Allegra said. "It's just that it makes me feel so…"

"I know. But it's making Peter feel bad too. Why don't you leave it to me? Go out. I'll stay."

"Maybe I'll do that. But you've got to tell Joachim – where's my list…?"

After another half an hour of fussing, by which time the child was uncontrollable too, Allegra left the house. Her mother watched from the window as she made her way up the road, stopping every few steps to turn round and wave. When she eventually turned the corner Hannah said,

"Now then young man, we better get you cleaned up before your father comes. Don't cry darling, it'll be all right, come on, hush now, hush."

Once she'd got Peter settled in front of a Magic Roundabout tape, Hannah settled near the window to keep a lookout. She hadn't seen her ex-son-in-law for eighteen months, and the last time they had met he refused to speak to her, averting his eyes and behaving as though she wasn't in the room at all.

As if Hannah gave a damn! As far as she was concerned everything had worked out absolutely for the best. Once Joachim had gone back to Germany, leaving his wife and son, Allegra chose to move in with Hannah. But the three-storey house in Marylebone inherited from Raymond Cunningham was inconvenient and with no garden was unsuitable for children. In any case, Allegra said she didn't like the atmosphere; whenever she went upstairs the dead body of her stepfather appeared before her eyes.

"No, mother, of course I'm not saying it's haunted. You know I don't believe in ghosts even if you do. I just remember rather too clearly."

So Hannah sold the house and found a pretty Victorian villa with a garden further west, near Brook Green. It was a lucky house, she could feel it. To dodge eventual inheritance tax she bought the house in Peter's name, with herself as the minor's trustee. The basement became a common kitchen-living room for all three generations; Hannah lived on the ground floor and the first floor was converted into bedrooms and bathroom for Allegra and Peter. They turned the attic into habitable space to use as an office.

Allegra reverted to using the surname Browne, so Hannah did too. They thought they might deed-poll Peter eventually, but meanwhile everyone assumed his name was Browne, and neither woman corrected the error. Allegra worked at home, neatly turning out 3000 words between nine and 12 o'clock when she printed out the day's stint, turned off the computer and went downstairs to meet her mother and her son in the family room.

Joachim had been granted access to Peter but it wasn't enough for him. He wanted custody. He wouldn't give up, making repeated applications and appeals, and as consequence Allegra and Hannah had endured numerous visits from social workers. Each one in turn concluded that this was a stable home and conducive to the child's happiness and recommended that the estranged father should have holiday contact only, particularly as he proposed to take the child to a foreign country to stay with relations whose language the child did not speak or understand. "Short visits only," the report concluded, and so the judge had ordered. Allegra Elizabeth Wenders otherwise known as Allegra Browne was granted custody, care and control of the infant Peter Joachim Wenders. The order was coupled with a grant of access to the father Joachim Maximilian Wenders and at times to be arranged with his ex-wife. Allegra announced that she intended to be civilized about the separation, she wanted Peter to know his father and his father's country. In private Allegra felt uncivilized, possessive and determined.

"My son's going to have a stable childhood with one home and friends he keeps for life, not moving round like a gypsy like I did."

"I did the best I could, Allegra," Hannah told her.

"I know that! You couldn't help it. But Peter's going to have a better time, that's all."

No doubt the arrangements would become perfectly smooth and regular, it was just something that needed to shake down and they would all get used to it in no time.

Peter would be three years old in August. He would spend his birthday with his father's family in northern Germany. It happened to be very convenient for Allegra who planned to go to a writers' and fans' congress in America, and for Hannah who wanted to get the house repainted while nobody was there. She let Peter believe that he had chosen the paint colours and promised there would be a nice surprise waiting when he got back. She and Allegra had repeatedly explained what was going to happen. He must be a good boy for Daddy and when he came back he could go with Mummy and Nan in a plane to the beaches in Spain.

"Pity we haven't got a picture to show Peter," Hannah remarked. "Did you really throw them all away?"

"There weren't very many in the first place." Joachim had always travelled light having grown up in a world where people had few possessions. He didn't leave many traces.

"That's a silly thing to say," Hannah rebuked her daughter. "Peter's a very solid trace, aren't you my precious?"

Like his father, Peter's features were large and made up of straight lines – the nose, the eyebrows, the line of the lips but in temperament Peter was his mother's child, she said. And his colouring was like his grandmother. As Peter grew out of babyhood the fuzz of dark hair he was born with was replaced by springy black curls.

Allegra had dressed him that morning in a little pair of denim dungarees and a yellow and white striped shirt. He looked, Hannah thought, good enough to eat. She picked him up and pressed her nose into the soft white back of his neck, sniffing out the delicious infant smell. She wished he didn't have to go to his father twice a year or even once or actually ever. She hugged the child tightly and possessively until he wriggled away.

There he was. She heard the chugging engine of a London black cab.

Joachim hadn't changed. There was the same gaunt, unforgiving pale face, the same short hair and strict clothes. I won't make it easy for him, she thought, and waited until the bell had rung twice before tapping her way down the tiled passage to the door.

"Joachim," she said, automatically pushing her left cheek forward. But he did not kiss it, nor did he say anything either to Hannah or even a word to Peter. He took the child by the hand, swung his small pack over his shoulder and turned and walked back to the taxi.

"Hold on, you've dropped his teddy." Hannah ran down the steps, picked up the shabby stuffed toy and went towards the cab. But the door was slammed before she reached it. "Joachim, he can't sleep without it, you must take it!" Joachim tapped on the glass partition and the driver put the cab into gear. "Wait, wait," she called again, but it drove away leaving her on the pavement clutching the slightly damp, deformed little object. Hannah could see Peter's appalled face, the wide mouth squared in dismay, but his cry was inaudible as the cab was driven away.

I'd published half-a-dozen novels when I started to be sent books for review, usually crime fiction and Aga-sagas. Why the literary editor sent me Schimmler's posthumous novel in a batch that included a police procedural and the story of a travelling menagerie I have no idea. It was quite inconvenient since I had a lot on at the time, but realized that I would have to read at least one or two of his earlier books if I was to write sensibly about this one. I cannot say that I enjoyed them.

From the Argus, Book Review Supplement.

August Schimmler LONG LOST reviewed by Isabel Arnold

The publicity accompanying this translated volume tells us that the story in it begins autobiographically but turns into fiction halfway through, or to put it another way, after the war. The author became one of the most popular novelists in Germany, and was the recipient of many national and international literary prizes for his novel, The Magic Soldier, in which a conscript is initiated into a sinister and secret Nazi cult.

Long Lost was found among Schimmler's documents after he died in 1991, unpublished in his lifetime, according to his agent, because he was ashamed of the actions described in it. Presumably this shame referred to the fact-based part of this partly autobiographical novel. It tells of a middle-class boy born just before the outbreak of the First World War into a relatively liberal but also relatively conventional family in Dresden. This boy, called Julius, was a law student in Berlin when the

Nazis came to power. Not himself Jewish, he had many friends who were and watched the increasing pressure that was put on them in the following years. He didn't join the Nazi party but he didn't do anything active to resist either, unless you call falling in love with a Jewish girl an act of resistance. To his family it seemed like an act of rebellion.

Julius's girlfriend became pregnant, they had a daughter and perhaps because, perhaps in spite of this, their relationship soured. But if they separated, what would happen to the little girl? He was her protection; in Berlin with her Jewish mother she would be in danger from the authorities but also, he gradually came to think, from the influence of her mother.

The way in which Julius's thinking changes is fascinating, as the society he lives in is taken over by prejudice, as he hears day by day and hour by hour more and more vehement, anti-Semitic speeches and jokes and remarks and explanations.

At first educated people didn't take much notice of the situation. Their Jewish friends were treated with delicacy like people who had been diagnosed with a fatal illness; but ordinary life continued. Even those who were aware of what was happening in the world, and in particular in Germany, still followed their daily routine. They noticed the disappearance of Jewish colleagues from offices and courtrooms, they had to find a new doctor when the family physician retired or emigrated, they were more cautious when talking politics over the dinner table, but their lives went on much as they always had.

But Hitler's education campaign against the Jews gained momentum. The populace were taught to consider them as at once subhuman and devilish and the infection of such thinking spread imperceptibly even to those who were intellectually in disagreement with Hitler's government, and wholly opposed to the anti-Semitic measures being brought in. So the reader observes Julius as he gradually and without even realising it begins to be affected by the anti-Semitic arguments. He would deny it if asked. But somewhere in his instinctive reactions, there grew suspicion of people whose differences he once didn't even notice. Perhaps, he finds himself thinking, perhaps there really is something in it, perhaps they are not trustworthy as colleagues or desirable as neighbours – or acceptable as the mother of one's child.

It's a dangerous direction for his thoughts. What is he to make of his own little daughter, innocent, endearing and being brought up by his Jewish former lover? Could he bear to see his child with a yellow star on her coat? What is to become of her? What is to become of him so long as she is his responsibility?

One day in November 1938, he learns that a rescue plan has been made. Jewish children can be sent to England. They are to travel by train (we are talking about the kindertransports here) in the care of volunteers. They will find open arms in Western Europe, and good homes. Better homes, Julius tells himself, than that slut his former girlfriend could possibly provide. Julius likes England. He likes the Low

Countries. He has always liked the French. What happier fate could befall his child than to be taken from her unsuitable home and her neglectful mother and to live in a civilised country until he can reclaim her?

He urges the idea on the mother, who is never given a name, always referred to as the girlfriend, the Jewess, the mother, the witch — depersonalised in advance of the depersonalising fate that awaited her people. The mother refuses to co-operate. 'The child and I are inseparable, we're moulded together,' she tells him. So Julius does a terrible deed. He informs the Gestapo that the mother has done something; he doesn't specify what. It's enough for a Jew to come to the authorities' attention. As the knock falls on the mother's door, the father takes the child. The mother whispers thanks. It makes a scene so poignant that it is painful to read or remember.

Julius carries the child to the station. The panic, misery and chaos on the platform, as parents part from their children, is so vividly described that I was breathless and sweating by the end of the chapter, when Julius has forced his way through the crowds and managed to thrust his daughter into a stranger's arms a second before the train pulled out.

As it happens, as hindsight shows, he has in fact done the best thing he could possibly have done for her. But guilt overshadows everything in his life. He goes through the war haunted by remorse, but at least he does go through the war, a survivor. He is an army officer who, in 1945, returns from France to find the devastation whose description we have seen so often in fiction and non-fiction. It is unusually beautifully rendered here by an author on whose mind it had clearly preyed. He is in Germany again but his former girlfriend is not — she died at Auschwitz.

In the novel, the daughter comes back to Julius after the war and the rest of the story has as its background the relationship between this guilt driven German and the motherless child. In real life, according to the blurb, August Schimmler never saw his daughter again and was never able to trace her. His fantasy about the lost child is painful and personal, and it exposes him as the perpetrator of a dreadful cruelty. The fact that it turned out to have been the right thing to do did not redeem him. No wonder Schimmler did not want the world to know this story in his lifetime.

The first thing Allegra saw when she came back that afternoon was Peter's teddy bear on the the living room mantelpiece. "You didn't forget it, surely!" she exclaimed in an accuser's tone.

"Of course not, he dropped it and Joachim wouldn't stop. I've been worrying about him going to bed without it, poor baby."

"What did Joachim say?"

"Nothing at all, he didn't say a single word to me. So rude."

"You could have posted it."

"There hasn't been time yet. Give me a chance."

Hannah took the stuffed toy and went up to the work room where she packed it into a padded envelope, addressed it to Peter at Joachim's house and went out to post it by special delivery. The next day Allegra set off to New York and the day after that a team of decorators moved in. Hannah applied to interior decoration the intelligence that had got her a degree, studying books and magazines about interior design, comparing quality and making notes She spent the next three weeks in a blizzard of paint charts and fabric samples. She chose formal designs, white on white damask patterned Cole's wallpaper for the hall, expensive makes of paint in an unusual blue-green – not the colour Peter had chosen, but he would never notice – and curtains made to measure with swags and tails in fabrics by Schumacher or Osborne and Little. Peter's bedroom was decorated with friezes of zoo animals and a soft floor covering on which roads and landscape features were printed in the right scale for zooming his toy cars along. It was highly enjoyable, now that Raymond Cunningham's estate had finally been settled, to spend his money.

Allegra's plane arrived at Heathrow in the early evening. It was still daylight when she got home and came into the newly elegant living room. She admired her mother's handiwork before going upstairs to see what mail had piled up on her desk. A few moments later Hannah heard her shriek.

"What's the matter?" Hannah ran up the stairs. Allegra was holding a torn envelope in one hand, and in the other was Peter's teddy bear.

"What's this doing here? In this parcel, no letter, just the teddy bear and this label look…" She held out a scrap of paper on which the words 'SURPLUS TO REQUIREMENTS' were written in black capital letters.

"He sent it back!"

"But Peter will be miserable, he can't sleep without it."

"Maybe he thought it was time for Peter to learn to? I mean, at his age…"

"My poor little boy!"

Hannah was trying to calm her daughter down. Unconvincingly she said, "Perhaps he should have grown out of it by now, Joachim could be right you know."

"No he bloody couldn't! It's unsettling enough for Peter to go away to a strange house and strange people not a single one of whom he'd remember ever seeing in his whole life before, without having to manage without his security toy. So mean, so unimaginative – it's really cruel."

"Well never mind, not much longer, he'll be back home tomorrow."

"Joachim obviously doesn't understand the slightest thing about children. Damned if I let Peter go there alone again."

On the way down to the living room Allegra went into Peter's room and put the teddy bear on his pillow, patting it gently. "I miss him dreadfully, now I'm back. It doesn't feel like home here if he's away, though I must say it was a relief not having to worry about him while I was away."

"So you didn't feel anxious all the time."

"To tell you the truth, it sounds awful but I was so busy I couldn't really think about anything except the next interview. It's been an exhausting trip. I am absolutely whacked!"

Allegra's jet-lag led to a night of sleeping nightmares and waking small-hour-angst. Hannah found her in Peter's bedroom at 6.30 in the morning, rearranging toys and plumping pillows, making the room her own.

"They're not due till lunchtime are they?"

"No, and that's if the plane is on time."

"Are you going to meet them?"

"I don't know which airline or airport, Joachim didn't tell me, otherwise I certainly would."

By noon Allegra was like a cat on hot bricks, walking up and down the living room, peering out of the window, going back to rearrange the pile of presents she had brought for Peter, pouring a drink, not drinking the drink. At 12.30 she had laid the table for lunch. "Only three places?" her mother said.

"Joachim won't want to stay."

At 12.45 she put the pizza in the oven. It was Peter's favourite food. At one o'clock she turned the oven down to its lowest to keep the pizza hot. At 1.15 she told her mother that the planes from Germany were frequently late. At 1.30 she turned on the television to make sure there were no news flashes about plane crashes. At 1.45 she started telephoning; first trying Heathrow, and eventually connected to somebody who was able to assure her that no flights from Germany had come in late; by five past two she had heard a similar assurance from Gatwick, by half past two from Stansted and from Luton too.

"Perhaps he decided to drive over," Hannah suggested.

At four o'clock Allegra called the number of Joachim's house in Germany. There was no answer nor was there an answering machine.

At five o'clock she rang the police to see if any accident had occurred to a three year old child travelling with a tall, blond man.

At five twenty five she called her lawyer who said it was too soon to panic, travelling arrangements were easily changed, have a drink, put her feet up and wait till the morning. Relax.

But Peter and his father did not turn up that evening; Joachim did not ring; nobody answered the telephone at the German house all evening. The police said they could not take on a missing persons enquiry at this stage. If the child was with his father he was hardly missing.

Allegra and Hannah spent the evening and the night in a state of hardly controlled hysteria.

"I'm sure it's all right," Hannah would say. "You'd have heard if anything had happened, someone would let you know by now."

"Nobody ever said Joachim was irresponsible."

"Of course not."

"I could trust him to take care of Peter, couldn't I?"

"They will be fine, I'm sure they've stopped off in a hotel somewhere on their way."

Neither woman went to bed. Allegra paced the floor. Her mother retreated to the top floor for a while, where she lit some candles and sat surrounded by them visualising her grandson travelling towards her, working out exactly what he would be wearing and where he would be sitting and directing her will towards ensuring that what she saw in her mind would happen in reality.

By eight o'clock in the morning both had fallen into an uneasy slumber, Hannah in an armchair in the sitting room and Allegra kneeling on the hearth rug with her head on the fireside stool. When the doorbell rang they both leapt up and ran to the front door. Allegra wrenched it open – to find on the doorstep not her son nor his father but the postman holding a recorded delivery letter. Like somebody walking towards the scaffold she took it slowly back into the living room. "I know what this is going to be," she said. "It's from Joachim. I can't bring myself to open it."

"A black cat crossed my path yesterday morning, I should have known something awful was going to happen," Hannah murmured. Allegra, who had never given up trying to persuade her mother that a black cat did not bring good or bad or any kind of luck wasn't listening. She turned the package over and over in her hands for a while but in the end did open it, cutting the sellotape with a sharp knife and lifting the flap to pull out a single page. There was one typed paragraph, not so much a letter as an announcement. It was from Joachim.

Peter was German and therefore must grow up in Germany. It had been arranged for the Youth Authority to interview Peter and find out which parent he wanted to be with. Joachim had applied for an order to allow him to keep the child in Germany. Of paramount importance in German law were both the interests and the wishes of the child. Peter was happy with his father. Boys needed to be brought up by a man. It was not good for the boy to grow up in a house full of women. It all added up to the single, dreaded announcement.

Joachim would not be bringing Peter back.

The nightmares concerned rituals, a church, a child. What I need, Fidelis told herself, is counselling.

It's far too long since I saw Benjamin. It was Benjamin who more than once had picked her up off the ground, dusted her off and got her back to work. Perhaps, also, it was conversations with Benjamin, or monologues to him, that laid the ghosts in her dreams.

Over-dramatising? She accused herself. Probably, but at least after talking to him she might sleep again. Benjamin was old enough to be her father. He'd been an old man for the last dozen years. He walked cautiously, like someone afraid of tripping and falling. His voice had weakened. He needed thick spectacles. But those were mere physical details. Those aside, he was eternally young if it is the young who have discoveries to make and come fresh to all ideas. Fidelis prescribed another quick course of Benjamin's conversation to banish the bad dreams.

Her increased involvement in Satanic abuse cases wasn't helping. Ever since she'd gone public with her scepticism Fidelis had been bombarded with unwelcome information. She knew better than to open unexpected parcels and letters that were addressed in handwriting, unless she recognized it. In fact her correspondents could be very interesting. She was sent numerous cuttings from newspapers and grew better informed than she wished to be about 21st century witchcraft. It was a difficult subject to discuss. "I can't get my head round it," she thought.

Benjamin was pleased to see her. He was affectionate and she was confiding, as always. She told him that she'd failed the annual voice test; having sung with the Bach choir since she moved to London, she would in future have to be audience not performer. Brightly, she added that not being able to sing in a choir any more was surely a very minor price to pay for the privilege of growing to a prosperous and compos-mentis old age. But she had never quite registered before what a difference it made to her mood to go to the weekly rehearsal, to join her voice in the unity, the collaboration of choral singing. "It will be a grief to you," he said gently.

She was silent, remembering how careful she had been, not to complain or argue or admit how much she minded. She'd had a good innings. The choirmaster had been sympathetic. Fidelis knew she'd failed the annual audition and only hoped she didn't let the disappointment show. "It comes to all of us in the end," she'd said lightly, and held her head high as she went down the stairs, greeting the singers who were on their way up to the first run through of the season. Of course they knew what had happened, but she kept smiling and smiling until she was in the privacy of her own apartment. But then gloom set in, a despondency that was not quite a depression but more like being in mourning. The calendar had told her for years that she was old. If she were in hospital, it would be in a geriatric ward. She was at the retiring age for members of the judiciary, which was already seven years older than everyone else's. She had a free travel pass, free TV licence and an annual subvention towards winter fuel. Today the objective fact became an emotional truth.

Walking past the mirror in the hall she asked herself fiercely, "what am I doing in this outfit?" and replied with the command to, "be your age." In her bedroom she tore off the 'fashion forward' tunic and the new shape trousers. They'd be a bonus for the charity shop. She opened the wardrobe doors and began to throw clothes onto the bed. A purple Jean Muir dress, a Nicole Farhi embroidered jacket, a coat of many colours bought in the seventies, a favourite sequinned evening dress with a neckline far too low for someone of Fidelis's age. All unsuitable, too revealing, not the thing at all if she didn't want to look like mutton dressed as lamb. She filled plastic sack after plastic sack. It was time to simplify her life. She ought to be like those Indians who dispose of all belongings and worldly ties and set off with a begging bowl, towards the end of their lives.

Towards the end of their lives. The phrase repeated itself in her mind. She thought, I'll just make sure…

Neurotically, since nobody else would have access to her bathroom cabinet, Fidelis reached to the back of the top shelf behind the insect repellent and sunscreen left from last summer, and took down a small plastic bottle labelled melatonin, which was what it had once contained, brought back from the United States at a time when it was recommended as the best remedy for jet-lag. But the red and white plastic capsules she shook out onto her hand were not melatonin. This was her secret stash of barbiturates. I might never use them, she thought. Morphine or even quinine would be the drugs of choice. Being a medic, she should be able to get hold of them, but in fact it was a long time since she had had a valid prescription pad. The Seconal was her insurance. She'd counted them, put them back in the bottle and put it back in its hiding place. But her hand had wavered, the hesitation of indecision. Perhaps the time had come. The roller coaster was speeding up, downhill all the way from now on. She'd always been one to leave a party while she was still enjoying it. *Fidelis, what are you like?* Physician, heal thyself.

Or let Benjamin heal you. She dressed carefully to meet him, in a black trouser suit that had escaped the massive clear-out, but was dismayed to realize that his once-observant eyes were unfocussed.

Benjamin seldom said, *I think, you should*, or *one must*; he advised by indirection, often by talking about things that seemed irrelevant or tangential; in fact he didn't even talk all that much. But by the end of a leisurely lunch or even a short conversation at a crowded party, he had somehow managed to plant solutions in someone else's mind and that someone was quite likely to believe they were self-seeded. But I didn't come here to talk about singing, she thought.

"Benjamin, I'm stuck. Do you remember years ago, that I came a cropper over black magic? Tell me there really isn't anything in it after all."

"Your problem, my dear," he said "is your inhibition about believing."

She knew that he was a practising Anglican, even a lay reader in his local cathedral. It was not a subject they had ever broached before.

"I'm a card-carrying agnostic," Fidelis said. "I neither believe nor disbelieve, I just don't know."

"Nonetheless, if I say there are more things in heaven and earth than we know of, your automatic response will be resistance, I think. You are sceptical and incredulous. This can be admirable, but it leaves you at a loss with the irrational. You have to get your head round the idea that many people believe impossible things and that belief in itself is enough to lend existence."

"Thinking makes it so?"

"If you think so!" he said. A joke, she thought. But perhaps he meant it.

For a novelist, Allegra thought, all this would in other circumstances have made good copy and in a brief moment of detachment during her first court hearing – when she had no idea how many would follow, over how long a time – she could see herself writing a courtroom scene, her heroine a desperate mother, her villain a cruel father, the hero, metaphorically galloping to the rescue – who? The barrister? No, not this one, a small and elderly man with dandruff on the shoulders of his gown. Or the judge? A tall man in a wig and black robe. Who was this stranger, speaking in an inscrutable vocabulary, from which odd phrases lodged in her consciousness – the Hague Convention, article 3 subsection – she never did notice which subsection – who was key to determining the future of Allegra's baby?

The legal argument passed incomprehensibly about Allegra's head until her solicitor tapped her on the shoulder and said, "Success! He's granted us an injunction!"

"So what happens now?"

"I have to inform the Child Abduction Unit – it's part of the Lord Chancellor's Department – and you're going to need a lawyer in Germany. I'll find out for you who would be good."

On that day, it seemed as though there was hope. But the order granted by the English court was useless. It couldn't be, or at any rate it wasn't, enforced. Joachim did not respond to it. Peter was not brought home.

The English lawyers talked about the Hague Convention, injunctions, wardship orders, illegal retention and foreign jurisdictions. A German lawyer was taken on. Before he had delivered any correspondence to Joachim, he received a document from a court in Saxony. Joachim had applied for the transfer of Peter's custody. Allegra had no idea that he had done so, had no means of knowing that the case was going to be heard and had no chance to put her own side of the argument. The German court granted him legal custody *pro tem.*

"It's a whole new ball game," the solicitor said. "We'll have to make another application to the High Court. It won't be easy."

It wasn't. The English judge was not willing to grant an injunction in contradiction to the decision of a German court.

In this new world, full of bewildering experiences, despair lurked like a predator, ever ready to leap out and sink its claws into Allegra. Daily despair, as she woke to a house without her child in it, despair when she went to Germany, to the dismal apartment in which Joachim had grown up and where his father still lived, and found that Joachim and Peter were not there. In fact nobody was there. A neighbour shouted from an upstairs window, but Allegra didn't understand the German.

"Away," the neighbour said. "From here, away."

"Where have they gone?" Allegra called, but the only reply was a slammed casement and a drawn curtain.

Allegra stood in the shabby street with tears pouring down her cheeks. There were few passers-by and those there were ignored her. Generations of fear had taught these people to keep clear of trouble, and a weeping woman in western clothes couldn't be anything else. Thrusting her hands deep into the pockets of her mac, Allegra found herself touching a small piece of stone. She took it out: a green, mottled pebble. This was one of Hannah's lucky charms. She must have inserted it secretly, knowing Allegra's perverse denial of superstition, maintained since her teenage years when she would upset her mother by purposely walking under ladders, spilling salt, putting shoes on beds and bringing bunches of flowering hawthorn into the house. Allegra threw the pebble angrily away, and strode off, her anger usefully, if temporarily, diverted from Joachim to Hannah. All the same, she'd have to go back to her. There was nowhere to go but home, if only it felt like home instead of something between a torture chamber and a waiting room.

Ever since she'd gone public with her scepticism about alleged Satanic abuse, Fidelis had been bombarded with unwelcome information. She had become more expert than she ever wanted to be about 21st century witchcraft. She had been present (by invitation) at several Wiccan ceremonies. Naked, shivering women, who undressed modestly, behind bushes, and carefully folded their clothes and moved into their circle bashfully, arms crossed tightly over their breasts, or with one hand over their pubic hair, and all still wearing shoes. It had been absurd and yet in some way admirable. The participants were asserting their right to individuality and self-determination. The ritual they used to express it had been developed in the nineteenth century by women who had no rights to anything. Discussing the phenomenon with post-graduate students, Fidelis found herself under verbal attack by a group of religious enthusiasts who thought ceremony was a good substitute for therapy.

"You don't see a difference between convictions that science can prove and those that depend on faith?" she asked.

"What's the distinction between science and faith? There wasn't one, until recently."

"Recently? The 16th century?"

"A thousand ages in thy sight are as an instant gone," one of the more enthusiastic girls sang. Fidelis suddenly remembered the line from the hymns in morning assembly back at school, the words meaningless to her then and meaningless still. She said mildly,

"Science is rational."

"My dad says that's what's wrong with shrinks. You just want things to make sense, screw making them better."

The discussion veered off in too many directions to reach a unified conclusion. It was towards the end of her assignment and Fidelis didn't see that group again, but the argument had stung. She was between books at the time, so dashed off a polemic on the subject. It was published in a professional journal under the impeccably academic title: The Influence of Preconceptions in Child Protection and the Avoidance of

Prejudice. Adapted and simplified, her argument was reproduced in a Sunday paper, titled 'Sense, Sanity and Satan'. It provoked a lively correspondence and as usual, changed nobody's mind. But it had a side-effect – a telephoned enquiry that Fidelis didn't expect to be followed up. But the written confirmation followed promptly. The letter was on cream paper thick enough to make a Christmas card, with a red embossed crest as solid as sealing wax. It invited her to become a member of the Royal Commission on Ritual Practices Concerning Children.

Fidelis's knew her views were regarded in official circles as slightly subversive. At the first meeting, at a boardroom in Whitehall, she realized that she was there to demonstrate impartiality. The other committee members included a Roman Catholic journalist, a Jewish financier famous for giving huge sums to good causes, an Anglican bishop and an Imam. There was a notorious 'full time mother' of ten children, who had become rentaquote about bringing up a large family, and a self-publicising lesbian mother who had made a movie featuring herself and a turkey baster. Numbers were made up by a retired missionary who never spoke, a retired social worker whose personal cause was the acceptance of revived memories: if, he insisted, after decades therapy leads someone to remember being abused in childhood, then that memory must be taken seriously.

Fidelis's ally on the committee was an agreeably cynical and incredulous headmaster who was also a historian, a broadcaster and writer. The chairman of the committee, a former senior civil servant, was professionally mollifying, and cleverly managed to avoid his members coming to serious disagreements.

At the first committee meeting members set out their stalls. More than half had no doubt that Satanists were flourishing and conducted rituals complete with animal sacrifice and the drinking of blood.

The Rabbi disagreed, saying that one could never believe the unsubstantiated statements of children. He quoted an example from California where children not only described ritual abuse, but also said that it had taken place in an extensive series of tunnels under their school building. Under interrogation techniques which were originally designed to trick adults into confessing, small children told police they had been sexually abused and forced to murder babies and drink their blood; some recalled being flushed down the toilet, or flying through the air, and seeing giraffes and lions in the underground caverns. The school was completely dismantled and the ground excavated to a considerable depth but no tunnels were ever found.

On Midsummer Eve the committee went on an outing to observe a celebration in Devonshire. They walked along a bracken-walled track to a circle of nine stones, natural and unshaped humps, each about two feet high. Set in the ground in the middle of the circle was a wooden totem or statue which seemed to be made of twisted roots. On the far side of the clearing was an open fronted canvas shelter held up by ropes slung between birch saplings. There were one or two benders, three small lopsided tents, two tepees and several painted camper vans. In front of the canvas shelter somebody had built a camp-fire, its sweet, illicit smell suffusing the area. "Don't breathe in, my guess is that even the smoke's hallucinogenic," the Chairman warned.

"I think I'm hallucinating already. Do those sheep look slightly pink to you?"

"It's Devon's red earth, it can have that effect. We Devonians wear rose tinted spectacles."

The participants were of both sexes and young as well as old; the music, augmented by live drums and guitar, blared from a stereo wired up to an old van and had more in common with Top of the Pops than any mass, black or white, and the dancing could have been in a club. Beside the fire about thirty young people were standing in a group. They wore ragged jeans or ground-sweeping skirts, three were holding babies or toddlers, some had tangerine coloured or emerald green hair. Somewhere somebody was playing a guitar, the insistent beat adding to the distraction of the intoxicating fumes from the fire.

As the chairman began, "Ladies and gentlemen, this place is called The Dancing Girls. It's…"

One of the young people came forward and held up his hand. In a disconcertingly posh voice he said, "As you've probably noticed, you've come into our home. We'd be glad if you treat it as such."

"A listed monument, open to the public."

"A sacred place. We're its guardians. As you probably know, legend tells of a dozen women petrified as they danced…"

The financier, standing beside Fidelis, whispered to her, "This is where they hold their Sabbaths – can't you feel the atmosphere?"

She shook her head, "I can't say that I do."

"You have to imagine the local villagers with their pipes and drums…" The young man was painting a dramatic picture.

"The trouble with you, Dr Berlin, is that you don't feel it because you won't."

The chairman directed a quelling glance at his members, but the instructor had finished and said, "Please feel free to look around but we must ask you to be respectful of the atmosphere."

"Respectful of your Black Masses?" jeered the former missionary.

"Our ceremonies are not Black Masses and we are not Satanists. Tonight we celebrate."

"What's tonight?" one of the members asked.

"Midsummer's Eve. We shall hold our revels. You may join in or leave, but we won't have an audience."

The Chairman looked round the group of his members. "Stay or Go?" he asked.

"Go!" The monosyllable, fired like a bullet from her own mouth, surprised Fidelis herself. It had been an involuntary reaction. Something in her head was repeating, *Get me out of here, let's go...* She looked round, surprised by her own...fear. That's what it was. She felt afraid. But what was there to be afraid of here? She looked round at the peaceful boulders, the calm pink sheep, the friendly landscape, the tents and – there was a small child peering out of a bell tent – a girl aged about two. At the sight of the child Fidelis felt her breath shorten, her heartbeat speed up. *I can't watch that child take part – I simply can't!* She backed away from the group, trying to be unobserved, but not really caring. *I've got to get away from here!*

Why? Her conscious, analytical mind demanded, but its logic was drowned in inexplicable urgency and fear. *Get me out of here.*

Watched by her mystified colleagues, Fidelis Berlin ran away.

Allegra became familiar with complicated arguments of Private International Law, with details of signatories to the Hague agreement on child abduction and about the enforcement of international treaties.

The days dragged on, turned into weeks, months. Allegra appealed for help from her Member of Parliament, from the Lord Chancellor, from the Foreign Office, from the Queen herself. She returned to Germany several times, begging and pleading with the authorities, the neighbours, the primary school staff, anybody at all who might be able to tell her where Joachim had taken her son.

Hannah said, "Surely they wouldn't keep a grandmother from her grandchild," and went to Köthen herself.

Doors were slammed in her face. Questions were ignored. On the third day she climbed the dusty concrete stairs to the ninth floor, wondering as she made her slow way up and whether the spray-painted graffiti cheered up the building's grey concrete, or defiled it. She was hammering her clenched fist on the locked front door of Peter's other grandparents' flat when two uniformed policemen leapt from the lift and arrested her. They were not gentle and her arms were still purple with bruises when, a few days later, in the office of Wootton Hardman, solicitors, she was warned against going back.

"But they assaulted me, look at the bruises."

"Well, Mrs Cunningham, complaints were made about breaches of the peace and refusing to obey legitimate instructions and – this is rather shocking – you seem to have scratched one of the officers across the cheek and drawn blood."

"They were the violent ones, that was simple self-defence – and it wasn't as though I'd been resisting arrest."

"That's as may be. But you are now *persona non grata*, which means, an unwelcome person…"

"I understand the Latin."

"Sorry. But it means you'll get the point. Don't go back to Köthen, Mrs Cunningham, it would be simply asking for trouble."

Peter's birthday came and went, marked but not celebrated, a day of mourning. They did not even know where Peter was.

"It is almost worse than if he were dead," Hannah said in a careless moment, and clapped her hands across her mouth, tears springing to her eyes, before she said, "I didn't mean it, nothing could be worse than that, he'll be back soon safe and sound you'll see, it's just the waiting, it's driving me mad." An unfortunate choice of words. Hannah might still be sane though sad, but Allegra's default state was one of uncontrollable hyperactivity and hysteria. She couldn't write, or sleep, or eat or even speak. She didn't wash her hair, body or clothes. She spent most of every day walking, but never walking to anywhere in particular, and at night huddled in a corner of the living room sofa touching and stroking Peter's abandoned Teddy.

Another flight to Germany, another law court and evidence that Peter had now lived with his father for long enough to feel at home there. There was a report which Allegra had not previously seen from the

'Youth Authority'. Its welfare officer asserted that Peter was happy in Germany with his father.

But how could anybody be sure? Neither Peter nor Joachim appeared. The case was adjourned, yet again.

—>>><<<—

In the early days of her career as a consultant psychiatrist, Fidelis's work was clearly separated from that of general practitioners. The patient would be referred to her, discharged back to him, and communication between them was distorted by the hierarchical (or simply snobbish) relationship. But by the 1990s she had begun to devolve some of her work from a hospital setting or from a consulting room, and occasionally provided consultation facilities in a general practitioner's surgery. She would even assess patients jointly with the GP.

So it was in a consulting room in south London that Fidelis found herself considering a woman called Daffy who was herself a nurse in that practice. It was highly unprofessional. Daffy was not a patient, she was the employee of Fidelis's friend, Dr Geoffrey Warner.

"I could really do with your advice, when she comes in, just have a look at her, see if you think there's anything one could pin down. She's a perfectly competent nurse but somehow she leaves trouble and chaos wherever she goes. She is just…what's the word? Manipulative."

"Was it Ford Maddox Ford who said some people are like fire ships on a crowded lagoon causing conflagration in their wake?"

"I suppose it's been a kind of conflagration. We've lost a receptionist and another of the nurses and she came to blows with a trainee doctor."

"But you've kept her on."

"One can't show that it is her fault. And you can't see me standing in the witness box saying that the other staff say she's a witch."

"Bitch is quite a mild word really, I can think of worse things to be called."

"Not bitch. Witch."

"Oh dear."

"I think she'd convince a tribunal that she was the victim. Frankly, I don't know quite what to do about her," he'd explained.

He left a file of documents for Fidelis to look at. Daffy – correctly known as Daffodil Foster, had changed jobs very frequently. Fidelis noticed that she had been working in North Somerset just at the time when Fidelis herself had been there. She felt an automatic revulsion from the town's name in the documents; it wasn't a place of which she had happy memories.

Fidelis had several patients to see that morning, two with postnatal depression, a child she diagnosed as autistic whose mother's symptoms of depression, guilt, apathy and stress caused her to scribble "burn out"; and no wonder, she thought as a child exhibited exhausting echolalia, repeating the times of trains to London Bridge over and over again, continuously, like a machine. As Nurse Daffy showed the patients in, Fidelis watched her too. A personality disorder short of psychopathy, she thought, scribbling in her own indecipherable shorthand "self-centred, frigid, suspicious." She guessed but did not write down that the woman had always been single, probably sexless, and was determined to control every last detail of her environment.

The last patients were a middle-aged woman whose 13 year old son had survived an attempt to commit suicide by cutting his wrists. The physical scars had healed but the psychic wound he had inflicted on his mother was still raw. As she spoke she picked at self inflicted scratches on her bare arms, lifting off the scabby tissue until her skin was running with blood. She talked about being a smother mother, said several times that it was all her own fault, she couldn't forgive herself, she loved him too much. "I'm the worst mother in the world to have done it to my own son," she kept saying.

Fidelis wrote a prescription for a heavy-duty tranquilliser, and as the patient left the room the nurse didn't follow but shut the door tightly and said,

"You know what they say she's done."

"No."

"Only used him as the altar boy at a Black Mass. That's why he lost the will to live."

"I beg your pardon?"

"There's a difference between using the ancient power of Wicca for the good, and black magic. You must know that."

"What are you talking about, nurse?"

"Did you not hear what I said?" Even in these more egalitarian days, it was an unusual tone of voice for a nurse to use to a medical specialist. "It's okay for Doc Warner to pretend it's nothing to do with him but you know all about the occult, don't you?" More unusual still: sarcastic, sardonic, in fact unacceptable. But Fidelis accepted it. She was interested to see how far the woman would go.

"It's only hearsay though?"

"Maybe, but I can tell, I know what I'm talking about. Better than you do probably, Dr Berlin. There's none so blind as those that will not see and that's something you've decided not to see. But I can. You can't take part without it leaving a trace on you. Night terrors, dreams, delusions – do you sleep well at night, Dr Berlin?"

How can she tell? I must be looking a wreck today, Fidelis thought. "Very well, thank you," she replied.

"In denial about that too!"

"Not at all," Fidelis replied. "I've never denied that these rituals take place. Indeed, I've been to them."

"You've been at the Black Mass?"

"I have. I've heard about the secret of the Holy Grail, the golden cup of fornication, the sacred vessel of our Lady the Scarlet Woman, the Mother of Abominations, the bride of Chaos, riding upon our Lord the Beast – you know about them?"

The other woman nodded and said, "Of course they only date from the 19th century, it is not the real traditional witchcraft."

"The rituals may survive but as an excuse for crime, they don't convince," Fidelis said, and refrained from adding that they did haunt. She had attended many variations of such ceremonies: amateur and highly polished, ritualized and spontaneous, suffused with sex and as chaste as a church service. They all gave her the creeps. This dreadful Nurse Daffodil was right. Fidelis had never been prey to nightmares until she had to learn about the occult, and the occasional co-option of children into its ceremonies.

"Are you involved with such things yourself, nurse?"

"And what if I am? The occult has been the refuge of the disempowered throughout the centuries. What's changed?"

Well, Fidelis thought, there is certainly one thing that has changed, which is that a job has become personal property. "You'd have endless trouble getting rid of her legally," she advised her friend. "Cost you a small fortune too. But you need to get rid of her, she's poison. I think you should cross her palm with silver. Buy her off."

Peter had been gone for nearly four years.

Another hearing in the English High Court, a different judge, female this time, with a warm, sympathetic voice and kind eyes. Allegra's lawyers had commissioned a second report from the psychiatrist.

"Dr. Berlin's worth every penny," Allegra was assured. "The judges take notice of her. She is an authority about relations between young children and their parents."

"It'll be interesting to meet her."

"Oh you won't actually meet her! Expert witnesses like that do everything off the papers."

Another closely argued document explaining the importance of Peter's relationship with his mother. More references to The International Hague Convention on the Civil Aspects of International Child Abduction 1980, to judicial cooperation between States, to the recommendations of Köthen's Jugendamt – the Youth Authority – to Child Trauma and Patient Alienation Syndrome.

The High Court in London confirmed the original order in Allegra's favour.

A brief moment of euphoria. It made no difference. Hope again dissipated into despair. The German court had made a contradictory order. This male German infant was happy with his male German parent and should remain in his charge. An order was made for supervised contact, for three hours one afternoon a month. But when Allegra turned up, Joachim and Peter were not there.

Court case after court case, consultation after consultation, endless frustrating treks to Germany. It became impossible to see an end to it. Weeks passed, and then months. Hearings were adjourned or deferred. Allegra would turn up and Joachim would unaccountably be absent.

If they actually got to court, the case was inevitably adjourned for some reason or another. Joachim's lawyer would be missing a vital document. A witness was unable to attend. Further information was required.

The German courts and the English ones worked independently of each other. One made an order for the mother to have access, the other determined that a visit would be disruptive or upsetting. One decided that evidence was needed to support the accusation that Peter had been at an occult ceremony. Another found the allegation alone sufficient to deny his mother access. As time dragged by, the authorities on both sides of the channel began to doubt that it would be in the child's best interests for his life to be disrupted again.

There was a brief moment of optimism when a psychologist who had personally interviewed all the parties recommended that Peter should see his mother again and the German court agreed. But Joachim immediately appealed against the decision. A new psychologist was appointed who did not even meet or speak to Allegra, but advised the higher court that seeing her would traumatize Peter. The access order was overturned.

Another application. Allegra had lost count of the times she had signed her name to documents she couldn't read. This time the response was more terrible than ever. Now that the child had spent well over half his life with the paternal parent, the English language had been forgotten and the mother would have been forgotten too. A visit from her could only upset the child. Access denied. Again.

"He wouldn't recognize me now. I might not even recognize him."

Allegra didn't formally move out but she could not bear to be in, and took to spending her nights crashing in a friend's flat rather than going home to her own bed. Weeks could go by without mother and daughter meeting at all. Hannah stopped expecting her daughter to turn up, and she didn't. But an even less expected visitor stood on the doorstep one fine morning, a face from the past.

"Daffy?"

"The very same."

"But how did you find me?" Hannah asked. "No, never mind, don't tell me: it's good to see you after all these years." Daffy still had the great mound of light red curls that had looked so unusual twenty five years ago, she was still a big woman, tall and burly.

"I saw you in Waitrose and followed you back here. Nice place."

"Yes," Hannah said. But to her the house had become a place to be, not a home.

"You've done well for yourself."

"Haven't you?"

"Yeah, right – living in a bedsit. Oh, I've had my ups and downs, there was a time when I had a nice little house in Bristol. But I've made a lot of mistakes in my time, as a matter of fact I'm still paying for my last one, she ran up huge debts on our joint account. But more fool me for not noticing till it was too late."

"What are you doing these days?"

Daffy was still a nurse, not having been able to afford the early retirement she'd hoped for. At the moment she was single. Hannah asked as delicately as she could if Daffy was still involved with Wicca, and Daffy said not really. "Would I be living in a six by ten box sharing a bathroom and a microwave with three strangers if I could work magic?"

"It's not the only way to get what you want," Hannah said. She made coffee, produced biscuits. Daffy blew on the hot liquid and scattered crumbs onto the carpet. Then she said,

"It's nice here. Pretty."

"It was pretty." The decorations were stained, with signs of wear on the once-expensive fabrics. The green wallpaper, Peter's choice all those years ago, was peeling away at the edges. Daffy looked interested and... what was it? Not kind, nor sympathetic – Hannah was still considering what word was apt when Daffy said,

"Not bad, is it, for someone who was born a slave."

"I beg your pardon? Did you say...?"

"Slave."

There. The word was uttered. Hannah had never said it, never told anyone. The keeping of the secret had defined her life and directed her actions.

"That's what you were, right?"

Hannah was breathing fast, her forehead and the back of her neck were suddenly dripping with sweat. Daffy said, "Come on, say the word. It'll make you feel better."

Suddenly uninhibited, Hannah said, loud and clear, "I was a slave."

"I read about the court case. They used the Slavery Act."

"It's true, they did. In the 20th century, in a society that had a welfare state and a national health service and free education for all, a child could be...I was born into slavery. But how did you find out?"

"You hear things, if you're a nurse. People talk like you're not there."

"But who knew?"

"That woman you worked for, that Mrs Payne – she said something to the doctor," Daffy, her face paler than ever, said. She sank onto the chintz sofa. "Go on. Spit it out. I want to hear it."

"I must have been one of the last ever. The very last, maybe. What a claim to fame!"

"Sorry, I'm not with you."

"I'm a living relic, it's over now, but there always used to be people like me in remote districts, some wretched girl would get pregnant and the child wouldn't be registered which meant it didn't have a legal personality, no school attendance officer came because nobody knew there was somebody who should be at school. Anyway, most of them – most of us – were half wits. It was the interbreeding. The master screwed his own daughters often enough."

Daffy said, "And look at you now!"

Hannah's grey hair was permed into a rigid helmet. She was dressed in a tweed skirt, tan tights, a beige twin set. She looked and sounded like a teacher. "It was a traditional source of free labour on the old farms, you'll find it mentioned in lots of 19th-century documents. They used to do informal home baptism and might even scribble the child's name on a scrap of paper, but there'd be nothing in the parish register and no real birth certificate."

"How ever did people get away with it? An unregistered birth! No schooling! No health checks or immunization – someone must have seen you!"

"Well, it happened. I'm the living proof. After all, what is a girl who has no legal personality or money or freedom? I belonged to that man, I was his property," Hannah said. Then she paused, and added, "Do you know, it feels very odd to say it aloud. To tell somebody."

"You do look a bit pale."

"So do you. I'm sorry if it upsets you."

"What about your mother?"

"She'd had died or disappeared before I could remember. They probably fed her to the pigs."

"Hannah!"

"You have to understand, people like my mother, or me, we didn't count as real people, not like the rightful heir, the child princess. She was pampered and protected, she was too young to touch sharp implements or do any work or go out on her own. But I was younger than she was and I was old enough to be treated like...a skivvy. A slave. A piece of property."

"Didn't anyone interfere? The vicar? The social worker?"

"They were probably scared of the master. I was afraid, for years afterwards, and ashamed too. I'd have died rather than tell anyone, or have anyone know. I've never mentioned it before, ever!"

"Your husband?"

"Husbands. Plural. Not a word. They had no idea."

"How did you escape? What happened?" Daffy was leaning forward across the table, her body tense.

"It was surprisingly easy in the end. Somehow the time had come. One day they got the doctor for the child princess. When people like that came, salesmen or the health visitor, I was always supposed to hide in the loft, I'd be beaten if they heard or saw me and not just beaten either. Chained and starved."

"But Hannah – is this true? You aren't exaggerating?"

"Really, I'm not. For years I had no idea there was anything peculiar about it. That was just the way it was. But then I was on the moors one day, there was an old woman – she must have had a name, I suppose – maybe nobody bothered to give her one. They called me the maidie. The old woman, I suppose she'd come from the same place as me, long ago. She scraped some sort of living selling charms and potions. She told me...she taught me things. How to see. How to be brave. How to hate."

"Who? Who did you hate?"

"Them. All of them. The child princess, I'd seen her room and clothes and toys and books – and he was so nice to her, so gentle. She'd sit on his lap or hug him like a monkey and he never touched her – you know. He didn't molest her, only me. I looked like her, and there she was, his baby, his princess, and I was a non-person. His toy. He'd never have thought of it as abuse because I wasn't a real girl, I was a blow-up doll, a thing – a slave."

"But his wife? The mother?"

"She treated me like she treated the dogs. You had to feed them and tend to them. And keep them tied up out of the way when visitors came. I don't think she ever really saw me, she wouldn't let herself admit who I was. What he was."

Daffy said hoarsely, "How did you get away? What did you do?"

"One day the doctor came to see the child princess. While they were all upstairs I climbed into the back of his car, and he drove me away. He stopped almost at once, because of the smell. I'd never had a bath and if I washed in a cattle trough once a month that seemed a lot. And I had fleas. But I was safely away."

"There must have been a law..."

"The master – I mean, the father – he was prosecuted under the Slavery Act, but he only went to jug for a few months. They were both fined for not registering a birth and not sending me to school. Nobody said anything about incest, or child abuse."

"They probably wanted to spare you from giving evidence about it."

"I would have done though, sent him to jail for life if I could,"

"What happened to their other daughter?" Daffy asked.

"The child princess? She hid at home and cried. As if she had anything to cry about. She should have tried living in the farmyard like an animal – anyway, she escaped as soon as she could, married at seventeen and emigrated to Australia."

"And what happened to you?"

"A kind childless couple took me in. I don't think they ever realized how much I wanted what they had, the comfortable bourgeois life. It was like a glimpse of paradise until..."

"Until?"

"They sent me away to school. It was probably necessary, at least until I'd caught up enough. I could read, I'd learnt to speak like the matron but I had to get away. They paid for me to go to a secretarial college in London, where nobody knew who I was. Or who I had been. I wanted to put it all behind me."

When Rosa married Benjamin everyone assumed that she and Fidelis would 'bond' because, as people frequently said, "the two of you have so much in common". In other words, Rosa was another child of the kindertransports. However, Rosa's mother had survived and the two of them were reunited after the war. Rosa had a conventional, English education and spent the early years of married life as a professional mother. But then she became active in local politics and turned herself into a 'professional survivor,' a popular speaker to audiences of school children or Women's Institutes or anyone else who invited her to talk about the loss to European culture represented by the lost Jews of Europe. She described sentimentally the mutually supportive village communities of the east, and boastfully the musicians, artists and scholars who had set the intellectual tone of pre-Hitler Germany. From historical generalities she always moved on to her own story: the horror of parting from her mother and father when they took her to the train, the shock of this sudden parting to a six year old – if she didn't reduce at least one member of her audience to tears it was an evening ill-spent.

Rosa's other campaigns – anti-abortion, pro-censorship, in favour of capital punishment – were all for causes which Fidelis herself opposed. It was even more alienating when she justified her stance on the grounds that she fought against everything that Hitler and the Nazis enforced. For Benjamin's sake Fidelis never argued with Rosa. For his sake she remained Rosa's 'friend' and even after Benjamin and Rosa were divorced, the two women would meet for lunch or go together to the theatre. But Fidelis hadn't noticed an unaccustomed silence from Rosa until she had a call from her daughter-in-law.

The dreaded plague, Alzheimer's disease, could creep up so gradually that nobody noticed its approach. Sometimes it hit like a hurricane. In that case the gap between total lucidity, and a consciousness hardly more reactive than a vegetable, could be bridged so quickly that nobody not personally involved would realize it was happening. Rosa in fact had noticed her own symptoms and believing them at first to be imaginary had consulted a psychologist, one who, as it happened, Fidelis knew because they were both tenants of the same consulting room space in Harley Street. Rosa was losing her short-term memory and rekindling memories from long ago. Memories? Or fantasies, inventions, things that never happened? One couldn't know.

Pointless though it probably would be, Fidelis knew she had to visit Rosa, who was staying with her son.

Fidelis had heard that Daniel was doing very well and in the current house price climate, the three storey, narrow terrace house within walking distance of Hampstead Heath was tangible proof. He was a merchant banker, Carole was an events organizer, their children were looked after by a pair of Polish girls who lived in the basement and between them worked all hours. Until Daniel's mother came to stay, the Prices looked like an example of the perfect modern couple who had it all. But now, things had changed.

Carole answered the door in stockinged feet with her finger over her lips. She whispered, "Rosa's asleep, for goodness sake let's not wake her, come in, come in."

Still holding the pink peonies she had bought outside the tube station, Fidelis followed Carole up the stairs. "Oh Fidelis, it's lovely of you to have come."

"Not at all." Fidelis would not have recognized Carole in the street. The big blond hair, the clear skin, blue eyes, the tight jeans and shirt moulded to the high round breasts made her attractive but also so much one of a type that she was difficult to distinguish from other high-flying mid-thirties Londoners. She and Rosa had never got on which made the young woman's bad luck even worse luck, as she was landed with her mother in law now.

"I'd say that Rosa would be thrilled to see you except that I've got to warn you she won't know who you are."

As Fidelis followed Carole up to the next floor, she sensed the tension emanating from the toned, lithe figure. "Look," Carole said, "we have to barricade the children's rooms, locks, keys, last week Daniel said he was going to have pressure pads installed – we can't be expected to live like this. Come in the nursery, you'll see the bolts on the doors. The older children are away, we've sent them down to my mother's in Somerset, but the baby's too little, I'm still feeding her."

It seemed old fashioned to call the children's room 'the nursery', but these extraordinarily rich city people were a survival, perhaps even a revival, from the time of social class distinctions.

"Come in, she's fast asleep." The room was large, elegant, a little chilly, and very different from the style Fidelis would in previous years have expected to be chosen by Benjamin and Rosa's funky, metal studded son. But then, last time she saw him, his transformed appearance, stout, pinstriped and red-faced was a surprise too. Neither incarnation seem to have anything to do with his gentle, unostentatious father.

Conducted in to offer her tribute to the goddess-baby, Fidelis laid a little package at the foot of the cradle which, like all the furniture in the room, was made of wood, first distressed and then stained pale grey. The painted floorboards and the walls were pale grey-blue, and going the whole way around the room at head height for a tall toddler was a decorative frieze. It showed a domestic scene in a series of rooms decorated exactly like this one, even including the image of this very frieze. It was repeated over and over again, on and on into a tiny distant infinity.

In its prettily coloured simplicity the room looked homely and snug, the high cot with its decorated bars, the round table with a dark green chenille cloth which hung down to the floor and protected the space underneath, where she'd hide in the safe cosy darkness until the corner of the material was lifted and a face, almost upside down, looked in, and the den would be filled with the safe, sweet scent of...

"Fidelis? Are you feeling all right?"

Fidelis felt a chair touch the back of her knees and sat down heavily.

"I'm fine," she murmured; but she felt a little dizzy, leaning forward with sweat breaking out on her forehead and the back of her neck.

"I'll get you a glass of water."

The baby was making snuffling noises. The room smelled of talcum powder and of Carole's flowery scent. A soft wind was blowing the curtains in from the window, billowing in and out. Fidelis pushed herself upright.

"That room," she murmured, "the room in the pictures."

"Aren't they lovely? I've always adored that series."

"I'm not familiar with...where did you find them?"

"Oh, they're still made, I doubt that they ever go out of circulation. We had copies at home when I was little, you must have seen them before."

"At home. Yes. Did you?" Fidelis answered automatically. She realized that she felt quite peculiar. She should go. But she wanted to stay in this room, this comfortable, familiar space that promised – but what am I thinking? She didn't say it aloud. Instead, her voice shaking a little she asked, "Who was the artist?"

"He was a Dane, Carl Larsson. I think the pictures are quite well-known."

"Yes of course. Quite well-known. They just for a moment took me by surprise."

Fidelis stood up. Pull yourself together, she thought. She sustained a sensible conversation with the younger woman as they went downstairs and drinks were poured, and then Rosa woke up and as her daughter-in-law had warned, she did not know her old friend Fidelis, she had become aggressive, unhappy and lost, and yes, Fidelis realized, Carole was right, it must be impossible to live with her.

"I don't have any strings to pull, Carole, because I've never had very much to do with geriatric medicine but I do know who to ask. I'll be in touch."

"But Fidelis, you really don't look very well, let me get you a taxi."

"Not at all, I'm absolutely fine."

I felt faint because it's a hot day, she told herself. Just a bad moment. She was going to ignore the episode completely, a temporary, peculiar aberration, not worth thinking any more about.

———>>>>><<<<<———

Peter had been away, unbelievably, for nearly eight years when a woman who had never seen her two sons since they were abducted by their German father published a book telling her story. It was launched in the House of Commons and widely publicised in magazines and newspapers.[3] "You see, you're not the only one," Hannah said to her daughter.

"Is that meant to cheer me up? Have you read the book?"

A few months later the author of that book became the wife of the United Kingdom's ambassador to the United States.

Allegra told her mother that it marked the end of hope. "If somebody in that position can't do anything what sort of chance have I got?"

She was living in a bedsit south of the river, and in that crowded space started writing again, a laboured work whose plot was constructed around a child's abduction by his estranged parent. It lacked the light-hearted high spirits of her previous books, so Allegra's publishers couldn't put it in their 'romantic novels' list. Instead it was included with crime fiction as 'a suspense novel' and the press release that went out with proof copies hinted that much of the story was based on the author's own experience. Allegra sent copies of that and her earlier books, with loving inscriptions, to Peter, care of his father's lawyer, in Germany. They were not acknowledged.

The book had sympathetic reviews. In fact it was treated with far more respect than the earlier work, and Allegra found herself invited to publicity events and literary festivals for which she had always been too popular and down-market an author in the past.

Her audiences asked about her life. Was it true her own son had been abducted by his father, was it true that she hadn't seen him for years, was it true that the German courts ignored the rulings of English ones? The question sessions were filled by other parents reciting their

---

3   Catherine Mayer. *These Are My Children Too.*

own tales of woe: lies the other parent told, how children were set against the absent parent, how little those busybodies the child psychiatrists and psychologists knew about real life – who were they to pronounce on the home environment, who were they to have such life-and-death power over innocent parents? No wonder people were driven to crime like the heroine of Allegra's novel. In the end there was consensus on only one fact: that the bereaved parent – and this loss was death-like indeed – had no legal recompense or hope.

As for illegal recompense: Allegra's book came out with a certain amount of publicity about her plight. It was not until three weeks after publication that Allegra had the energy to look at her own website. On it she found several messages from readers, told herself that she must answer them and immediately forgot about them. But there was one message that she printed out, intending to show it to Hannah. On second reading she decided to keep it to herself. She'd heard of Restoration & Co through whispers and hints from other people met at protest groups and mutual self-help organizations. It was amazing how many people were in the same position as Allegra, their children abducted or kept from them by the other parent. Women who had married men from Islamic societies in which wives had no rights, men and women whose children had disappeared into the impenetrable mist and fog of changed names, disguised appearance and geographical shifts; people whose children had been kidnapped by the other parent and the majority of these parents, who had lost their children through some legal process.

As far as the outside world was concerned Restoration & Co specialised in ancient buildings, and when she went to the office in west London, Allegra saw that it was decorated with pictures of derelict cottages and desirable residences – before and after.

She was beginning to wonder whether she had made a mistake. Perhaps she had misunderstood the message. She was gathering her things together to leave again, when the door opened and a bustling, cosy looking woman came in.

"Allegra?"

"Yes."

"I'm Sandra. Now, tell me all about it. You've got a little boy…"

"He was little when I lost him. But it has been years…"

"You should have come to us before."

"I didn't know about you – anyway I was scared. The lawyers tell you – such frightening 'awful warnings' – I'm still scared actually, but what can they do to me now?"

Within moments of beginning her story Allegra was in tears and – which made her feel irrationally comforted – so was Sandra.

Relating the saga of losing Peter, so often told and retold before, Allegra felt at once detached, as if she were on automatic pilot, but also revived, her anger and grief as fresh as when the injury was new. Sandra made it clear that this was the one and only such tale she was thinking about – but also that she'd heard many such before. While Allegra was talking a man came quietly into the room, and stood by the door, listening carefully. Then he came across to Allegra, hand held out.

"This is my husband, Keith."

"How d'you do." His hand was dry, warm, steady, a comfort.

"He does the dirty work," Sandra said.

"Got to tell you, it costs," Keith said.

"We'd do it for free if we could," Sandra went on smoothly. It was a practised spiel.

"It's labour intensive and slow," Keith warned. "Makes it expensive."

"I'll pay anything. Absolutely anything. Though I might take a while. Somebody told me it's not…it doesn't have to be…"

"Not all up front," Keith agreed. "We'd never get a single client if that was what we insisted on. But there are a good many costs. The travel, the wages, the waiting, the car hire…"

"I understand that. I know it will cost every penny I've got, but I'd promise every penny I ever make if only…"

"Won't be quite as bad as that. We need some up front, enough for our expenses, and initial wages and travel."

Allegra pulled out her cheque book.

"We prefer cash," Sandra said.

"But you won't get a receipt," Keith added.

"I quite understand. No paper trail."

They nodded and smiled in unison, like proud parents at a clever child. Later that day, when Allegra came back with a carrier bag full of banknotes, she handed them over without a qualm. Maybe they were crooks. If so, so what? How could things be any worse?

From The Argus, Book Review Supplement

Aaron Hondhorst NEW FOUND
Reviewed by Isabel Arnold

Long Lost, a novel by the prize winning German author August Schimmler, appeared three years after his death. It described a non-Jewish German good father and a Jewish bad mother. The father commits the dreadful deed of informing on his girl-friend who is immediately arrested by the Gestapo, so that the father can save the life of their small daughter by getting her away from the mother and sending her to England on the kindertransport. Since its publication there have been many discussions about the characters' actions. The general consensus so far is that the father's behaviour was understandable and indeed forgivable; everything must be sacrificed to save a child.

Now the Dutch writer Aaron Hondhorst, who has been researching the life of Schimmler for many years, has published a book which casts a very different light upon this story. The principal piece of information which has dismayed Schimmler's fans, is Hondhorst's discovery that Schimmler was an active, indeed devoted, member of the SS from about 1935 – never admitted in his lifetime – and still more secret, that he become involved with the Hitlerian version of Satanism.

Hitler had repudiated Christianity. Instead he embraced the paganism of the early Germanic tribes. What were thought to be their beliefs provided a historical basis on which a structure of repulsive concepts could be built. In this farrago of sinister nonsense, Hitler becomes a substitute for God himself, seen as saviour – the saviour of the Aryan race. It may not be the conventional notion of devil worship but of course that's what it was. In their Black Mass ritual, they used the swastika as a focal point, replacing the crucifix, upside down or otherwise, and Hitler's book Mein Kampf took the place of the Black Book of Satan.

In 1934 Heinrich Himmler took a lease on Schloss Wewelsburg, near the town of Paderborn. This book's illustrations include a picture of the ancient fortress and the surrounding landscape, heavily wooded, full of giant, weirdly-shaped rocks, all apparently standing in a fog-pocket. Clearly it was the perfect place to educate novices in the pagan mysteries that had been adopted to underpin National Socialism. Most students were in the SS. They came to the Schloss for induction courses after which the pupils were initiated into this brotherhood.

Meticulous and arduous searching led Aaron Hondhorst to records showing that in the early months of 1938 August Schimmler was a pupil there. What's more, he heard from a witness, now dead, that on at least one occasion Schimmler had travelled to Paderborn with a child and a nursemaid who had been lodged in an inn down in the town.

This information gives rise to horrible thoughts.

It never occurred to any contemporary critic or reader that the story in Long Lost could be based on fact (although in that book it is the mother who attends the nefarious ceremonies) but the question arises now: did Schimmler take his little daughter to the castle? Was she made to participate in obscene ceremonies? Certainly in one of his later novels, The Magic Soldier, the hero takes his own daughter, an infant in arms, to attend a Black Mass. It's a terrifying, disgusting, description, vivid enough in itself to justify the numerous prizes that book collected. In purely literary terms ....(review continues).

You didn't need to see a detailed invoice to understand why Restoration & Co was so very expensive. What was not spelt out in their brochure could be read between the lines. "We can't discuss specifics of how we conduct investigations but there are many steps we can take as private investigators that may not be possible for law enforcement. We can assist the authorities and give them useful information. But the main aim is to expedite locating your missing child(ren) and then to get them home." As Allegra realized, she was about to become complicit in illegal behaviour. She was also about to bankrupt herself, or at least to mortgage the rest of her working life. She didn't give a damn.

The Extraction Procedure began with two people, a couple in their late 20s purporting to be – and perhaps actually they were – postgraduate students. They took a room conveniently placed between the house where Joachim officially lived, and the tower block where his parents really did live. They kept an unobtrusive watch; gradually they got to know neighbours; they made themselves useful, carrying the rubbish downstairs for old ladies, keeping an eye on a baby while the mother did some shopping, repairing a broken window.

Fifty years of repressive government had left their mark. The inhabitants of this little town still seemed cautious to the point of para-noia. Nearly every conversation was carried on as if secret police were surreptitiously listening to every word. Residents spoke only in guarded terms about their neighbours and there was still an atmosphere of fear, unfocused and by this time unnecessary, but deeply ingrained. It took the two young people six weeks even to identify a likely informant and another fortnight to get some information. But in the end they did, and on a Sunday took a picnic and a music player and a rug, went off for an outing and came back in the late afternoon having had a sighting of the child. He lived in the country now, in a restored and enlarged cottage, with his father and another woman, presumably the fathers' girlfriend. He was a thin, pale, quiet little boy, not easily recognized from the photograph of a plump and jolly toddler, but the watchers were sure they had found the right person when the father came out to bring the child indoors. No doubt as to whose photo that was.

They kept an eye out for a while longer. Did the child go to school, to church, to sports fields? Did he have toys and if so, what? What were his interests, who were his friends?

The contract had been running for two months when the young couple faded out of local life as unobtrusively as they had entered it, and were replaced by an operative who had been carefully chosen once all the information about the child's present place of residence had been collected. It is inevitably more difficult to lurk in the country than in a busy town, but it was necessary to get an idea of the routine of the child's carers. In the end a watcher was chosen: an elderly man who took a room in the village inn in order, he said, to complete a musical composition. He was in fact a composer of modern classical music. If anyone had checked his credentials they would have found plenty of confirmation, and, as Sandra had told Allegra, one had to work on the assumption that the watched were watching.

The composer spent two days at in his room working, wearing headphones attached to the roll-up electronic piano he'd brought. He took no interest, as far as anyone could see, in the hotel or its guests or its proprietors, merely ringing down from time to time to ask the porter to tell a waiter that he wanted coffee, then a larger pot of coffee, a hot-plate as the coffee was getting cold too quickly, then a kettle so that he could make his own, twice as strong as the hotel provided. His little eccentricities were repeated in the bar that evening and again, exaggerated, the next.

On the third day it became clear that his work was not going well. He ventured out for a walk round the village. That afternoon he went for a long walk, striding briskly past the house in which the Wenders now lived without apparently looking at it. The next day he ventured into the woods. It seemed to help. That evening he covered several pages with his peculiar notations, as the chambermaid reported to her colleagues. They were pleased for him. He was a polite and generous hotel guest who gave very little trouble, just the sort of person the staff hoped would stay for a good long time.

"I'm married to my work," Fidelis once told an importunate suitor.

"But don't you want children? A family of your own?"

"That just shows how little you understand me," she replied. To another man, she had said, "My patients are my family. And to yet a third, she'd asserted that her articles and books were her children. She was wounded by a review which suggested that her life work's involvement with the relationship between children and their mothers was a direct consequence of her own lack of a mother or child of her own, but that very lack meant she was incapable of really understanding the reality of the tie. And with the swing of the pendulum, from crediting behaviour to nature, and back again to nurture, to and fro, by the early years of the second millennium people were again attributing importance to heredity, and Fidelis had to recognize various facts that it had been more comfortable to ignore. She was struggling with an article for a colleague's Festschrift, on the subject of inherited behaviour patterns, when she received a bolt from the blue. It had a much greater effect than if it had come earlier in her life.

The letter was headed with an address in Weimar.

Dear Dr Berlin,

I write to you though I am but a stranger. To explain: I am Gerda, daughter of Dorothée (always called Dorit) Fuchs (born Rosenthal). She is dead since 1989, but I did not at first read the many papers left to me. Now I learn the story, how was discovered the novel Suite Francaise. Author: Irene Nemirovsky, of her you have surely heard, the Jewish woman, novels writer in France, who was murdered during the war. Then for 50 years her children read nothing of her notebooks. They spare themselves the pain. This gave ideas to me, and I examine the writings, though our story was quite otherwise because my mother has survived the war. In the Hitler-time she was first hiding, but then taken and she is in camps until peacetime but then the Russians come and she is still in camps, ever further east, and with child. She give birth to me in Siberia but I am sent away until in 1982 Dorit is free. For seven years we live together, when she is already 75.

Now I am sent her notebook, by a miracle survived, many years guarded by an Aryan friend. To begin I do not understand. Dorit was student in Berlin, she will become referenda (that is judge, in Germany then). She has a man, his name never written, only the letter A, and with this 'A' in 1937 she has a child. This she never mentioned, I am never told that there should be a sister, her daughter, who is named Gisele. Dorit since 1931 is sincerely communist, and is also Jewish. She and her daughter are in the Hitler-time in mortal danger. Now she writes little, it is not safe. She has fear of the man, the father. When he takes the child she fears for her. Comes she back? Every time she asks herself, has he taken her for ever? In 1938, November, 'A comes. Argument again. Bad. Danger. Finally I must do this. I take G to train.'

No more is in this journal, for now she is arrested. She is taken to Buchenwald, this she has told me, although she has not told me of her first child, her Gisele that she sees never again.

But later, when she is old, she reads about you, Dr Fidelis Berlin, that you are orphan kindertransport-child, and she sees photo of you and cries out "Fidelis" and then she weeps, and later she says that you are the mirror image of her own mutti, my grandmother lost in 1944, who is called Gisele Fidelis. Still she does not tell me her story, I know only that she wills to write to you but this from East Germany is a problem and she dies before it is time, and now I read of you, in the London Argus, that you know not, and nobody knows, if your true name was lost on the voyage perhaps. So I think you are perhaps my sister Gisele; and so I write to you this letter.

Fidelis had held and fingered the letter so much, and had passed it round between so many of her friends, that the computer paper looked tatty and the signature, *I greet you, from Gerda Fuchs,* was half concealed by a smudge.

"I'd have been so happy to get this when I was young," she said.

"And aren't you happy now?"

"It doesn't seem to matter any more."

"All the same, it might be worth investigating," a tentative suggestion from a much younger woman. Fidelis's friends were divided. Some at one extreme thought it was a scam and didn't believe a word of it.

"It's perfectly simple to discover every detail about you online, even without the recent interview. Sounds pretty unlikely to me I must say. You want to be really careful about this."

Others friends were equally vehement in insisting that Fidelis should go immediately to Germany and meet her half sister. "Your sister, Fidelis, after all these years."

"You spent all your life thinking about the relationship between mother and child, you can't pass up this chance to discover whose child you were."

"Just imagine, having a family, having relations! What are you waiting for?"

Fidelis replied drily that she didn't feel all that alone and if she did, she should be used to it by now and it was a bit late to change.

"I didn't mean it like that. You know we love you like a sister." It was a sign of the changing, more demonstrative times that Tina got up to put her arms round Fidelis, holding her close, her hand cupped round Fidelis's head. Even five years ago they would never have had closer contact than the formal kiss on meeting and parting. Some of Fidelis's exact contemporaries were becoming noticeably more emotional with age. Films and plays would bring tears to their once cynical eyes but Fidelis had never learnt to feel completely comfortable with physical displays of emotion. She really preferred a conventional cheek to cheek, or from her god-daughter Clodie, an affectionate but brisk hug on greeting and parting, but none of the hand holding and stroking that were becoming the norm as society became less inhibited.

Clodie took a balanced view of the letter from Fraulein Fuchs. "It could easily be a scam but just suppose it's not! Couldn't you go and see her if you are in Germany anyway? Where is it, Weimar – sounds ok – I mean, you could go there for a holiday or something."

"Actually I've never been to Germany."

"For God's sake – why not?"

"No special reason, it just never happened."

"Well I can tell you, Berlin's the most exciting town in Europe, I know quite a lot of people who moved to live there. Wouldn't you like to see it?"

"Maybe. One of these days."

"You'll have to send this woman some sort of answer."

Fidelis said she knew that and she would. Soon. One of these days.

When some weeks later, Clodie enquired what she'd said to Gerda Fuchs, Fidelis muttered something evasive. There was no need for her to admit to Clodie that in fact she had not replied yet. Once or twice she had sat down at her desk intending to compose a letter. She sat there looking at the words, Dear Gerda Fuchs, thank you for your letter, and couldn't think what to say next. That part of her mind was suffering some sort of temporary paralysis. Did she want to meet a woman who might be a blood relation? What did she want to do about all this? It was very unusual for Fidelis to be indecisive. She had little experience of the 'on the one hand, on the other hand' kind of argument with others or with herself.

"What would you advise me, if I were in your shoes and had asked you what to do?"

"Oh Clodie, I really don't know. I think it's one of the occasions when you wouldn't advise, you try to winkle out what the other person actually wants to do."

"And so?"

"And so I just don't know what I want to do. If I stopped thinking about it the answer might come to me but it is rather hard to forget at the moment."

The next time Clodie came round Fidelis was simultaneously cooking dinner for 10 and laying the table, which was in fact her desk pulled lengthways and made larger with two folding card tables, all covered with an Indian bedspread showing the pattern of the tree of life. She had borrowed some chairs from her upstairs neighbour.

"Fidelis!" her god-daughter exclaimed. "You shouldn't be doing all that. Here, let me." While it was true that the furniture moving and rushing to and fro was a little bit much for Fidelis, there was nothing that annoyed her more than being treated like somebody old and infirm. Clodie knew it perfectly well and immediately backtracked, apologising so nicely that Fidelis immediately asked her to help, smiling inwardly that Clodie had got her way.

"You're not a mind doctor for nothing," she said.

"And how did I learn to be one?"

"Stop it! Here, you can cut up the vegetables."

"Oh look, you've got a new picture."

"Just a reproduction."

The new picture was of a section of a comfortable living room. It showed a wide shallow window with one of the casements open, and the windowsill covered with plants in terracotta pots. There was a sofa covered with a blue cloth and upright dining chair with a blue and white seat, and a multicoloured striped rug on the floor. On either side of the window were candelabra, each hanging above a little black framed portrait. On the round table lay an unfinished piece of knitting, laid aside for a moment by a girl who stood in half profile by the window holding a watering can.

It was a charming, comfortable picture of secure middle-class life but it looked oddly out of place beside Fidelis's brilliantly coloured Philipson, a vibrant Whitchurch and her recent extravagance, a small Peter Lanyon.

"It's quite different from your usual line in art," Clodie remarked non-committally.

"I know, but it looks like…well, I know it's a silly thing to say, but it looks like home. It makes me feel comfortable."

"Where have I seen something like this before?"

"I did quite recently, in Daniel Price's house. You know him don't you? I was there to see his mother – she is in a bad way and poor Carole's bearing the brunt. Anyway I just happen to see a reproduction of one of Carl Larsson's pictures when I was there and it really appealed to me." The younger woman and the old one stood silent side by side for a moment looking at the evocation of a happy, cosy nursery and the secure life led by the middle-class European bourgeoisie before the sky fell in. Then Clodie said,

"What's that tune, Fidelis?"

Fidelis had not even noticed that she was humming. She repeated the sound, and then sang in a low voice,

"Hoppe hoppe Reiter/de dum de dum…"

Clodie took up the tune. "Wenn er fällt, dann schreit er/fällt er in den Teich/find't ihn keiner gleich…"

"I don't know the words. It came into my head."

"Bumpety bump, rider/if he falls, then he cries/……"

"Clodie, you know more German than I do. It's just a sound in my head."

"From when you were a baby."

"For heaven's sake! Here, let's listen to a Brandenburg and pour me a gin and tonic. People will be coming any minute now."

"You want to know what I think is going on here?" Clodie said.

"No, but I can see that you're going to tell me."

"Yes I am, because Carole Price rang me up the other day and she said that you had a funny turn…"

"How dare she! The interfering…"

"She was worried about you."

"Oh really!"

"Anyway she told me what happened, she said it was when you were looking at the Larsson picture. Well I didn't say anything to her – I know you aren't all that keen on her so I didn't want to discuss you, but I did talk to Mum."

Clodie's mother was Fidelis's close old friend Tina. Fidelis grunted but did not interrupt, so Clodie continued, "Mum wondered, and so did I actually, we thought maybe it was a memory you had suppressed. Those pictures, people probably had them in their children's rooms all over Europe. I mean, perhaps before you were…well, you know."

Fidelis was vexed but knew it was irrational, knew that her friends only discussed her from affection and concern. She stopped herself from saying something churlish and ungracious. Instead she admitted, "It was funny, actually, because when I saw that picture I had this incredibly vivid image of being under the table in the shelter of the dangling tablecloth. I could see myself sitting under there in my den, crouched in the darkness, with voices outside and then somebody lifting it to find me – it was like a dream or vision or something."

"Or something? Like a memory, is what you mean. You remembered, after all these years. Perhaps something else will come back to you soon." Clodie's voice choked. She felt far more emotional about all this than Fidelis herself.

Allegra had been counting the days to hear something from Restoration & Co. When they invited her to call into the office she knew that it would be to say either that they had found Peter or that they were going to give up their search for him. She sat on the shabby, cretonne covered sofa. Sandra came and sat down beside her. Allegra clasped her trembling hands and bit down hard on her lower lip. Sandra handed her a sheaf of photographs. Allegra looked at the first one and looked again, and instantly, involuntarily, burst into tears – violent, juddering sobs and wails, and quite unconsciously she tore at her hair.

Her words were just distinguishable in the storm of grief. "What have they done to him, oh my baby…"

The pictures showed a schoolboy, his hair cropped so close as almost to be shaved, his face pale, his eyes suspicious and timid.

"I take it this really is a picture of your Peter," Sandra said.

"Yes," Allegra whispered.

"Well, we know where he is living and where he goes to school."

"Can we get him? How soon can we leave?"

"Not so fast. These things take a lot of organization, they have to be carefully planned. It will take half a dozen operatives, we have to recruit them and get them to Germany and practise and rehearse. You'll have to travel separately, no visible contact. They will be watching you."

"Whatever you say. I'll do anything you tell me. Anything at all."

Following Sandra's detailed timetable, Allegra checked herself in to a health farm in Somerset. She arrived by car and handed the keys over to the receptionist, who said, "You won't be needing those for a week."

"No nipping out for fish and chips in the village?"

"Not if you want to come back here afterwards. The doctors are very strict."

The hand-outs Allegra took along to her room reinforced that message. Guests wanted to get fitter/thinner/better. This could be achieved through diet, treatments and cooperation. Those who had chosen to come made a bargain with the staff: considerate, caring treatment in exchange for genuine, willing cooperation. Nobody needed to stay here, but everyone who did was expected to observe the house rules.

For two days Allegra followed those rules in a daze. She swam, she sat in a steamer, imprisoned by bolted metal doors, she underwent massage on face and body, she tried to eat the miniature meals that came to her room on a tray. She was summoned to the doctor on day three. He didn't bother to open the brown paper file lying beside him.

"I'm going to prescribe bed rest," he said.

"But…"

"In case one of the other patients notices your absence. Be ready by midnight."

"But my car…"

"Leave it where it is. You'd hardly leave without it would you?"

"No. No of course not."

He unlocked the desk drawer and brought out a plastic triangle. "Here, you'll need something more solid than…"

The Sainsbury's sandwich packet contained salmon and watercress, both ingredients Allegra hated, but back in her room she was hungry enough to gobble them down eagerly. Now was the time for the emergency chocolate she'd hidden in between unused blankets in the top of the wardrobe, along with her passport and purse full of Euros.

They had allocated a ground floor room to Allegra. The window was supposed to have a block on the frame, preventing it from opening more than 5 inches, but the little piece of metal was missing so Allegra was able to open it wide enough for her to climb through the gap. She waited eagerly, not knowing quite what she was waiting for. It turned out to be the man, Keith, who appeared so silently and suddenly that Allegra had to stifle her own squawk of surprise with her hand. She climbed out of the window and obeyed his gesture to crouch low, below the sills of other ground floor windows, and follow him quietly through the flower garden, past the indoor gymnasium and the outdoor pool, and out onto the public road through a narrow doorway flanked with dustbins. A car with engine idling was waiting for them.

"Do you really think they were watching me?"

Keith was looking out of the rear window. "Nobody there, we should be okay," he said.

"But do you?"

"Sure of it," he replied. "We do, in similar circumstances. You'll want us making sure you're safe, once you've got the little chap back living with you."

They drove for about an hour, with Allegra too excited and nervous to do as Keith suggested and get a few minutes shut-eye, so she was alert and ready to go when they drove in to the entrance of a private airfield, and through a maze of trucks and huts to a small plane. A tiny section of her mind was whimpering, *I've chartered a plane! How will I ever pay for this? I can't afford it.* But most of her consciousness was concentrated on a single thought: Peter. I'm going to get Peter back.

They landed at an airfield indistinguishable from the one they had left. The passport Allegra and been so careful to bring was not examined. A large estate car with darkened windows was waiting and she got in beside Keith. As it drove off he began to speak.

"Okay, now listen up. It's 6:30a.m. At 7.45 precisely the car taking your son to school and will approach the bridge over a small stream. We'll be very unlucky if there's any other traffic around, there hasn't been the last three days, but we'll operate a roadblock anyway. The idea is to stop the car, lift out the child and bring him to you in this car."

"You mean I've got to wait?"

"That is exactly what I mean, you keep absolutely clear. You'd only be in the way. Wait here until someone comes. Got it?"

She nodded, not really listening, not really caring about the detail. What did it matter so long as Peter came to her?

The car was turned off the road onto the flat sandy countryside. It was light by now so she could see the forest of conifers, planted just far enough apart for the large car to be concealed between them.

"Wait here."

The driver went with Keith.

By the car clock it was 7.30.

7.32.

7.35.

Time crawled. Would the clock hand ever move?

Still seven minutes to wait.

Allegra made a sudden decision. After all, she said aloud, who's paying? She opened the door as quietly as she could and carefully let it fall back without actually closing. I haven't made a sound, she thought. The pine needles were silent under foot. She moved from the shelter of one tree to the next.

There was the bridge. Nobody to be seen. Silence.

She waited.

There – that's a car coming. Where are they, where's Keith?

Then at the same time she saw a red car driving along the straight road towards the bridge, and heard another engine from the opposite direction. A monster four-wheel-drive people carrier roared towards the bridge and stopped suddenly just as the red car reached the same place and squealed to a halt. Suddenly there were people everywhere. Three men with balaclavas pulled over their faces leapt from the four-wheel drive. There was Keith, he moved to the driver's side of the red car. The driver – was that Joachim? No, another man with a shaved head and holding – he's got a gun! But behind the outstretched arm, a face pressed to the rear window of the red car.

"Peter," Allegra gasped. Instinct took over. The long-lost child, the gun, those terrifying thugs. Peter had to be protected. *I've got to get him out of here.*

She ran towards her son. Her arms itched and ached to hold him, *My Peter, so big he's grown, they've shaved his hair, how could they, his lovely black curls, he's terrified, poor child, he doesn't even recognize me!*

What was that? A shot? Another?

The boy, no longer so little but still tightly strapped onto the rear seat, was white, trembling, silent. Traumatised, she thought viciously.

"Peter, my darling, it's your mummy, it's me!"

Two men were collapsed on the road. The man with a gun was crouched by the wheel of the four-wheel drive, peeking and peering for other targets.

Automatically, without thought or plans, Allegra leapt into the driving seat of the red car.

"It's all right now darling, mummy's here."

The engine was still turning over. She rammed it viciously into gear and jammed her foot on the accelerator. The metal scraped horribly together as she forced her way past the black car. And then she put her foot down.

The police rang Hannah's bell just as she was thinking it was time to fix something for supper. They weren't in uniform, but one of them held an identification card up to the camera, so she buzzed the street door open. They walked up the stairs, a man and a younger woman.

"Mrs Browne? Mrs H Browne?"

"You've caught up with me at last," she said, almost flirtatiously.

"Can we sit down?"

In fact the woman didn't sit down but turned towards Hannah's kitchen. "That's right, Constable, make us a nice cup of tea," the man said and then turned towards Hannah. "I'm afraid I have some bad news."

"Hannah! What's the matter? What happened?"

It was a dismal evening, rain pouring down outside and the central heating on the blink. Daffy was working for a temp agency and came home early. She was wrapped in a pink macintosh and walked directly from the front door towards the utility room to hang it up, her short-sighted eyes blinking against the bright light. At first she didn't notice that her landlady was sitting at the kitchen counter clutching something in her closed hand and trembling. The calm efficiency of a nurse on duty slid automatically across. Her stance and expression seemed to change as she took control.

"You've had a shock, I'll make you a cup of tea. Won't take a minute." She bustled around the room: from kettle to sink, back again, across to the cupboard for the tea canister, to another cupboard to get a cup, to the fridge for the milk, to the larder for the sugar and a biscuit, babbling quietly all the time: the wind, the weather, how early it was, everyone else was still asleep, strong sweet tea, drink it up, it'll make you feel better.

"Now then, what we got here, what's this in your hand? Mmmm, I've seen this in your room. A fetish? Your lucky charm?" She peeled Hannah's fingers away and set the little wooden object she was clutching on the table. It was not exactly a doll, not exactly a figurine, but a piece of flat wood about 6 inches tall, crudely carved into the shape of a woman. It was very dark, impregnated with the grime of ages.

"It's my Joanie."

"It's your lucky charm."

"To keep me safe."

Another long pause. Hannah didn't speak and in the end Daffy said, "You needn't tell me, I can feel it. Death. Who's dead, Hannah?"

"Everyone dies. And now Allegra's dead too."

"Allegra? Your daughter? What…?"

"She tried to take Peter back. It was a car accident. Head on collision. Not wearing a seatbelt. Died instantly."

"Oh Hannah. I'm so sorry."

"She's better off dead," Hannah said in a harsh, hostile voice.

"Hannah!"

"She was too unhappy. And there wasn't any hope for her."

"Her little boy…"

"He was in the car."

"No! Is he…?"

"Perfectly all right, according to the police. He was tightly strapped in."

"But to see his mother…"

"You'd think so, wouldn't you? But all he said was that a lady had driven him away. He didn't understand what she said. And he didn't know who she was."

And now, she didn't add aloud, he never will.

The Times, 20 April 2010

SECRET ARCHIVES OF HOLOCAUST TO BE OPENED AFTER
60 YEARS
from Roger Boyes in Berlin.

One of the most comprehensive sources of information about Jews killed or lost in the Holocaust is to be thrown open to historians after an about-turn by Germany. For 60 years a wall of secrecy has surrounded the archive at Bad Arolsen in Central Germany, which contains 50 million documents and the names of 17 million Nazi victims. Germany had claimed that opening the files would break its strict privacy laws. Now, under pressure from Holocaust researchers in the US, it has relented. As a result, the documents could be made available to help historians, family members and others to establish how the victims of the Holocaust met their fate.

The files, mainly German papers impounded by Allied forces, are a testimony to the Nazi obsession with documentary detail. Among the papers stored in an old SS barracks, there are lice inspection reports from concentration camps and insurance policies signed by German companies when they took on slave labourers. The many documents form a remarkable mosaic that shows the lives and tribulations of Jews as slave labourers and other victims. The archive has been used since the war as a tracing service by the International Committee of the Red Cross. As Holocaust victims die out, the service has become less important. Even so, it succeeds in reuniting dozens of families every year...

The director of the museum's Centre for Advanced Holocaust Studies said: "It makes it possible to learn a lot more about the fate of individuals and about the Holocaust itself, concentration camps, deportations, slave-enforced labour and displaced persons." The executive secretary of the Task Force for International Cooperation on Holocaust Education, Remembrance and Research, said: "This is about the memory of the most appalling event in human history and about respect for the survivors today. It is extremely important for the archive to become open as soon as possible and give survivors and their families relevant information before they die. Now that Germany has bowed to pressure the 1955 treaty limiting access to the archives could be revised within the next six months.

This information was obviously important. I would find out whether or not clients I hadn't been able to help before would commission me to pick up their cases again. I would do it out of – what should I call this emotion? Guilt? Fear? Empathy? No, it was the same impulse that provokes people into making charitable donations: there but for –

luck? Good judgement? The grace of God? – go I.

There went I too: not into a kindertransport or a cattle truck, not into a concentration camp or the gas chamber, but into the land of the free and the life of the comfortable bourgeoisie. I read that news item in The Times, counted my blessings and began to make a list of previously disappointed clients I should contact with the information that their questions might be answered after all.

Fidelis's not-quite-god-daughter Clodie Byrne was a senior registrar, overdue for promotion but waiting in a queue because of health service cuts. Fidelis had loved Clodie since she was her best friend's baby. These days she sometimes felt that Clodie treated her like a child. It made her worry that there might be a good reason for her to do so.

Clodie was coming to dinner this evening bringing the pudding with her.

"You don't trust my cooking?"

"Of course I do. I just thought this would save you trouble."

She paused for a moment and then went on, "I've got something to show you. It's from The Times last week. The Germans have changed their minds, you can get someone to search the archives."

Fidelis read the cutting slowly. Clodie followed the movement of her eyes and as she came to the end said, "It's not too late, you see. I know you didn't answer that woman who claimed to be your sister but you could still find out…"

"Now? At my age?"

"Never too late."

"This really isn't something that's been preying on my mind all my life, you know."

"Maybe, but it's beginning to now, isn't it? Like all those patients whose past begins to haunt them when they're…after they…"

"When they are old."

"Well, yes."

"But my past isn't haunting me, Clodie. I'm living in the present –

look, I'm laying a table and cooking dinner (could you just give that sauce a stir?) and finishing a book…"

"And denying your feelings."

"You're trespassing, Clodie. Keep off the grass."

"If trespassing is what it takes…"

At which point someone pressed the flat's buzzer. "Saved by the bell," Fidelis said.

Next morning Clodie rang from the ward. In her indefatigable determination to find solutions for all of Fidelis's problems she shouted her idea into the phone, her enthusiasm reminding Fidelis of a puppy offering its owner a bone.

"You can go over there!" It sounded like, *Cinderella shall go to the ball.* "I've got this brochure, this travel company programme, you can go to Germany really easily like this and have a lovely time and even if you don't go and see that woman. I've got it in front of me now, I'll bring it round later."

Clodie punctually turned up that evening bubbling with encouragement. "Look," she said enthusiastically, "this is a terrific programme, three concerts and a lecture a day, all about Bach, I'd pay a small fortune to not have to go but you could have an orgy."

It was certainly true that the wide-ranging musical tastes of Fidelis's earlier years which swung wildly between the Beatles and Bach, jazz, pop, rock and baroque, were narrowing down. It must be quite a long time since she had put anything by a different composer on her record player. Even as the two women were speaking, the secular Coffee Cantata was belting out in the background.

It was difficult to know how to deal with the occasionally puppyish enthusiasm of a woman now in her thirties and highly qualified in a demanding profession – Clodie was on the verge of becoming a consultant psychiatrist herself. Yet when talking to Fidelis Clodie seem to have forgotten everything she had ever learned about not being prescriptive, about nudging the patient into suggesting for himself or herself what the doctor knew perfectly well should be done.

"You shouldn't have taken so much trouble," Fidelis said formally.

"No trouble, I just want to see you happy."

"My dear girl, what a remark for someone in our profession to make!"

"Well, I can't just be objective and professional about you. There's too much history."

Fidelis was torn between pleasure and a slight feeling of being crowded; was it possible that Clodie perceived some failing or falling off that made her feel the need to take care of Fidelis? The older woman watched the younger suspiciously. Would Clodie always have leapt up to get the kettle when more hot water was needed for the tea? Had she always been so assiduous in passing biscuits or offering cake? Did she do the same thing when she was at home with Tina? Or was she being – dread word – *kind?*

"I really don't see myself on a package holiday," Fidelis said.

"That's just prejudice speaking, blind prejudice. Why ever not?"

"Well, how would you like it?"

"I do like it. Lovely having somebody else having to find parking places and be responsible for getting me to the airport on time. Gavin and I have been on more than one together."

"But being told where to go, when and worst of all, who with!"

"Well, I can tell you that this trip is full of people who could perfectly well be part of your own gang. A friend's mother-in-law did it last year and she said it had an incredibly high professor count and more than half the people were following the score – honestly Fidelis, if it counts as a package at all it's a pretty upmarket one. And just think of the music! What I thought was, you could go to Germany for the first time and have a really nice holiday and you could look at places like Dresden and Weimar or not really, as you like, but it wouldn't have to be so formal or such a big deal."

Fidelis fingered the elegant brochure. The programme sounded almost irresistible to someone who was nuts about the music of J. S. Bach. There were going to be four concerts in Weimar so it would be possible to pass the two days there without really looking at anything or meeting anybody. No one would know one was there. Gerda Fuchs was hardly going to recognize her in the street. Fidelis could call on her or not as the fancy took her. Alternatively she could skim the surface, listen to the music and quite simply pass on. Or, alternatively, not.

"Imagine," Clodie enthused, "two or three concerts every day, really high quality musicians, nice places to be in between, a bit of sight-seeing, potential friends…"

"That does sound good."

"And if the fancy takes you, you could drop in on the woman who wrote to you."

Clodie said, "I'll leave it with you, shall I? Give you a chance to make up your mind. I have to say, it's not my idea of fun."

Hannah picked up and re-read the letter that had arrived this morning. To think how excited she'd been to see the stamp and the postmark. She'd actually supposed that it was the ice breaking, there'd be contact at last, after all these years. Without Allegra she was surely no threat. After all, she didn't want to take the boy away from Joachim.

Her hands were trembling as she opened the envelope. At first she did not take in the formal words. She expected to see Joachim's signature, news of Peter, a photo perhaps, even the promise of a meeting.

Far from it. This was an eviction order. Notice to quit.

The letter was written in English but came from a firm of lawyers in Germany, it was addressed to Mrs Hannah Cunningham otherwise known as Mrs Hannah Browne. It pointed out that the house in which she lived was the property of Peter Wenders, who was a minor in the charge of his father and legal guardian Joachim Wenders. Now the said Joachim Wenders hereby gave her notice that her licence to occupy the property was now terminated. Any necessary repairs should be carried out speedily in order to give vacant possession in good condition. The deadline would be Easter next year.

How had Joachim found out?

Hannah and Allegra had agreed from the outset that this was some-thing Joachim need not be told. And Peter wasn't supposed to know until Hannah was dead. In putting her grandson's name on her title deeds, Hannah meant no more than to promise a legacy. It was an inheritance tax dodge, that was all. Hannah's name was on official documents, it was Hannah who received demands for council tax and utility payments, Hannah who paid the service charges. The notion that Peter's grand-mother occupied her own home at his will was as absurd. Offensive. Unacceptable.

Hannah was still sitting holding the letter when Daffy came back. She hung her wet coat in the hall and came straight to the kitchen. The notion that she was going to be an unobtrusive tenant, as she'd initially promised, had dissipated very early on. Without anything being said, their relationship was not that of landlady and lodger, but of a couple of superannuated flat sharers. How did that happen? Hannah wondered. It wasn't quite what she had intended. All the same, she almost automatically handed over the letter.

Daffy read the correct, impersonal words slowly, and then again. At last she said, "Well, there's one thing about it, at least you know his lawyer's in Weimar. Maybe they've moved there."

"Could be."

"Should be easier to track them down, I'd have thought. Maybe you should go and talk to Joachim in person."

"Talk? I'd spit in his face."

"After all, your Peter must be how old, twelve? Thirteen? He's old enough to have a say."

"I don't suppose he even remembers I exist."

"Time you show him then. Why don't you write to this lawyer and say you'll be coming to Weimar yourself…"

"But I can't!"

"Why not?"

"I'm not allowed within fifty miles. They said I couldn't go back again, the German court, they said I made too much disturbance. I did too and I would again. So there."

"That was years ago, surely."

"The injunction lasts till Peter's eighteen."

"I can see that presents a difficulty – let me just think about it a minute, something I heard the other day…"

Later in the day Daffy rang Hannah from work.

"It's come back to me, it was Clodie Brook, Dr Brook, I heard her telling someone – listen, Hannah, I know exactly how you can get in to Germany without any trouble at all. It'll all be all right, believe me, I can feel it."

The guide, dressed more formally than his passengers in a tie and tweed coat, was probably even younger than he looked. The convulsive events of the previous century surely seemed as distant from him as the Napoleonic Wars did to his audience. They listened politely to his dispassionate account of the recent history of this part of eastern Europe, but the average age of package tour passengers being somewhere in the high sixties, most of his audience took the facts rather more personally. Fidelis Berlin, for one, had thought it quite possible that she'd be overcome by emotion. So far, she wasn't. In fact she felt as phlegmatic as her companions looked, all dozey or dopey in the warmed air and the steady rumble of the bus thundering eastwards along the autobahn.

The first day had been exhausting, with endless shuffling queues to check in and get through Heathrow's security, only to find flights to Frankfurt delayed. When they finally arrived they were shepherded onto coaches and driven for three hours through vast dark stretches of impenetrable trees. Fidelis listened to a professorial figure in the seat in front of her, discoursing on the Roman army's superstitious fear of the alien German forest and the barbarian tribes that inhabited it; in another part of the bus a fluttery woman was going on and on about the strangeness of being behind the Iron Curtain. "Well, I know there isn't an iron curtain any more, but after taking it for granted most of one's life…"

As in the fading light they came into Mulhausen she changed her tune. "It's like being a time traveller, look, look, there's a hairdresser with helmet dryers, when did you last see those? It's like an old movie!" The hairdresser was in a narrow alley labelled *Judenstrasse*.

"I don't suppose that's what it was called for most of the last 50 years," someone said. As he spoke the coach turned into Karl Marx Allee, which had not yet been given a name more suitable to the new capitalist system, and pulled up outside a hotel. A motley crowd on the pavement: unaccustomed group-travellers waiting by the bus's luggage bin to make sure their own cases were still there, others, tobacco dependent, lighting up with sighs of relief. A group of young people went by, some chattering, a few singing. Fidelis knew the tune but couldn't name it or remember where she'd heard it. She found herself panting with sweat running down the back of her neck. They were speaking German. Of course – what else, in Germany? She hadn't understood a word, but something in the sound had affected her. This is a fear-reaction, she thought. Question: Why am I frightened? Answer: I am *not* frightened.

"The witches ride out."

Fidelis jumped at the sound, and when she had taken in the words stared at the speaker in bemusement, an elderly man whose left hand beat time to the diminishing sound. He said, "Don't let it worry you. You have gone quite pale. They were performing a skit on a traditional magic song, quite sinister if you credit such things. It's sung at the Black Mass."

"But those were children!"

"There's a young people's fad, or movement if you prefer, for debunking every tradition. They sing comic versions of that one, and the anthem – Deutschland Über Alles – and some of the old Junker hymns. Not unlike defacing portraits."

"Oh. Thank you. I thought I recognized...I must go in. Good-night."

She went in to collect her key from the reception desk, once in her room ate her emergency rations (a nut bar and some dried apricots) and went to bed.

Day two: a lecture, an organ recital and two cantatas after lunch, 78 and 79; a delight. Fidelis, who believed in neither Jesus nor the existence of a soul, was humming the introductory motif of 'Jesu, der du meine Seele' as she boarded the bus to travel onwards to Ohrdruf and Arn-stadt. The party was beginning to gel, but most of them were experienced travellers, wary of getting landed with a bore in the early days of a group journey, so new friendships weren't being made yet. Three concerts on the third day, and on to Weimar. Fidelis sat alone in a rear seat and nodded off, waking with a start when the overhead lights were turned on as they pulled up in front of the hotel. It took a little while to gather her wits and belongings, so when she reached the reception desk most of the group had already checked in and gone upstairs. Nearly all had come as couples, either married or merely friends. The woman who was just signing the form was another of the few people travelling without a companion. Fidelis stood behind, waiting her turn.

The clerk handed the credit card back and wrote three figures on a little envelope.

"Third floor, elevators round the corner."

"I hoped that..." She cleared her throat and went on, "Is there a message for me?"

"Mrs..." He turned to check the name on the form.

"Browne."

"I will see." As he disappeared into the back office the woman turned to Fidelis.

"Sorry to hold you up, but I'm expecting...I told someone I'd be coming, it's really important."

"That's all right," Fidelis said.

"Don't I know you?"

A patient? "I don't think so."

Too florid. High blood pressure? The woman had turned away, her attention concentrated on the door through which the clerk would bring something vital. A love letter?

Fidelis realized, actually I've seen her somewhere before. Where was it?

The clerk came back to the desk and said,

"It is here, a package has come. H. Browne to await arrival."

"I...oh – here, let me – thanks." She started to tear at the resistant brown paper and then the shiny tape.

An image flashed into Fidelis's memory: this woman in a black suit. A schoolboy's voice, a picture – yes. Benjamin Perkins' memorial service. That's right; she'd been sitting behind that wiry iron-grey bob, with the scalp showing through where the hair had thinned. The woman had been in the pew in front in St. Mary Abbots, Kensington, standing room only for late comers as colleagues, patients and pupils crammed in with that varied gang of friends, hardly a dry eye in the house. Benjamin had been the victim of a hit and run driver, never identified.

Waiting at the hotel desk, Fidelis was taken by surprise, brought up short by a flash of genuine grief, which was partly a wholly selfish emotion. Benjamin would have been the person to advise her now. The physician who could not heal herself needed her mentor. Why? Because she didn't see herself confessing to a mere friend. Confessing! Why had she thought that word? It wasn't an expression usually used in the context of therapy. She slotted that thought into a mental pending-tray as the clerk picked up a pair of scissors, leant across the desk and made a neat snip. H. Browne pulled the wrapping apart, scrabbling at it eagerly until an envelope was revealed, snatched and torn open. "Oh!" She took out a plain white postcard on which three words were written in large red capitals. Fidelis could not help reading: 'SURPLUS TO REQUIREMENTS.'

"The lady should sit down," the clerk said. H. Browne had gone from florid to unhealthily pallid. Fidelis took her arm. "Come, there's a chair just behind you. Here's your parcel, I'll just put it..."

"I call the doctor maybe," the clerk suggested.

"I'm all right. It's just that I didn't...I was expecting something else, not this – whatever it is."

"Books, it is books," the reception clerk said.

She tore away a strip of the brown paper to reveal that the parcel contained several fat blockbusters in gaudy colours. *The Moving Statue*, Fidelis read, and *Ministers of Grace*. The author's name was above the titles, embossed gold lettering: Allegra Wenders.

Hannah Browne sat down heavily, knocking a couple of books to the floor: *Home Sweet Home* and *The Prince and the Pea*.

Fidelis picked one up. The author photo was glamorous, with a wide dark gaze, a great cloud of black curls, even, white teeth.

Hannah grabbed the book from Fidelis and held it tightly to her chest with both arms.

A waitress arrived with a glass of water and set it on the low table. Fidelis exchanged complicitous glances with the clerk, sat down on the other low chair, took a small packet of tissues from her bag and put them on the table. Then she folded her hands, waiting as she had so often waited for a troubled patient to be soothed by her unthreatening presence. After a while the woman took a loud, deep breath, sipped the water, put the cold glass against her forehead, put it down and then took one of the paper hankies and blew her nose. She said,

"It was the shock. That's why I felt so...I had a shock." She laid her hands, one still loosely holding the crumpled paper, above where she supposed her heart to be.

Fidelis's receptive attitude was no more than an automatic reaction; this was the last thing she wanted on a journey undertaken anxiously and after a lifetime of dither. "Well," she murmured, her intonation implying closure.

"That's all I have left of her, her books. He might as well have taken a dagger and stabbed it – stabbed it straight through my heart."

"Are you sure you're not reading too much into it?" Fidelis suggested.

"How can you say that? I mean, to reject her books – it could hardly be clearer, kill her creation, kill her. Kill me."

Fidelis said, "Perhaps the note just means what it says. Maybe whoever it is already has other copies."

"Not like these." She opened a book to show the flyleaf. 'For Peter, from his affectionate mother, Allegra W.' The handwriting was regular and small, but the signature was less controlled, larger, more flamboyant with the tall rising stroke on capital W turned into an elegant pattern. The first Queen Elizabeth had indulged herself with a similar flourish.

"Your grandson sent the books?"

"Oh no, not him." She paused, hands clenched white-knuckled on a book called *Ask, Tell*. "It's his father. He's the one who...who..."

"His father," Fidelis repeated. She had just had an awful thought. It had come to her who this woman was. Of course. James, Hannah, Allegra Browne. "The name means happiness," the young voice had said.

Now she had remembered who H. Browne was, it was easy to see the traces of a lively young woman in that lined, lived-in face. But if there was going to be a moment for mutual recognition, this was certainly not it.

This was the H. Browne who had been married to Raymond Cunningham, about whom he had consulted Fidelis. The same Hannah Browne Fidelis had briefly met in Edinburgh a long lifetime ago; the young wife who had suspected Fidelis of seducing her husband. Of course she had been at the Memorial service for Benjamin. Raymond Cunningham and Benjamin had been friends and associates for decades. Oh God, Fidelis thought, I don't want to be stuck with her for the next fortnight. I don't want to be stuck with her for a single evening. Don't let her have recognised me!

What a hope! Fidelis had been recognised, but it was for yet another connection, one that Fidelis herself had not recognised.

"Yes, his father!" The words came out as a kind of shriek. "Dammit, you wrote the reports, you decided where he should live, without ever seeing him, or us, or the father. Your signature's on them! And now you're asking all these questions! As if you didn't already know!"

Hannah was careful to leave the hotel half an hour before the morning excursion was due to set off. She didn't want to explain herself to the agency's staff. And she felt quite keen on avoiding Fidelis Berlin, who surely soon or later would realize who she was. Though Fidelis couldn't have known of the connection when she wrote her "oh – so balanced" reports to the courts about child Peter W. Which just showed how silly the system was, silly and cruel and destructive. Why did people get away with it, why were they allowed to ruin other people's lives with their baseless judgements, not even setting eyes on the child in question, or knowing his real name, behaving like little tin gods…

Stop, Hannah. This was not the moment for such thoughts. She switched her attention to the programme for today.

She found her way to the lawyer's office easily from the directions the porter at the hotel had given her. She walked through narrow winding streets of houses with high pitched gables and roofs, a townscape left over from the Middle Ages. She passed the cultural monuments outside which other visitors were queueing, the homes of the poets and philosophers and composers who had lived in this town. Their names meant nothing to her.

Nor, as it turned out, did her name mean anything at the office of the lawyer who had signed the letter she showed the receptionist. "Can I see him?" she said.

"English?" a young woman said. She picked up her telephone and gabbled incomprehensibly, then gestured to Hannah to sit down on one of the leather benches and wait. So far so good.

Eventually she was conducted with waves and words into an interviewer room. She was joined by another woman, middle aged, formally dressed and with a fluent command of English. She put her file down on the desk and said,

"I am an associate here, how may I help you?"

"I'd like to be put in touch with your client please," Hannah said firmly. "I have personal business with him. He is the husband of my daughter. My daughter has died."

As she had intended, this remark provoked condolences. She went on, "I must break the news but I have lost his address." She made herself look old and fluttery and helpless. The associate said,

"Just let me check. I'll only be a moment."

A moment was all Hannah needed. She quickly opened the file, turned a couple of pages, saw a copy of the letter which began Liebe Herr Wenders, scribbled the address on a post-it note and pushed the file back to the other side of the table. When the associate returned Hannah was sitting in her chair with her handkerchief in her hand as though she had just been wiping her eyes. She accepted without comment the fact that addresses could not be given out, agreed that she would write a note which the firm could deliver to her son-in-law, thanked the associate for her help, wiped her eyes again for the sake of verisimilitude and made herself shuffle as she went out into the street.

Round the corner she found herself in a wide pedestrianised boulevard. It was buzzing with activity. She pushed her way through a crowd of young people and sat down at a table outside a café.

She stared out in the street. Peter might be one of those young people. He wouldn't recognize her even if he knew her of her existence.

"Would I recognize him after all this time?" she wondered. That dark boy over there with tattoos on his arms, could that be Peter? Or the one who was so passionately entwined with an Indian girl? Could he be the busker belting out an Abba song with a collecting cap for coins on the ground beside him?

There was one of the nutters on the music tour. Hannah pretended not to recognize him. She'd been beside him at the second concert, an endurance test she had forced herself to sit through. It had been held in a church, the church for which the dirgy tunes were composed and where they had first been performed, as the participants were told.

She'd watched a man cross himself and kneel in his pew before sitting back expectantly. She managed to keep still during some interminable organ music. She looked around at the other passengers and saw that at least half of them had bought books with the music which they followed on the page. Show-offs, she thought. She didn't believe that anybody could really enjoy this racket, nor did she believe that anybody could sit on these pews without longing for release. They were all putting it on. Must be.

Luckily after that concert she'd realized that nobody was checking the travellers in or out and nobody would notice if she simply skipped the concerts. The tour had been a good mechanism for getting herself into the country but there was no need to go over the top.

That had been in Eisenach, where passengers had been escorted through the mean streets of a small poor town to a Bach Museum. Hannah had repelled a couple of mild attempts to make friends with her. She was here with a serious purpose and didn't want to be distracted. In any case the idea that one could have anything in common with intellectual snobs who went on this sort of holiday from choice, was absurd.

She ordered a second pot of coffee. She needed fortification. The address she had copied was not in Weimar but in Arnstadt. The tour was going there after lunch tomorrow because it was where J. S. Bach had been the organist and where his father had lived and his son had been born. According to the programme it was only about 20 miles away.

Peter might be here. Probably he came to this place for its shops and big-city life. They might be close now, this very minute. Joachim would have delivered the package of rejected novels as an insult. He meant to hurt her. But instead it proved that she had come to the right place. Peter could be nearby.

Unless Joachim had sent him away.

Joachim knew she was coming, because in her first acknowledgement of the lawyer's letter she had said that she hoped to be on her way through Weimar in May. She hadn't explained the circumstances in case Joachim had enough influence to exclude her from this place as he had from his home town.

Lost in a resentful reverie, Hannah told herself again, as she had so often before, that it wasn't Peter's fault. It was his father who'd deprived him of contact with his mother and his grandmother. It wasn't his fault that he would have little memory of his earliest life. He probably didn't even remember any of the English language, let alone any of the people who had taught it to him.

"Enjoying yourself?"

Hannah did not hear the question the first time. When the woman repeated it she was jerked back to the present moment: a sunny pavement café in a foreign town. She said, "Yes, of course."

"Wonderful performances, aren't they?"

"Wonderful."

"I'm so looking forward to this evening's."

"Absolutely."

"And tomorrow. I do so love the organ music."

"Oh yes, me too," Hannah lied.

"Hearing the music like this, it seems so fresh and new, I feel I'm on a voyage of discovery, d'you know what I mean?"

To that question at least, Hannah was able to reply truthfully. "Oh yes, I do. That's just what this is for me, too."

What to see in Weimar:

Goethe's house, Fuchs's House, Lizst's house, Goethe's Garden house and the Goethe National Museum; the Castle Museum; the Bauhaus museum, the Nietzsche archive, the house of Cranach the Elder.
Wittumspalais, fully furnished town-house of a leading member of Weimar's 18th-century aristocratic intelligentsia.
The Herderkirche (church of St. Peter and St. Paul).

The list, which was in the handout given to travellers on the package holiday, was incomplete. It omitted any mention of Weimar's 20th century monument.

Fidelis had brought with her a more subversive guide which told her that this civilised city, the home of Germany's great poets, had also been the site of the very first and one of the worst concentration camps. Goethe and Fuchs used to walk together through the forest up the Ettersberg to the hilltop they called The Court of the Muses. On that very spot, Buchenwald was built. Nearly a quarter of a million people, Jews, Slavs, gypsies, homosexuals, political prisoners and others, were confined there. One was Dorit Rosenthal. Nearly 60,000 people were murdered there, some suffering atrocities that have made the name of Buchenwald synonymous with human iniquity. Even after the war the atrocities continued. After 1945 the Soviet occupation forces sent thousands of prisoners there to be tortured and murdered.

The stables beside the castle were used by the Gestapo to hold and interrogate prisoners, a tradition carried on unchanged by the East German communist regime that followed. Fidelis was at this very moment in the Elephant Hotel – next door to Bach's one-time home – from which Hitler had addressed an enthusiastic mob.

Her room, furnished with leather Bauhaus furniture, decorated with prints of paintings by Lyonel Feininger, looked out over the old market place where a dried up fountain, dedicated to Neptune, was already at this early hour festooned with tourists taking the weight off their feet. And there was Hannah Browne.

She was a stout, tall, square looking woman with a dark complexion and wiry grey hair, walking with her legs quite far apart, plonking her feet on the pavement as she barrelled her way forward. She had a piece of paper in her hand and glanced at it from time to time; presumably a map. Fidelis wiped the woman from her thoughts. *She's not my problem*, she told herself.

The official programme for the day was less full than the previous two. Most of the time would be free, apart from a talk about J. S. Bach in Weimar. Because she had her personal plan, Fidelis had decided to miss the lecture and instead read about this period in his career: the Dukes whom he served, the music that he wrote, the ignominious end of his career there when he was passed over as successor to the Kapellmeister, and when he took a job elsewhere was held under house arrest until his dismissal in disgrace.

Fidelis thought, I'll go and see the monuments. It would be good to see the interior of the writers' houses, and the Bauhaus museum. I'll wander round the streets. I've always said it's my favourite thing, getting to know a new town.

"Stop it!" she said sharply, aloud. Addressing herself like a naughty child, she thought, *You know perfectly well what you've come here to do today.*

Moving slowly and reluctantly, she extracted from her folder the letter signed Gerda Fuchs. The coincidence of names struck her. Was she connected with the poet who had lived in this town?

Or should I go and make a pilgrimage to Buchenwald?

"But I'm on holiday," she whined to herself. She looked at the programme again. They were not leaving Weimar the next day until mid-morning. There would be plenty of time to call on her correspondent tomorrow.

But by the evening Fidelis arrived in the mirrored hall of the castle, where the concert was to be held, feeling obscurely dissatisfied with herself. She had had the kind of culture-filled day the holiday's organisers had planned. She had not had the day of revelation which had been the purpose of the holiday. I wimped out, she thought. Whatever would Clodie say?

I haven't been to visit Gerda Fuchs. I didn't go to Buchenwald. I have done nothing unpleasant or difficult except brood on what unpleasantness and difficulties tomorrow may bring.

Tomorrow morning's programme was to be cheerful chamber music. Fidelis would miss it. I should have gone today, she thought, and remembered her own shuffling feet, her heavy unwilling limbs, as more than once she had turned towards a taxi rank with the address on the tip of her tongue, and each time had swerved away at the last minute, putting it off again. I'm afraid of what she may tell me, she thought.

Courage. That's what Benjamin used to say. Fidelis remembered what his grandson had said at his funeral.

"You felt braver after seeing him. Okay, so he had white hair and wrinkles. But he never told us what to do, he never thought he knew best. He gave you courage."

Fidelis remembered her last lunch with Benjamin. She hadn't mentioned her newly revived interest in finding her lost family, but as so often he had sensed what she was thinking about. No, she admonished herself, don't be silly. However sensitive, he wasn't a thought reader. His reminiscence, which she'd heard before, was spookily relevant but that was pure coincidence.

1938: Benjamin was an ardent young graduate volunteering at a YMCA in Amsterdam where, because his mother was Dutch, he had done a postgraduate year. He answered a call for volunteers to go to Berlin and look into the circumstances in which Jews were living. He travelled with a moral rearmament clergyman who had the embarrassing habit of offering to share Benjamin's sins, and going down on his knees in the train compartment to pray. "The floor was covered with smuts and ash and cigarette stubs, I don't think his trousers can ever have recovered."

Benjamin and the clergyman stayed in Berlin for a week. Benjamin had been given a package of new books to take to a famous Jewish collector and benefactor called Wilfred Israel and never forgot the stupendous wealth of the Oriental antiques displayed in his house. But he looked desperately sad and more exhausted than seemed possible. When Benjamin left his house he found the street was full of SS cars and men in black uniforms who made no pretence of not watching him and after that followed wherever he went in Berlin. He never forgot the atmosphere of suspicion and terror and the certainty that every word was being overheard. When he left Berlin, still in the company of the clergyman, he travelled on a train full of Jewish children escaping from Germany. "It was the most tragic thing I ever witnessed. Those children, their parents – some of them knew it was forever. And yet the parents were so desperate to get their children on the train, fighting to reach it, to get through the crowds, to hand their babies and children over to complete strangers…"

"I might have been one of them."

"I know. That's why I mentioned it."

"I don't think about it. I can't quite bring myself to."

"Do think. The courage of your mother or father, to send you off – they deserve your thinking of it. Be brave. Courage!"

A world of meaning in the words. Now he was dead, but Fidelis still heard the exhortation. *Courage.*

I came, didn't I? I'm here.

The Castle had a neoclassical façade. Fidelis went on through the Doric portico and up the ceremonial staircase, through an ante-chamber and into the gilded ballroom.

Fidelis had heard live performances of the St. John Passion many times and many more recorded ones; she had even been in the chorus, at least twice, when her choir's annual offering was this greatest of choral works. So there was no sense in her reaction this time, as she sat in the beautiful mirrored hall listening to the well known sounds.

She knew the words well, if parrot fashion, since she didn't speak German. She was intimately familiar with the music. The sound crept into her awareness like the slow embrace of an old friend, all the separate strands audible together and separately. Why could she not give herself over to the pleasure of it? She opened the score and followed the music and text on the page. Word after provocative word seemed fresh and new. There were the innocent Romans, the scheming Jews, the bloodthirsty mob crying 'kreuzige, kreuzige' – 'crucify, crucify'. Just for a moment it almost seemed possible that the story might have a different ending after all. But no, punctually, hideously, beautifully, there followed the tragic climax, the inevitable death.

Why had Fidelis never been horrified by the message of this music before? The message that told a murder story, the message that identified the inevitable culprit? I am the culprit, Fidelis thought, this finger is pointed at me. And if I'd been a mediaeval peasant listening to it here, I too would have been inspired, encouraged, provoked into going out to revenge myself on the murderers: the Jews.

At the museum in Arnstadt was a princess's life work: a series of miniature tableaux and doll's houses, at one-sixth scale, showing how people lived in the sixteenth century. Filling in the long hours of an aristocratic lady's day, everyone probably thought she was wasting time. "Can't you find something more useful to do?" her mother or husband would have asked. But her hobby had proved more worthwhile than most.

Hannah had followed the rest of the party in to the gallery. She listened coldly to the exclaiming and cooing of the other women in the party.

"So sweet, look at this, it's so lifelike. The charm of the miniature."

Hannah slid behind two women who were arguing about the point of it all. Had the Princess wasted her life? Or had it been better spent than her contemporaries'?

Who cares? Hannah thought. Who cares what someone long dead did? She crossed the open space, not meeting the eyes of one or two stragglers from her party. They would have assumed she was going to the hotel where lunch had been laid on. She walked on behind the hotel and went round the corner before moving into a shop doorway to get out of the rain and unfold her map. It was not a big town but the information was hard to follow. How was she supposed to decipher unfamiliar street names in a language she didn't understand? It took three quarters of an hour to find her way to the address she had written down. It was in a wide street, with pollarded trees at regular intervals, and bollards and paving stones so clean they could have been scrubbed. The houses looked pre-war but one could see from the rows of bells that they were in multi-occupation. Conveniently on the far side of the road from the house Hannah was looking for there was a bench, a flat sheet of stone without arms or back. There was no response to her ringing of the doorbell so Hannah plonked herself down on the wet surface to wait. She was exhausted.

Hannah passed into a kind of reverie, her mind a blank, her eyes open but unseeing, her hand clutched around the wooden Joanie in her pocket. The light drizzle thickened, her coat became saturated, her hair spiralled into corkscrews. The drivers who passed looked at her curiously but she didn't notice and they didn't stop. There were no pedestrians. Everybody was out at work. Somewhere far away a bell marked the passing of each quarter of an hour and somewhere in her abstracted mind Hannah registered the approach of lunchtime. Perhaps he would come home for lunch. She didn't know whether in this country there was such a thing as school dinner.

One o'clock. Quarter past one. Half past one.

She waited and waited, her eyes closed, immobile. She could have been an art work, a woman turned to stone.

Giggles, words, an excited movement around her. She came to and found she was looking at a cluster of children of different ages standing close to her. One of them had put out his hand and touched her wet coat and then jumped back nervously as she stirred. It had stopped raining. A girl with red pigtails was skipping in a puddle, splashing water with each bounce. Two small children in very short shorts with leather satchels high up on their shoulder blades stood at a safe distance giggling. Closer, were several teenagers.

They were all talking, but she couldn't understand a word. They were pointing at her, saying things. Their voices were harsh, half broken, full of a kind of cruelty, a hatred of the outsider.

She said, but unvoiced until she cleared her throat and repeated, "Peter? Peter Wenders?" They looked at each other and giggled and then turned their stares back on to her. "Peter?" she said again.

And then he came, lolloping along the road, unmistakable. Dark hair, not in curls now but cut brutally short, topaz eyes, tanned skin. Hannah felt a thrill of recognition.

"Peter!" she said. But he didn't reply. Other children had followed him like a Pied Piper, and Hannah found herself in the middle of the group. The children surrounded her, moving, jumping, giggling. She stood up and moved towards Peter as he turned away with a gesture of disgust. She tried to follow him and found that the other children were following her, suddenly many of them touching her and pulling at her, still though more violently, jostling and pushing. They said incomprehensible words, the tone however easily understood. Rudeness addressed to her. Peter had disappeared. She was being pushed, pulled, chased – he went in that direction, she thought, and walked after him, but suddenly she was not the pursuer but the pursued. Then something hit her on the shoulder. A pebble. And then another. She turned and shouted, "Stop it. Don't do that!" but they laughed at her. More people were joining the crowd. They started chanting. "Aus, aus, aus."

You didn't need to know German to understand. Out, out, out.

She stopped and turned on them, holding up her hand that still clutched the wooden toy. "Stop it," she shouted. "Stop."

But it didn't protect her. One of the girls, a little yellow-pigtailed creature, jumped up and grabbed the doll, took it out of Hannah's hand, threw it to her friend, and it went on to another.

"Give it back," Hannah shouted. But her words had no power, any more than in the end the magic figure had. It didn't protect her. She couldn't take care of it. It fell into a puddle and then it turned into a toy to kick around, shoved by trainers into the mud as Hannah flailed her arms and ran and slipped and missed, and sobbed "Give it to me, give it back."

The crowd of children was like a pack of animals that had smelt blood, they'd sensed her helplessness.

Where were the adults? Where was somebody to control this mob? Where was Peter? And where, lost in this scrum of people, where was her Joanie?

She closed her eyes as though if she couldn't see them they wouldn't be there. And when she opened them the noise had died down, the children were backing away. There were two officials in uniform. There was Joachim. He'd got fat. He'd gone bald. His flat folds of cheeks were bright pink under grey stubble. "Du. You," he hissed, "you cannot be here, it is forbidden." He bent with difficulty and picked the doll delicately out of the mud.

"Thank you, Joachim," Hannah said humbly.

"Now you will go."

"Peter," she said, but the word didn't come out properly and she cleared her throat harshly and repeated it. "Where is he? I've come to see him."

"He has no wish to see you." She looked desperately around. The children had melted away. "You could observe it yourself, Hannah, he was disgusted at the sight of you, that is why he called me. You may not be here, these men will take you."

It was true, Peter hadn't wanted to see her, he had been the one who showed the children he was disgusted, he stirred them up into a mob. He had become cruel, like his father, full of hate and hostility. The policemen came on either side of her and she began the automatic movement to shrug their arms off her. "They're going to take you to the airport. You'll be deported. You are not allowed to be here," Joachim said again.

Weimar is not a large town and Gerda Fuchs's address seemed to be quite near the centre of it, so Fidelis could walk through the pedestrianised streets, past buildings, monuments and open squares named for the poets who had lived there. It was beautiful weather and the tourist crowds were already out, queuing to enter the houses where poets and philosophers had lived, filling the pavement cafés.

Perhaps I'll just stop for some coffee.

The thought was like a devilish imp in a mediaeval painting, labelled 'temptation'. Sternly Fidelis made herself walk on. She had timed her excursion carefully: walk to this address, have meeting, return to coaches and set off again for the afternoon and evening concerts. She had arranged to meet for lunch the agreeable couple she had been beside at dinner the previous evening, the woman a banker, her husband an academic. They had discovered friends in common and a shared interest in obscure contemporary classical music.

Fidelis was humming – what was it? She concentrated for a moment on the automatically produced tune. Dies Irae, she realized, The Day of Wrath. Suitable for a singer who felt uncomfortable and tense. I can't concentrate, she thought, trying to banish an undefined feeling of oppression.

Nearly there. Would the house she was aiming for be 18th-century and elegant, would it be full of Bauhaus bentwood and bold designs, would it be plain white from IKEA? Suddenly there she was, facing an ugly, blocky building with a row of bells, another row of wheelie bins, and newly painted cycle racks in the front area. She looked up at the blank windows. Was somebody watching her from behind the net curtains or Venetian blinds? And was that somebody the first relation she would ever know?

Fidelis had a DNA kit in her handbag. She was equipped to take a cheek swab. The truth could be determined nowadays. If she was sure that she wanted to know it.

Her footsteps faltered as she walked up the steps to the front door, and her eyesight blurred as she tried to read the names on the row of bells. Fuchs: third floor. She moved her finger to the button, withdrew it. She felt her lips trembling. She dropped her hands to her side and took several deep breaths.

"Frau Doktor Berlin? Fidelis?"

The door had opened. somebody was standing there: stout, tall but hunched, a burly, undisguised old woman, with thin piebald hair permed into rigidity, with mottled, broken veined cheeks and gaps in her teeth. She wore a beige track suit. Fidelis had a sudden vision of how the two of them would have looked to somebody who was watching, like a different species of being. She had dressed with thought and care for today's encounter, businesslike, expensive: a successful professional who had made a good life for herself, and could afford Armani suits, the softest, most perfect leather boots, the bag that shrieked of money carried and money spent.

"Ich bin Gerda, die tochter…"

Gerda, the daughter. Or should she say, 'a daughter'?

Her voice was hoarse but the other woman did not seem to need a reply, instead drawing Fidelis inside towards a small coffin shaped lift.

They stood in uncomfortable proximity as it creaked upwards. Should I feel it? Fidelis thought. If this is my sister, or half-sister, is there some subconscious recognition of shared blood? Don't be ridiculous, the inner doctor rebuked the inner child.

Gerda Fuchs lived in a one room flat, tidy, monochrome beige, with a smell of lavatory cleaner exuding from the bathroom, whose door was a folding plastic screen that slid loosely into the slot. The cooking equipment was in one corner of the room, the bed in another, backed up against the only cupboard. There was one chair.

Gerda's voice was harsh, the consonants clipped. Her English was just halting, words rather than sentences or even phrases. "Kaffée," she said, and "sit you." Arranged on the bed was a photograph album, and a notebook bound in mottled black fabric.

Fidelis found herself guided – no, pushed – into the chair, a cup of weak coffee on her lap, a gurgle of incomprehensible sound in her ears. Then the odd word made her realize that the other woman was speaking English, or believed herself to be doing so. Mother, she made out, and Journal, and picture.

Fidelis put out her hand to the album and Gerda picked it up, opened it at a marked page and held it so that Fidelis could see the photograph.

"Dorit?" she cleared her throat. "Is that Dorothée?"

"Ja, ja, meine mutti – see."

The photograph showed a woman standing in a doorway. She was tall, like Fidelis, but stooped forward, leaning on a stick. She wasn't smiling, but stared at the camera as though it was taking a mugshot for police records, her thin mouth in a straight line, eyes hooded by folds of lid. The eyes seemed dark. The hair, tightly drawn back behind the head in an invisible bun, was grey. She looked fierce, but was marked by suffering. Is she like me? Fidelis wondered, suddenly panic-struck? Do I look like this impoverished, subjugated daughter, or this inimical, alien image of her mother?

Gerda was looking at Fidelis with…what? Suspicion? Pleading? What did she want – a long lost sister, a blood relation, or something else? Money? Contact with the rich and privileged?

Fidelis opened her bag and fumbled in it. I can't give her money, she thought in a panic. Her fingers knocked against the plastic box containing a spatula, a sterile container.

I could find out. Or at least I could know if we're related. DNA testing would give me that much of an answer. Incontrovertibly. There'd be no need to look for any other clue.

She turned pages in the albums: black and white pictures held in place with transparent triangles. Photocorners – the obsolete word came into Fidelis's mind. The photos showed streets and houses, groups of people awkwardly posed. Strangely, no infants, no grinning kids. A depressing record of a depressing life. The marked picture seemed to be the only one of this woman. Would enlarging it show more detail? Family traits? Perhaps the shape of ear lobes or fingers, Fidelis thought, staring at the wary, suspicious face. Are you the woman who put a child on a train and sent her away for ever? Was I that child? Did my hand clutch that finger, did that hand enclose mine?

It was a flimsy building. The lift sounded as though it were in the room itself. Gerda looked at her door which promptly opened. A young-ish man came in, or perhaps not so young, late 30s or early 40s. Stubble, a leather jacket, jeans, earrings, chain round his neck, tattoos, but harm-less ones. Two generations ago they would have been swastikas, Fidelis thought.

"Hi, what's the old woman been telling you? The story of her life?"

"I don't know, I don't speak German."

"Ha! Well then, she doesn't speak any English. Guess I'll have to do the talking."

"Are you her son?"

"No way. I am her hairdresser and now I'm her interpreter. And you're the famous doctor. We read about you."

"Where did you learn to speak English so well?"

"I didn't learn, it's German I don't speak so well."

Fidelis realized she knew the accent. "You're South African?"

"Ya, but only a couple of generations away from this place. What a dump, eh? Don't know why I bother. Look at her."

It was true that Gerda didn't do his skills much credit. He went on, "She can't do without me. It's love." He pronounced the last word with a long, descending vowel, with a mocking undertone.

He hadn't so much as glanced at Gerda who was motionless, like a stage prop.

"Here, you'd better see her credentials. I might be conning you."

You might indeed, Fidelis thought. She said, "And are you?"

"Here's the famous diary."

Bound in black mottled fabric, the paper flimsy, lined, writing on both sides making it hard to decipher in any case, but as far as Fidelis was concerned it could just as well have been written in hieroglyphics. The handwriting was even and orderly, furiously slanted towards the right, sometimes in pencil, sometimes ink, but it was tiny, the letters crammed close together and Fidelis could not read a single word. A piece of folded tissue paper marked the spot. Fidelis couldn't even read the date. "Which year was this?" she murmured.

"It was 1938, obviously."

Three lines, written faintly in mauve indelible pencil. Fidelis knew by heart the words that Gerda had written to her. *A comes. Argument again. I take G to train.*

That was indeed a letter A. and this could be a G, though it could equally well be a C, O or Y. "G for Gisele," Fidelis murmured, pronouncing the name as though it were French, and the young man said,

"Hard G. Geese-er-la. That's how you say it in German."

Suddenly disgusted by the situation she found herself in, Fidelis pulled around herself the psychic armour of a non-believer, of somebody who was experienced in being told things that weren't true. "Will you just ask Gerda for me, or perhaps you know the answer – if Gerda's mother was a prisoner during the war, and was in Siberia afterwards, how did this survive? Does Gerda know where the diary came from? Her mother can hardly have kept it with her all those years."

"I think a friend kept it for her."

"But this entry that you have shown me, it isn't the last one. If it is true that she was arrested in 1938..." Fidelis turned over the pages. There was writing before the entry she had been shown and after. Opening a later page she squinted at the date written at the top of it. "Does this say 1970?"

"I'm not sure. It isn't easy to read."

"No. But it's written in biro, so it can't have been written before the war."

He spoke to Gerda in German and she replied.

"She says somebody returned it to her mother after the war, a friend from the old days. She doesn't know who or why because her mother never mentioned it, in fact before she died Gerda had no idea this existed. But she guesses that the late entries were put in many years later, after it was sent back to her."

"What do they say, these late entries? This page, for example."

He took the book from her hand and squinted at the page. "It's something about food. Shortage of...I think this word is milk."

"Have you read the other pages? The ones earlier than this? Does it say anything about A? Who was A? and does she mention G?"

"I haven't read everything. But most of it is about politics, I didn't come across anything personal."

"Except that one entry." Fidelis didn't try to hide the incredulity in her voice. But there was no point in talking about it. This kind of thing was easily checked. She said briskly, "Will you ask your friend if I can take the notebook for tests?"

He spoke in German, and Gerda shook her head, seized the book in her hands and held it to her chest. "It is of my mutti," she said.

"Well, a handwriting expert would need to see it, obviously." Fidelis put her hand in her bag, took out the little polythene envelope, through which the spatulas could be seen and said, "And of course DNA testing."

Gerda was shaking her head violently. A white dusting fell onto her shoulder. I could hold the polythene bag open and catch that dandruff, Fidelis thought crazily.

"Nein, nein."

Fidelis stood up, visualising herself as she did so, a tall elegant figure incongruous in this squalid environment. "Well, in that case…" she began. The young man spoke rapidly and Fidelis could read the changes in Gerda's mind through her gestures, expression, and the way she stood. What was he saying? *She'll slip through your fingers if you make difficulties? Don't let her get away?* His body language labelled him as a sharp operator, but was he a conman? Was Gerda? And why? What was in it for them?

That last was easily answered. The loose change in Fidelis's shoulder bag was probably as much as this woman's monthly income. If this is a scam then I'm the mark, she thought. And if it's true – I don't want to know. Or do I?

Fidelis told herself, If she doesn't let me have the notebook and a sample I'll forget it.

Her body language must have been readable too, for at this moment Gerda spoke. "You take," she said, "Your Mutti too."

Hannah hardly noticed the music as she let herself into the house. My home, she thought. The proceeds of her hard labour. Taking care of a man, being a wife, that was really work. *If ever someone deserved a proper recompense...* In any case, Raymond had been going to make another will, Hannah was sure of it, so one could certainly justify her doing on his behalf what he'd meant to do himself. Okay, so he'd made a trial version. It was an experiment. He just wanted to see what it looked like, leaving the loot to his children. As for getting the two foreigners to witness it, that didn't signify anything. He never intended that one to stand, he'd been going to change it when he got round to it.

"He set me a good example," Hannah had told the two witnesses. The man, a Pole, was surprised, delivering a small consignment from Selfridge's Food Hall, to be asked for his signature again, but he'd cooperated willingly enough, writing his consonant-rich name at the bottom of the document he believed to be Hannah's will. And so it was, in a way: a manifestation of her will-power. *I deserve this*, she'd told herself, carefully copying his signature. And *His children are doing fine, my need's much greater than theirs.*

How right she'd been. She had needed the legacy, she deserved her own home at last. Her own home: a house of women. What dreadful things a woman had to do, to get a house. She still shuddered to remember. James crouched about her like a battering ram, defiling her with bodily fluids, sweat, semen, spit falling from his loose mouth. How ever had she born it for two years? Or Raymond, older, drier, but intruding everywhere, inside, outside, touching, stroking. If only he'd got it over with quickly. Really, one couldn't be expected to endure it. And it was entirely his fault in any case. He thought he was so clever, using his special non-latex condoms but letting himself off for the days after her period. No need to take precautions tonight, he said, probing playfully with his long penis, hard and thin like a wooden stick, stroking and rubbing inside her, deeply touching, scraping against her inmost privacies. If he'd left her alone he'd never have come into contact with the latex cap. He might still be alive today.

Propping her case by the hall table, hanging up her coat, Hannah was thankful to be home. Except that she'd given it away. It wasn't her own home any more and she would soon be evicted from it. Don't think about it. No judge would let Peter evict her.

Somebody was here. If Daffy was entertaining in Hannah's absence, her guests could jolly well be told to leave. She wrinkled her nose at an disagreeable smell and there was an insistent beat and thud coming from the living room, an unpleasant noise in Hannah's ears. She'd never been keen on music.

She opened the door to find that the room was dimly lit by the gleam of four candles in each corner. Black fabric was tacked over the windows at both ends of the room, the carpet had been rolled back and on the uncovered floorboards somebody had painted a pentacle. The swoony, intoxicating fumes of some incense mingled with smoke. Hannah had never enjoyed cannabis or experimented with anything stronger, so could only guess that it was what newspapers called 'illegal substances.'

The room seemed full of people – well, she corrected herself, there were six of them, five naked women and a tall figure in a robe with the hood pulled over its – no, his head; looking down the long body, she saw the erect penis poking through the black cloth. Other paraphernalia stood around the room. A silver dish, the skull of – was it a goat? – decorated with silver paint.

One of the naked women was Daffy herself. She saw Hannah and spread her arms wide. It was meant to be a welcoming gesture but what Hannah noticed was the chicken wing upper arms, the round and sagging belly, the dangling breasts. A hot bubble of rage and frustration rose up in Hannah's gullet. I've had it, she thought, and put out her hand to the light switch, smacking on the overhead light and the spotlights on the wall. The sudden brilliant illumination was a shock. The naked women automatically crossed their arms over their breasts. The man pulled the black robe to hide his nakedness.

How sordid everything looked once it was properly illuminated. What a squalid mess these people had made. What a waste of time Hannah's credulity had been.

"Do you know how idiotic you look? This is all nonsense, it's crap…" Her voice rose to a kind of screech. "Don't you understand? It doesn't work!"

"But…"

"I've spent my whole life trying to make it work. I have tried in groups, I've tried alone, I've tried ancient rituals, I've tried modern Wicca, and voodoo and Satanism – the lot. I know all about spells and ceremonies and the Black Mass, I've joined groups, I've read books, I've used charms – none of it works."

Daffy, now clutching one of the draperies round her nakedness, answered with characteristic know it all superiority. "That's because you haven't committed yourself to it. You don't really believe. You've always been like a butterfly, flitting from one belief system to another, never really committing yourself to any of them. How can you expect it to work? You need to study for years, you need to suffer, you need to become adept, don't you understand?"

"What I understand is that it's a waste of time. It's been a waste of my life, all those years of trying to find the secret. Well listen to me. This is the secret: that there isn't one! There's nothing there. This is all there is."

As she was speaking the other women were pulling clothes on. One of them absent-mindedly quenched the candle flames. Another picked up a messy looking lump of cloth and straw, and held it in a protective position against her.

"Charms and fetishes – all that crap. It's a cheat, I tell you, a trick!" Hannah was still clutching her handbag. Now she opened it, took out the blackened, hardened carving that had travelled throughout life with her, and threw it violently into a corner of the room. "I've had it up to here, it's over. Done with, the lot of it!"

"Hannah…"

"Don't you Hannah me! I'm not Hannah or Mrs Browne or Mrs Cunningham – no more pretending. No more play acting. I'm the wild child without a name, the pisky in the farmyard, the farmer-father's toy."

Her audience had evaporated as she spoke, sliding silently out of the room, and when she opened her eyes on the ruined space that had been her drawing room, she saw that she was alone. Suddenly calm, she whispered, "I am the wild child without a name and I can kill."

Fidelis had been to a meeting which ran late, so had to rush home in time for the one hour time slot when her supermarket delivery had been booked. She put on some music and sorted the mail, which had been delivered while she was out. In it was an envelope from the laboratory to which she had sent a sample taken from Gerda Fuchs.

Fidelis's hands were trembling so it took frustratingly long to open the package. A stack of impersonal forms listed incomprehensible figures and showed baffling graphs.

Then she heard the knuckle-knock on the door of her flat. The delivery. One of the neighbours must have let the driver in at the street door downstairs.

For a moment she could not take in the sight of a person in black leathers from neck to foot and with the helmet's visor drawn down. Nor did her brain really register that a large black revolver, held in both gauntleted hands, was pointed at her chest. Instead she noticed irrelevant details: the discarded take-away bag on the floor by the stairs; the lift door left open so that nobody else could summon it; the smell of scent. Chanel Number 5, she realized, incredulous. This anonymous apparition was female.

Fidelis stepped backwards, obedient to the gun's slight gesture. A kick of the booted foot slammed the door closed. Retreating as far as she could across her own hall, Fidelis felt a chair at the back of her legs and collapsed onto it. She made herself speak, though her voice came out in a whisper. "What do you want?"

"Retribution."

"Retrib...from me?"

The muzzle moved slightly upwards, and down again.

"Why? What did...?"

"You're dead."

Fidelis was shaking violently, her lips trembling, every limb in motion. Suffused with physical terror, a part of her mind remained cunning and aware. She tried to clear her throat but it closed up against the words. She mouthed,

"Welcome."

"What?"

"Welcome death. I've been waiting for you."

As she spoke the music surged towards its tremendous chorale, *dona nobis pacem*. Give us peace. A purely animal, physical terror surged through her, almost drowning the competing voices in her mind: *I don't want to die*, wailed instinct, while the still functioning part of her brain reminded her that she knew death could not be far away in any case.

Yes, but not yet! Not quite yet!

A pause. Fidelis's words were not what had been expected.

"What do you mean? How can you have been waiting for me?"

Get them talking – patients, patients' relations, muggers – the shrink's universal remedy.

"I just meant," Fidelis replied carefully, her voice almost inaudibly husky, "that you would save me doing it myself."

"You? Killing yourself? But you've got it all. Why would you..."

The black muzzle was still pointed at her but the finger on the trigger had slackened. You could see the gun was heavy.

She cleared her throat harshly and adopted the attributes Isabel Arnold had given her alter ego. She'd been disconcerted at first when her fictional self acquired an incurable illness, but gradually came to think of it as her portrait in the attic. Isabel's heroine was diagnosed with Parkinson's disease and wrote a bestseller. The real woman was perfectly well but had never been paid for any of her published work since academic journals didn't reward their contributors. She muttered,

"I've got an illness. Incurable. Getting worse." She wasn't sure if it was taken as an explanation or a bid for pity.

There was a pause. Then the woman moved backwards to sit on the other hall chair and rest the weight on her lap. The revolver was still pointed at Fidelis, but in the short time taken by the utterance of three sentences, it had become clear that it wasn't going to be fired. Not immediately anyway.

Physically still consumed by animal terror, Fidelis had already moved forward in her thoughts. It was not, after all, the first time that she had been threatened. The pattern of events unfolded in her imagination, weakly and unconvincingly, but in a parallel strand to that rumoured, unimaginable moment of her own death. With her twitching body still cringing away from a bullet's impact, almost consumed by the fire of fear, she could still see in the corner of her mind the alternative future in which she talked this aggressor out of her murderous intent, helped her to identify and then to come to terms with whatever experience it was that had driven her from an acceptable behaviour pattern to this transgression.

"It's too hot." The voice was fretful, aggrieved. "I can't stand that rumpus."

"It's Bach."

"Is that the remote? Turn it off."

In the sudden silence Fidelis could hear her neighbours going about a normal evening, running taps, arguing.

The woman didn't let go of her grip on the gun but moved her left hand to the face-mask and helmet, pushed one up, pulled the other off. "You're not going to be telling anyone."

The leather had left forehead-grooves even deeper than those incised by age. The wiry iron grey hair stood out around her head like Shock-Headed Peter's.

It was the woman who had been on the Bach journey, Fidelis realized slowly. Hannah Browne. What harm did I ever do her?

She'd disappeared after Weimar and although the staff hadn't said anything, a couple of fellow travellers had seen her being delivered to the hotel by people in uniform. "She looked a complete wreck, I think she'd been mugged. At least, something dreadful had happened to her. They got the hotel doctor round. Somebody told me she'd been driven off first thing, gone home early I suppose." Fidelis had heard the words and immediately forgotten them. All her thoughts were on her own dilemma. But now, remembering only the woman's violent disappointment on unwrapping the parcel of her daughter's books, Fidelis thought guiltily of her own indifference and the speed with which she had put another person's misery out of her own mind.

"Hannah Browne," Fidelis murmured.

"Remember me?"

"We knew each other years ago, in Scotland." She'd used a light, social tone, her voice trembling only a little. "Of course I remember." The woman stared inimically. But at least she had not pulled the trigger.

The whites of the woman's eyes were slightly jaundiced, her skin grey-brown and deeply furrowed. There had been something about her unhappy childhood. James Browne had spoken of it all those years ago, telling Fidelis about his wife's background and his own. Suddenly she could hear his voice, as clear as though he were speaking to her now, deep and with a pronounced Scottish accent and intonation, telling her, as men always did, about himself. He'd been in the Army in Germany and brought back "a medal, a scrap of stone from Hitler's bunker, an army revolver." He'd been matter-of-fact. It was nothing unusual for those days.

"All these years…" Fidelis said.

"What about it?"

"You've kept it. His souvenir."

The round black hole no longer promised certain death. This woman wasn't going to fire the gun; Fidelis felt almost sure of it. It's probably too old to fire straight anyway. The bullets must have deteriorated. All the same, the lethal weapon was still pointing at her.

"Look at you, you're terrified. Frightened of me."

She likes that. Wants me scared. Fidelis said huskily, "Yes."

"And so you should be. I have powers…" The woman's face crumpled, the corners of her mouth turned down like the mask of tragedy, her voice broke. "I had, I should have, I thought I had. But in the end this is it, after all those years of searching and trying, and this is what it comes down to every time. Take it into my own hands. Do it for myself. You can't rely on anyone else."

Fidelis was not a psychotherapist; her professional weapons were conventionally medical. The syringe, the tablet, a hospital bed. All the same, one didn't choose to become a mind doctor without accepting the efficacy of the talking cure. She said gently, "Tell me about it."

"What?"

"What's happened. It's been most of a lifetime since we met in Edinburgh." A silence. Had she forgotten her weapon? Perhaps now is the moment – no, not yet Fidelis told herself. "With James…" she prompted.

The gun pointed at her again. "How do you know about…oh yes, I remember, you were one of them, all thinking he was so wonderful, war hero, pillar of the establishment – right?"

"But he died." *Get them to talk.* Fidelis suddenly remembered the instructor's voice. A huge bruiser with a gentle manner, advising the new intake of housemen (Fidelis the only woman among them) nervously beginning a stint on a high-security ward. *They won't hurt you if you show you're really interested.* She clasped her hands tightly together and assumed the practised expression of sympathetic interest. "Won't you tell me about it?"

The woman shifted her buttocks backwards on the chair, crossed her legs, rested the hands holding the weapon on her knees. It still poin-ted at Fidelis.

"You saw how he treated me, first he wouldn't leave me alone and then he wouldn't touch me, then he said he was going to leave. He said I should go and live somewhere else, some place where there'd be no men. Like a convent! I don't think so! I have been out on the street without a penny! What did he expect, that I was going to let him get away with turfing me out? Anyway, it was his fault, if he didn't have the sense not to eat – it was his choice. I left it for him. He was just greedy. Served him right."

Fidelis made the therapist's grunt, that indeterminate sound that suspends judgement and encourages more bean spilling, that shows the listener is neither asleep nor shocked, but simply waiting to hear more.

"Same with Raymond, if he'd not been so…If he'd left me alone, he'd never have had contact with the latex. I'd not have gone and got fit-ted. He drove me to it."

"Latex?" Fidelis prompted.

"He was allergic to it. He said it could kill him. Such a fuss he always made. Once he ran away from some kids with swimming rings, literally ran across the lawn and into the car. Actually," she added primly, "it became positively embarrassing."

"Your diaphragm…?"

"I ask you, a Dutch cap at my age! It was all so unnecessary. If he'd behaved himself he'd have been fine. All that stuff about teaching me to relax, and not to worry – well, he was the one that needed to be worried."

"Anaphylactic shock," Fidelis murmured, thinking of her friend's anxiety about his new wife. Frigid, he'd said, wondering how to help her. Poor man, he only wanted to help.

"They thought he'd had a heart attack. It was neater than…do you have any allergies?" The gun was pointed at her again but without conviction. She's not going to shoot me, Fidelis realized, and noticed that she felt only relief. She'd never chose to take those hoarded pills, she realized. Death would not be so welcome after all. But this was an uncomfortable way to learn that she valued her life. The woman said, "What does it feel like?"

"What?"

"Being about to die. Is your whole life running through your mind?"

"I'm wondering what I did to you."

The voice raised, but the hand didn't move. There was a hideous kind of laugh. "Apart from sleeping with my husband, you mean?"

Should I deny it? No. Keep quiet.

"Apart from helping them steal my grandson? Your lying reports, you self-styled expert, you had no idea…" She paused and said more gently, "But I've come out top in the end, haven't I?"

"You have," Fidelis agreed. Her voice was almost inaudible. She cleared her throat and said, "You know, we could get comfortable, you could tell me all about it, get it off your chest. Go back to the beginning."

"Go back to the beginning," she echoed. And now her accent was different, in Fidelis's ears it sounded rustic and the cracked, elderly voice could have been a teenager's. It was a chilling change, almost a transformation, as though the elderly woman was suddenly possessed by a long-dead spirit, her own, or not. "That's what Gillian Butler said, those were her words. Exactly the same. *Tell me all about it, go back to the beginning*. Like I'd have told anyone! Would you tell anyone about being brought up a slave, living like the animals, with them in fact – would you have admitted that? Or let anyone know? She'd have made sure people knew all right, knew what I'd been and where I'd come from. Nobody could put up with it. You couldn't. And I wasn't going to. I shut her up all right. Never could say a word again, could she? What's that? A bit drastic? Best do things properly, I say, they just come back and haunt you otherwise."

The doorbell rang loudly twice. "It's only the supermarket delivery," Fidelis began, but the sound had fractured the tenuous relationship. Suddenly Fidelis had no thoughts, no rationalisation, just animal terror as Hannah tightened her finger on the trigger.

Then Fidelis realized she was still alive, still in the chair facing the other woman. There had been a loud click and then a pause, but no explosion, no bullet, though Fidelis had jerked herself sideways in an automatic attempt to escape. Her elbow, perhaps, or some other part of her, must have hit the remote control for suddenly the music started up, the CD player jerking into motion. It had jumped to Bach. Magnificat, magnificat. My spirit shall glorify the Lord.

Music to die to? Fidelis thought madly. The woman pulled on the trigger again, and the barrel moved round but the ammunition had deteriorated – or something. Again, nothing happened.

Fidelis was sitting on hot wetness. She'd peed herself. Hannah turned the revolver towards herself, peering into the barrel. Fidelis had time to think that she ought to grab it now as the woman muttered "What's wrong? It ought to work," and pushed a catch back with her thumb – but it wasn't the safety catch, it was the trigger, and of the six bullets in the revolver, one was still functional.

The noise was deafening, followed immediately by the sharp thud of the weapon falling to the floor, and a little more slowly, by the other woman's fall from the chair onto the carpet, her face disintegrated, a spout of blood splashing up and over Fidelis, and onto the walls, and then pouring out, a sticky red mark on the pale floor, hot, acrid. A harsh gasping sound.

Fidelis was out of the habit of dealing with bodies. Almost as helpless as a layman she pushed herself painfully down and knelt on the floor, a professional denuded of her qualifications and qualities. Where was her courage, and capacity to cure, where was competence or even cleanliness? Her hands were shaking so violently that she could hardly grasp the wrist. As she did so another gout of dark blood poured out of the ruined mouth. And then the sudden stillness of death.

I'd been excited to read about the – long overdue – opening of the Holocaust archives. I'd had several clients whose search for German-Jewish relations had been fruitless, because there just wasn't enough information accessible. I went through my list and realized there were five of these clients still alive. Should I get in touch with them? Or was it a mistake to raise their hopes? I decided to keep quiet for the time being, which turned out to be a sensible decision because there was a wait of many months before the Bad Arolsen archive was eventually made available to the public and by that time one of my clients had died and another succumbed to dementia.

After two negative responses my optimism was quenched. But then – a result! I called Fidelis and arranged to go and see her that very afternoon. As far as she knew, it was simply for a friendly visit. But in fact I had a tale to relate: an unfinished story.

Dear Madam,

In accordance with your request to find references to Child F. Berlin or to unidentified infant passengers on the Kindertransport trains, we confirm that we have consulted the archives at Bad Arolsen on your behalf. We have also sought information from the International Red Cross, which has used the archive as a tracing service. We can confirm that the name Fidelis Berlin does not appear in any of the documents or registers that were made available to us. However you also enquired about Dorothée Rosenthal or Fuchs, about whom some facts are recorded.

Dorothée Rosenthal was Jewish, a communist, a lawyer and the mother of a daughter, registered as Gisele Augusta Fidelis Rosenthal, born in December 1936.

Dorothée Rosenthal was arrested on 4th December 1938, sent to Buchenwald and later to Ravensbrück. The daughter Gisele was unaccounted for at the time of arrest. The details of Dorothée Rosenthal's interrogations are on the record.

I paused at this point, thinking about that record. German bureaucrats had been meticulous even in the torture chamber, recording how many buckets of water, how strong and how frequent the electric shocks, which weapon was used for beatings on which part of the prisoner's anatomy, and how often. Better not to tell my clients those details.

The prisoner held out against all forms of questioning, refusing to divulge her daughter's whereabouts. She reiterated that the child's father would never find her. His name was given as August Schimmler.

August Schimmler? It can't be, I say aloud. Then I get up to fetch my own cuttings books and go back to reread my review of Schimmler's book, and the other one of Aaron Hondhorst's exposure of the famous writer, the book that suggested Schimmler had not only been involved in disgusting occult ceremonies himself but that he might have taken his baby daughter to them – for what purpose, even Hondhorst could not bear to think.

I remember that Mr Katzenellenbogen had been sent to check into my client's history and he'd failed to find anything. But I also remember, very vaguely, reading and even tearing out to keep, an article about him. Had it been headlined The Clerk with Vengeance in his Soul? Perhaps it was The Vengeful Clerk. If I had kept it, I'd never find it in the prevailing mess. No need: it was on Google.

Katzenellenbogen, who had been a student in Berlin himself before the war, caught sight of somebody he had known in those days. They spent one of those long evenings of 'do you remember?' Nearly everybody they spoke of was dead. The friend, in his early 30s still, had turned prematurely into an old man, privation and suffering still etched on his body. "It doesn't matter," he'd insisted. "If only the children had survived." At one point in the conversation the friend talked about a neighbour in his building, a woman of great brilliance, insight and indeed beauty. She was called Dorothée Rosenthal and was a lawyer. The speaker described her with love and longing, though he had admired her only from afar. "A truly remarkable person," he'd explained. She had a child, a little girl who looked like a miniature version of her mother. He described her home, a happy place, away from the increasingly threatening outside world. He spoke nostalgically about nursery meals, at a round cloth-covered table with the little girl underneath in her cosy den while the grown-ups ate; the gaudy Bauhaus design of the bedspread, the contrasting traditionalism of the framed pictures on the wall, comfortable, peaceful interiors by a Scandinavian artist. It was a refuge, but not a safe one, for the woman was of Jewish descent. Her lover was not.

In fact the father joined the Nazi party. Then he went further: he became an active member of the SS. He was a loving father, if one can call his misuse of the child love. But as for her mother: he accused his ex-girlfriend of bewitching him. It wasn't a metaphor. Like many Nazis he believed in the occult.

When they came for the mother – as of course they did – the baby was missing. The neighbours heard the shouting, the questions, the blows and screams. They'd all been interrogated, but not very roughly. The Nazis had no reason to suspect that one of them had discussed with Dorothée how best to manage getting out unseen; what dose of pheno-barbitone would ensure that a child of nearly two would be silent; what to write on the luggage label, when to pin it to her clothes. They never guessed that her neighbour had helped smuggle the child out in a laundry basket, and in his imagination watched as the mother put her child, asleep and alone, on the train and somehow found the strength to leave her there and then walk home alone.

I read on and find that the father had become a war criminal as bad as the worst of them, but escaped trial when his death was reported in 1945. In brackets, Katzenellenbogen had written, "some doubt as to veracity of this report. Possible, even probable, that X is one of the many such who survived and has assumed a false identity."

As for Dorothée, she was sent to Buchenwald. The story Mr K had been told was that her former lover himself had come to arrest her and had her tortured but not succeeded in discovering where she had hidden the little girl.

Dorothée herself apparently survived the war in concentration camps but Mr K had been told she perished at the very end, during the Russian advance.

The Magic Soldier is one of the most famous novels by one of Germany's most famous writers, August Schimmler. The hero takes his own child to celebrate the Black Mass in a castle. It's a terrifying, disgusting, obscene description, vivid enough in itself to justify the numerous literary prizes that book collected. I'd read it when it came out and hated it. The infallible Google worked its usual magic and I found this deplorable episode quoted, presumably in breach of copyright, on a so-called 'pagan' website.

Only the previous year I'd reviewed Schimmler's posthumous novel, in which he told, as fiction, the story of a father sending his daughter away on the kindertransport against her mother's will. The story had been treated as autobiographical by critics and commentators.

Was it possible that he told a true story, only reversing the mother's and the father's roles?

Just suppose you were Dorothée, knowing your days were numbered, knowing that your child's father was – what Schimmler was; that he had exposed the little girl to corruption already. Wouldn't you risk anything to protect her, to get the child away from her father? Life, limb, liberty – the lot. But what could you do? He'd track the child down wherever you hid her. On his side, all the might of a lawless state, on hers, total, abject powerlessness. Even if you sent your baby away, put her in the charge of strangers and let her be taken to refuge in England, even then, the father could travel freely, follow her to England, find the kindertransport children, prove his paternity, get her in his power. Nothing could have stopped him – except one thing. Not being able to identify or to find his child.

Dorothée must have sent her daughter away to safety in another name, her true identity hidden, irretrievable. Better to lose her forever, but know that she was safe.

Imagine what it must have been like at the railway station in Berlin. The scrum of people, the parents saying goodbye to their children knowing that they might never see them again. The children excited, not quite understanding the dangers they were escaping, the babies clutching on to their mothers until they were prised apart; and Nazi police and spies, always watching, noting names, condemning.

On arrival in Britain the children were taken to disused holiday camps where, on Sundays, a 'cattle market' took place. They were herded together in a large hall and prospective hosts arrived to look them over and choose which, if any, to take home. The sweet and small children were picked first. Fidelis's foster parents were lucky to take home a little girl.

A little girl who was probably Gisele, the daughter of Dorothée Rosenthal and her lover August Schimmler, once an SS officer and in future to become a famous author. Gisele, who was in fact the woman we knew as Fidelis Berlin.

François comes up to Edinburgh with me this time so we stay in a hotel and I'm flanked by husbands one and three at the Procurator Fiscal's inquiry into the death of Gillian Butler. François is supportive and Hector a protection. Newly appointed as a Justice of the Supreme Court of the United Kingdom, his presence might have been at least a little intimidating to an adjudicator so far below him in the hierarchy if intimidation had been required. But it isn't. Fidelis Berlin gives evidence of what she had heard Hannah Browne, sometimes known as Hannah Cunningham, say. Hearsay, admittedly, but what else could it be when all the protagonists are dead? It's all too long ago. Nobody really cares. In fact the verdict is hardly reported even in Scotland. It was murder, of course, even if nobody knew the exact details of how Hannah Browne had lured Gillian Butler out of Edinburgh or how she had killed her before weighting the body down and hiding it in the deep water. As for motive – well at least there isn't much doubt about that. It was because Gillian knew who Hannah was: the illegitimate, unregistered, un-christened, unacknowledged daughter of a farmer who had served a prison sentence for his treatment of her.

"Hardly surprising that she went to the bad," Liza remarks.

"Is the farm still there, do you suppose, and the family?" I ask, wondering as I speak why I never went to see for myself. But, perhaps not surprisingly, Fidelis has.

"I've been to west Cornwall before, it's always seemed a very dramatic place to me. But this visit was calm and undramatic. I drove out to the farm expecting to see something very primitive – on the way to it there are several cottages and walls built out of those huge granite boulders, so they look as if they have somehow grown out of the ground. But Hannah's birthplace has gone."

"Razed to the ground?" I murmur.

"Possibly. I didn't ask. There's no farm buildings or animals now, just a sea of tents and caravans. It's become a huge holiday park. And nobody I asked remembered the family that had farmed there. They've all died or moved away." We are all silent for a moment. Then Liza says,

"And that poor boy? What happens to him?"

"He grows up a good German – and one day, probably, comes looking for his maternal relations."

"And does not discover the truth about all of them," Hector says loudly. He looks round, meeting eyes. We're all agreed. Peter Wenders is to be protected by ignorance. He may learn, if he ever asks, about his straight-up Scottish grandfather and the names of the great clans in his ancestry. "Montrose. A connection on the distaff side," Liza says, remembering the quotation after all these years.

But Hannah Browne's life story will be forgotten. Her savage childhood and the murderous life it explained haven't been disclosed, and there doesn't seem to be any point in our doing so now. Let James Browne and Raymond Cunningham rest in peace.

We re-assemble that evening, not this time in the Dorneywoods' place but in Hector's – which had also once been mine. The bricks and mortar have retained their beauty far longer than he and I have. The flat looks as comfortable and infinitely more elegant than it did in my day when Hector was not yet a high earner, and I made the curtains myself and painted the woodwork and learned to hang wallpaper and hunted in junk shops for furniture and fittings we could afford. I can see only one item that has been there ever since, a small revolving bookcase I had found in a junk shop, polished up myself and given Hector for Christmas.

"Of course you'll be moving to London now," François remarks.

"We get a grace and favour in the Middle Temple," says the current Lady Drummond. "But we're keeping this as well."

In that first novel of mine I had described our two floor apartment, with its graceful internal staircase and glass cupola. I didn't disguise it at all though I hid even from myself the fact that some of the characters I included were described not invented.

I am suddenly taken aback to realize that the revolving bookcase holds books by only one author, myself. Fidelis, elegant in a velvet tux, is sitting beside it. I watch as she makes the shelves turn. She pulls out a book, my first. She opens a page at random and reads a couple of paragraphs. Then she turns to me and says,

"I've happened upon your description of this very room, haven't I?"

"Yes."

"And of these very people?"

"Until recently I'd have answered, no. Now I probably have to admit it. I'm afraid I didn't know I was doing it – can you believe that?"

"Yes, easily, since you also didn't know you were describing me in your later books." She flips over some more pages and something catches her attention. She reads it carefully. Then she says, "You write from instinct, Isabel, you use different qualities and different abilities from those you employ in your other profession. Instinct and insight."

"I'm not so sure about the insight," I mutter.

"Perhaps you've forgotten the passage I've just read."

I suddenly realize that everyone is listening. Hector's deep voice says, "Why don't you let all of us hear it, Dr Berlin?"

Fidelis replies, "I will. It's a description of one of the characters." She smooths the page and takes a deep breath. "She was small and dark, wore conventionally pretty clothes, uttered received opinions and deferred prettily to her husband and any other male. But underneath this acceptable façade was a seething mass of desires. She wanted – it might be easier to say what she didn't want. She wanted husband, children, status, safety, wealth and well-being; she would stop at nothing to get it all. And if anyone got in the way she'd kill them. Alternative methods were planned out in detail in her head; she would drown him in the bath, push him over a cliff, trick him into eating a lethal pie. Or would she take her husband's own ex-service revolver and force her victim to drive to a remote loch or quarry, and then to get into the water, and then to drown?"

Fidelis looks up from the page. My husbands, present and ex-, my friends old and new, are staring at me.

"Isabel, how ever did you know?" Liza Dorneywood whispers. And I reply,

"I didn't, I don't. It's all imagined. Made up. I wasn't thinking of anyone."

"Some of that was positively visionary," Hector says.

"And some of it was...as if you knew what had happened," Liza adds.

"I didn't know," I say. "I had no idea. But that's what writers do. Imagine things. And sometimes," I add, "just sometimes, they come true."

Author's Note

Isabel Duhamel (born Arnold) appears in my first novel, as the wife of Hector Drummond. I am grateful to Martin Edwards, who suggested that I should look at A Charitable End again and inspired me to write some kind of sequel, forty years on.

Fidelis Berlin was introduced in A Private Inquiry, reappeared in a minor role in Under a Dark Sun and was featured as one of the principal characters in The Voice from the Grave.

I have several people to thank for their kindness in helping me with this book: Imogen Olsen, Diane Johnstone, Joanna Hines, Chris Bond, and, again, my daughter Lavinia Thomas Buhagiar. I am most grateful to them all.

Jessica Mann is the author of 21 crime novels and 4 non-fiction books. As a journalist she has written for national newspapers, weeklies and glossy magazines. She is the crime fiction critic of *The Literary Review*. Jessica and her husband, the archaeologist Professor Charles Thomas, live in Cornwall.

Lightning Source UK Ltd.
Milton Keynes UK
UKOW04f2235051213

222449UK00001B/91/P